Ten Minutes in the Sin Bin
by
M.J. Schiller

DEDICATION

This book is dedicated to five very important men in my life. Four of them I've never met.

If you were to ask me why I'm a rabid St. Louis Blues fan, I would first say because hockey is the best sport in the world, bar none. Then I would point to the fact that I was born in 1967, and so were the Blues. (Don't do the math on that. It means I'm way old!) My parents were season ticket holders that first year, so, yes, I bleed Blue.

When I was in second grade my parents divorced. I moved with my mom from St. Louis to Iowa. On those rare occasions when we got to visit my dad, we did a lot of special things. The zoo, the botanical gardens, Kirkwood Park...but best of all were those nights I would cross the bridge over Highway 40, with cars whizzing by underneath me at a terrifying speed, not scared at all because I was holding my daddy's hand and we were on our way to the Checkerdome to watch a Blues game. My dad would patiently explain the finer points of hockey...as long as I waited with my questions until a period break. He has since passed, but this book would not exist if it weren't for him. If it weren't for him, I wouldn't have a signed Brett Hull jersey hanging in my basement, along with a hockey puck that holds melted ice from the year we won the cup. If it weren't for him, my brother, sisters, brothers-in-law, husband and I wouldn't text each other constantly during practically every game with our wisdom concerning what the team is doing wrong and what they are doing right. (It's quite obvious to us.) If it weren't for him, I wouldn't have gotten my first tattoo while in my fifties, a Blue note on my ankle, after we won the Stanley Cup. (We had a longstanding family bet that if the Blues won the cup we'd all get tattoos. For a while it was a pretty safe bet that wouldn't happen, but it did! Some have welched on getting those tattoos, but I won't name names.) So, this one's for you, Daddy.

Four other men are also responsible for my love of hockey. Chris Kerber and Joey Vitale are the radio voice of the Blues. They have rescued me when I've been on the road and could not watch the game. And John Kelly and Darren Pang, the TV broadcasters, are the Blues, to me. What a team! John Kelly is the lovable straight man to the enthusiastic Darren Pang, or, as every-

1

body likes to call him, Panger. While on air, Panger seems to be the jokester of the two, but I love how JK plays off him, serving up some great one-liners in his fabulously rich voice. And as fun as they are, they are also very intelligent and insightful hockey commentators. They taught me what chiclets were, and what someone is talking about when they refer to a twig or a bucket. They helped me recognize when a play was offsides and understand what constitutes icing. I've been listening to them for so many years their voices would be much more recognizable than some family members' voices are.

So how do you thank the men who have given you something that has brought so much to your life? I guess the best I can do is dedicate a hockey romance to them.

Because life without hockey ain't no life at all.

Copyright © 2022 Mary Jean Schiller

CHAPTER ONE

Scott

There was only one thing to be done about a guy taking your parking space. Drive him into the nearest hard surface with as much force as humanly possible. This time it happened to be ice. The fact Sergei's obnoxious snoring kept me awake last night simply meant further retaliation was a matter of course.

"Uhh...McCord. We need him. Please do not injure teammates."

"But, Coach, he took my parking space."

"Oh, by all means, then, take him out."

I eyed my prey, currently trying to pull himself up the boards and onto his skates.

"Kidding, McCord. Cease and desist."

Sergei scowled at me and spit. "He purely lets you get away with that shit because of your Conn Smythe trophy."

I grinned. "Yeah. Ain't it great?"

"You won't think so when I poison your food tonight."

"All right. Knock it off," Coach said wearily, for the hundred and eightieth time.

Sergei's focus shifted to something behind me. "Holy shit! I'd love to get ten minutes in the sin bin with her."

I twisted to see who he was ogling.

Down the steps of the stands of our practice arena came a pair of legs, topped by one of those short, tight suit skirts, a silky white blouse, and red blazer. I'd have been drooling myself if said legs hadn't been connected to one of my best friends in the whole wide world.

"Ain't happening," I commented absentmindedly to Sergei.

At the same time, Elise, who had been searching the ice, apparently spied me, as she released a high-pitched squeal and yelled, "Scottie!" She ran over the concrete stairs in those heels of hers, bound to turn an ankle and face plant against the glass like someone had checked her into it. I tore off without thinking about anything besides Elise being there. It had been too long.

4

I picked up speed before my skates bit into the ice at the rink's edge. "What are you doing here? I thought we were meeting at my place."

She bent over the half-wall and wrapped her arms around my neck. I responded to her hug with such exuberance I almost pulled her out of the stands and onto the ice.

"Oh my gosh. It's so good to see you," she whispered in my ear. "It's been too long."

I squeezed her. "I was just thinking the same thing."

One of my teammates whistled appreciatively and we broke apart, Elise sliding until her heels met the steps. She glanced in the guys' direction sheepishly, but she still glowed with excitement, which, I'll admit, gave me a little high.

I stole a peek at the guys too. Blane Mansford was leaning over the boards, clearly winded but still leering in our direction without pretending to do anything else. Tommy Rosetti was shuffling his feet back and forth to no doubt alleviate the tightness in his crotch. He was married, but in name only. He was probably the horniest bastard on our team and the guy most likely to score with any woman we met, even though he looked like a pug with bad genetics. Our newest pickup, a goalie from the Czech Republic named Ctirad Malý, had his mask pulled up, and although he could barely speak a word of English, apparently he could appreciate a hot American woman. He must have been the one to whistle as his fingers were still in his mouth. I guess whistling at women was an international thing. He'd already earned the affectionate nickname of Shit-turd because that's what his first name appeared like it would sound, even though it was pronounced like Tirad, with a long "i". Rounding out the group was my roomie, Sergei Duskin, or The Douche, if one knew him well. He had both hands on the top of his stick as he ogled Elise with the rest of them. Obviously, I would need to make it clear Elise Scofield was permanently and irrefutably off the table for anyone wearing a Fire jersey.

"I'm sorry." She gave me a shy smile I didn't recognize. "I didn't mean to interrupt your practice. I just couldn't wait." Tucking a piece of her straight blonde hair behind her ear, she added, "I needed to see you." Her eyes were misty. Something was wrong.

I searched her face. "Are you okay?"

"Yeah. Yeah. Fine," she said. But her voice sounded weird. "I'll go. Let you get back to what you were doing." The smile was there, but not right somehow. "See you tonight."

Coach blew the whistle and circled his arm at me. I skated backwards. "You've got my address, right?"

She straightened. "Yeah."

I glanced at my teammates, then at her. "I told the doorman to expect you," I shouted as I was a distance from her now. "His name's Jimmy."

She waved. "Got it."

I spun and returned to my team. I was lighter and knew I would own the rest of practice.

I bent my head and let the hot water beat between my shoulder blades and on my neck. It felt incredible. The water drowned out the others' voices, so I felt rather than heard the communication going on around me.

"So, McCord...who was the hot blonde?"

I straightened, twisted the water off, and gave them a glare meant to end conversation. "The 'hot blonde' was my sister, so I suggest you stop talking about her."

But as I turned and grabbed a towel from a nearby bench, Mansford spoke up. "That didn't look like any brotherly hug you were giving her, 'Scottie.'"

I don't know why he said it like that. A lot of people called me Scottie. Hell, he'd called me that, the press called me that, I probably was called that more often than Scott. I shrugged. "I was happy to see her. It's been a while."

"I was happy to see her too," Sergei said snidely. "At least parts of me were." He thrust his hips forward and ogled his dick like it was his pet dog. This was the guy I shared a bathroom with at home. Sick bastard.

The others chuckled, staring at me with what felt like hostility.

I'm telling you all to keep away from one girl and suddenly I'm the enemy?

"I thought you only had the one little sister, McCord. And that chick today didn't seem no five years younger than you, or whatever. And we've already met that older sister of yours, who is equally fuckable, but not the gal we saw today." Rosetti smiled smugly and I mentally tallied an illegal check coming his way whenever I got a chance. My muscles tensed and my blood began to boil in the same way it did when I met a Redwing on the ice.

I worked my jaw. I didn't owe these guys any sort of explanation, but I offered one anyway. "Elise's mom and Dani, my stepmom, are best friends, so we were together all the time when we were younger, like brother and sister."

"Elise, huh?" Sergei's mouth slid into an oily grin. "Pretty name." He twisted off his water. "Pretty lady." His eyes had a glint in them. Was he still mad because of the check I gave him? Pussy. He snatched a towel hanging from a hook behind him. "So she's not blood-related. You won't mind if I tap that then." Again, the intensity to his glare seemed over the top. I'm sure I was spitting fire back because he was pissing me off.

I took a step forward. "Not if you don't mind me screwing your sister."

He quit rubbing his hair with his towel. Faucets squeaked closed and the sound of water running stopped. "Go right ahead. Maybe it would lighten her up some."

A low murmur of chuckles bounced off the walls. My fists clenched reflexively. The league had asked me to take the guy in. Mentor him. Show him the ropes. So I had. To get the captain's badge. But I was ready to toss him out on his ass. C or no C.

"Well, you may not give a shit about the women in your family, but I do. And you don't want to mess with me, Douchskin." We both moved toward each other.

Lucas Barbeau, our resident nerdy, Canadian centerman—every team needs one—squeezed between us. "Let's take it down a notch, guys. No need to let things get out of hand."

Sergei clapped him on his shoulder. "You were there, Luke. Did that seem like a brother hugging a sister to you?"

"Uhh." He tilted his head. "To be honest, no." He looked at me. "There seemed to be a lot of chemistry between you two."

Chemistry?

"You guys are full of shit." I connected gazes with Sergei one more time before turning to leave.

Sergei's voice followed me. "So, if you're not into the girl, then you'll have no problem with me doing her."

I stopped in midstride, clenching my teeth, then took a deep breath and spun around. "You know what? Go for it. But Elise is smart on top of being beautiful, so she'll see right through all your crap. You haven't got a chance."

"That's right," Joey Hoskins inserted, "she may buy a lollipop from my nephew," —Joey's nephew was selling candy for a school fundraiser— "but she won't be sucking anything of yours."

The guys busted up.

"Is that right?" Sergei replied without looking away from me. "Want to put your money where your mouth is?"

Hoskins was always down for a bet. In fact, he probably had a gambling addiction. "What do you have in mind?"

"A grand says I can get sissie dearest into my bed."

The thought made me want to puke. Elise was way too good for him. He wasn't even fit to touch her.

"You're on."

Sergei folded his arms. "You in, McCord? If you're so sure she won't let me jump her bones, then it would seem like an easy grand."

Don't take the bait.

"Oh, I'll take that bet, all right," I said hastily. "She won't even let you close enough to smell her perfume."

Shit. Why'd I do that?

He jutted his chin out. "We'll see." Pointing at me, he added, "You can't say anything to her, though. You can't tell her bad things about me or discourage her in any way. And most importantly, you can't tell her about the bet."

"I won't have to," I said with utter confidence.

He extended his hand wordlessly, and I shook it in kind. It felt like I was making a deal with the devil.

Spinning on my heel, I left the jeering and crap behind me to get dressed. I was often the first one in the locker room after a game or practice. Sometimes it was hard to remember that I worked with professional athletes because they sat around and talked like a coffee klatch of old women. Not I. I had better stuff to do.

I'd been used to having a sweet storage setup since my college days in Omaha when I was a Maverick, but I still always loved walking into my NHL locker room. Since we were the newest team in the league, ours was topnotch. Open wooden cabinets stowed our gear, with locked drawers beneath where players could store their wallets and charge their phones or iPads—which was good because we were always looking at plays on our tablets during period breaks, studying what worked and how we messed up. LED lighting, that ran along the floor and illuminated our name plates over our areas, gave the place a kind of Starship Enterprise feel. My favorite part, though, was the giant, backlit Fire logo hanging from the ceiling. We also had a lounge area that was equally nice, with recliners displaying the logo, and lit action photos from our early games. They even went all out with the visitors' locker room, despite the fact that many of the other teams did not treat their visitors well, as far as the accommodations they provided.

Mike Fazini (or Faz, as we called him) was sitting on the cushioned bench in front of his locker, his crutches resting beside him. Faz was probably my closest friend, besides Elise. We both were from Lincoln—although he attended Denver University and I went to school in Omaha—and were drafted to The Fire the same year. He usually played as the winger opposite me, the spot that Sergei, unfortunately, was now filling, while Faz was on injured reserve with an MCL tear.

"What the hell was going on in there? I couldn't hear everything, but it sounded intense."

I rolled a shoulder. "Oh, nothing. The guys were giving me a hard time about hugging Elise."

"Oh, she got here fine, then. Good." He scratched his chin—which he often did when he was deep in thought—while I pulled underwear and my pants on. "So...uh...what kind of hug was it?"

I glared at him. "Don't you start."

He waved his hands. "Oh, I'm not starting anything. I was in the training room. I didn't see it."

"Well, there was nothing to see," I snapped. "They're full of shit."

"Maybe..."

I exhaled and twisted to stare at him.

He laced his fingers behind his head and leaned back against his locker. "I'm just saying, something made you go off on Sergei and now you're jumping down my throat."

"I'm not—" I inhaled slowly. "Wouldn't you be upset if the guys were talking about your sister in a crude way?"

"Yes. But Elise isn't your sister."

"She practically is," I said defensively.

"I mean, wasn't she the girl you had a thing for in like...junior high, or something?"

I turned away from him, focusing on getting dressed. "No. I never had a thing for her."

"Hmm...odd. Because I recall you mentioning making out with her."

I slammed my deodorant onto my locker shelf, but grinned, shaking my head. "Dude. How do you remember shit like that?"

"I remember because I was jealous as hell. I'm not afraid to admit I had a thing for her. Who didn't?"

What the actual hell?

I narrowed my gaze on him. "*You* had a thing for her?"

He laughed. "Yeah, man. You gonna deck me or something?"

Not a bad idea...

I snorted. "No. No. I don't care." Staring blindly at the closet in front of me, I tried to remember what I needed to do next. "Whatever."

He laughed so hard he almost fell off the bench.

"Dude. Don't fucking mess up your rehab or I'll kill you. Another day with Sergei and I'm gonna—"

"Hi, Sergei," Mike said loudly. "Looking good out there."

"Yeah," he responded cockily. "You nervous you won't get your spot back?"

Mike slid a glance my way. He was pissed. "No. Not at all."

The conversation went a different direction, and it was enough to distract Mike for a while.

It's like these Neanderthals don't think a guy can have a relationship with a girl without there being sex involved. Bunch of oversexed adolescents.

CHAPTER TWO

Elise

My heels *click clacked* across the rink's parking lot. I would be late for practice. Not really the best way to start out, but I'd invent some excuse about having a hard time finding the place. Although the enormous art performance center was kind of hard to miss. But I didn't care if I made a good first impression or not. I just needed to see Scott. There had been so many changes in my life...I needed something solid to land on, and that was Scott.

Literally. Man, he had really beefed up since I last saw him. When he pulled me against his body, it was like hitting a brick wall. A beautifully sculpted brick wall.

Stop. You can't think of him like that.

I'd promised myself I would not renew my teenaged infatuation with my best friend. That would obviously make me more miserable than I already was. I checked around the almost-empty parking lot before opening the door to my rental and sliding behind the wheel. Closing my eyes, I drew in a couple of deep breaths. I'd felt so lost since my breakup with Hunter, and I was beginning to think moving away from my family to the West Coast wasn't the best idea. Nothing made a person any lonelier than moving to a new city. A new state. And taking on a new job. A job I knew I wasn't qualified to fill. But the offer hit at the right time, providing a reprieve from seeing my ex, my first and only boyfriend, with his new girlfriend.

But I wouldn't think of that now. I started the engine, typed Davies Symphony Hall into the GPS, and left the lot. As I drove, I shook my head, wondering over the fact I was even here at all. Two nights ago, I had performed at a gallery in my hometown of Lincoln, Nebraska. Before the day my mom remarried, I had never played for anyone other than Hunter. Not even for my mom. Being semi-coerced by Hunter and my stepfather, Kyle, I decided to put my musical skills on display at the reception. After all was said and done, I was astounded I hadn't one, fainted, or two, gotten sick.

So, riding high on that little victory, I guess, and again with Hunter's pushing, I accepted the invitation a woman from the wedding had extended a few years later and played for a small crowd of strangers in a chic gallery across town. The newly opened studio was featuring up-and-coming musicians and artists. I amazed myself by agreeing to perform, sensing I needed to push myself out of my shell and mature a bit. After my part was concluded, I had tried to slip off unnoticed, but was accosted by two women. The older of the two women, an Ophelia Prentiss, couldn't stop gushing over my playing, while the other, who introduced herself as Claudia Van Hoof, was fairly quiet on the subject. Ms. Van Hoof told me she was the director of the San Francisco Symphony. Eventually she agreed I'd be "perfect" to fill a position in her orchestra suddenly vacated by a woman who had been in a car accident and was hospitalized.

When I protested, explaining I had never played with others, not even in the high school band, the older lady said, "Stuff and nonsense." She argued that I had played with the band at the reception, which I couldn't refute. But it had only been for a few songs, hardly the qualifications for someone who would be part of any symphony, let alone one in a city as big as San Francisco. But the woman simply refused to take no for an answer, and so here I was, far from home and far from equipped for my new job.

When I pulled into the lot of Davies Hall, I almost turned around and headed back to the airport. The hall was part of this massive, beautiful performing arts center whose façade was a tad intimidating, to be sure. Giant windows spanned the front, and inside it was quite breathtaking, with marble floors, carpeted stairs with brass railings, elaborate chandeliers, and amazing views. I followed the directions in the text I'd been sent and found the entrance. I took a deep breath and got a tighter grip on my violin case, my hands being sweaty. I'd survived bullying, being attacked by a gang of girls wielding weapons, and had been brave enough to open up to Hunter and let him see the real me. Of course, that hadn't ended with success... Enough of that. I would not let myself be beaten by it. I had a fresh start, and that fresh start lay behind the doors in front of me.

Here goes nothing.

I pushed in the door and stood frozen in a room as big as a hockey rink, but *far* more refined. I felt dwarfed by the immensity of it all. Plush seats fanned out to my right and to my left, interrupted at intervals by radiating aisles with matching carpet, bathing the whole area in a copper color, accented by creamy walls with a yellow tone to them. These pathways for symphony patrons spoked away from a massive stage made from a light-colored wood, its honeyed tones melding with the upholstery and carpeting to offer an uninterrupted flow of opulence. Numerous lighting fixtures were suspended from a ceiling that seemed to touch the sky, adding to the beauty and elegance of the facilities design, which I could tell focused on the acoustics it provided. Tiers of balconies stretched along the walls with additional seating to the rear of and above the stage. With wonder and appreciation, I scanned the vicinity, soaking everything in.

Then I realized someone was calling my name. I focused in the direction the sound was coming from, and a woman was waving her arms. The stage was like an anthill with busy black shapes scurrying around. So much for sneaking in unnoticed. As I got nearer, I could hear the hum of people talking to one another accented by the occasional note being played on an instrument as someone tuned up.

"Come on. Come on. Don't be shy," the director said as she continued to flag me in like an errant airplane.

I slapped on a smile and hurried toward the stage, being careful to not trip or get thrown by the way the aisles were tilted. I wasn't the most graceful person in the world; some might even go so far as to say I was clumsy. I continued to take in the details of what was to be my new workplace. While the platform they were on was elevated above the audience, it still had a pit-like feel to it as the musicians' seats were in a three-tiered semi-circle, with a small raised area for the conductor in the middle. As I got close, I realized there were no stairs to their level.

Ms. Van Hoof looked down on me with a pleasant expression. "Welcome, Elise." She lifted her arms out to her sides. "I wanted you to get the grandeur of the place right off the bat. After we're finished, you can follow the others to the parking lot the back way, which is how you will normally be entering." She gave me directions so I could join them, and I listened nervously, afraid I'd get lost in the cavernous building, but it was really quite simple. As I finally stepped into the bright stage lights, the director tapped her baton against her metal stand. "Attention, everyone. Please take your seats so we can begin."

I located the string area and waited for everyone to sit so I could determine where I was supposed to be.

A woman with long, black hair leaned forward in her seat, smiled at me, and patted the seat next to her before saying something to the woman on her right.

"Thank you." I took a seat and started to remove my violin from its case.

"Excuse me?" Someone said in an indignant voice.

I looked up. Another dark-haired woman, whose tresses were drawn into a bun, stared down at me with arched eyebrows.

"*I'm* first chair," she spouted regally, her dangling diamond earrings swinging angrily like a pendulum from her lobes.

"Oh, I'm sorry. She just said..." I turned to the lady who'd indicated which seat to take, and she drew back, gaping at me like I was out of my mind. I scrambled to my feet. "Uhh...it was unintentional. I apologize."

The prima violinist only glared at me.

I bowed my head a little, like a servant to her master. "It won't happen again."

I took my case and scooted farther along the line, feeling the heat that was no doubt making my cheeks red, the realization of which caused me further embarrassment. The outraged woman continued to rail behind me.

"Did you see that?"

"How rude," someone replied.

Good job, Elise. It took you less than five minutes to establish yourself as a social pariah. That has to be a new record for you. Way to go.

I had barely taken a seat when the director addressed me. "Elise. Why don't you come here for a second?"

I immediately had flashbacks to my first day at school—after we moved from Bloomington, Illinois, to Lincoln, Nebraska—and the teacher called me to the front of the room, swamping me with an almost paralyzing apprehension. We had changed in the middle of the year because I was being bullied so much I was showing physical signs of it affecting me—I couldn't eat, my hair was falling out, I developed weird sleeping habits... Funny thing was, switching schools didn't help. I seem to have an inner bully-shaped beacon, kind of like the bat signal for Batman, but not in a good way. I considered protesting that there was no need for me to come up front, then I remembered I was trying to be pleasant and fit in. Damn.

I rose from my seat, turning to my violin on it, and scurried to the front. My palms began to sweat again, and a familiar sick feeling rolled in my stomach. One anyone with anxiety would recognize.

"Come on. Come on. Don't be shy," the woman scolded. I stood next to her, and she slid her arm behind me, clasping both of my biceps like she was ready to throw me into a lion's den, which she probably was. "I would like to introduce you all to the newest member of our group, Elise Scofield. She will be taking the place of poor Sophia." I kind of nodded, not looking directly at anyone. "On a recent trip to Lincoln, Nebraska, for a wedding, Ophelia Prentiss and I—you all know Ophelia, of course. Prentiss Steel and Machinery International is one of our biggest patrons—anyhoo, we discovered this rare gem at an art gallery." She smiled at me and something in her expression set off alarm bells. I don't know exactly what it was, but it was like the smile she was giving wasn't reaching her eyes. She narrowed them on me and kind of raised her brows, then released me and stood back. "Elise, why don't you give everyone a demonstration of what you do."

What? "I'm confused. You mean play the violin?" Wasn't that what I was just about to do?

"Yes. Like you did that night for us." She waited a beat. "Oh. You don't have your electric violin, do you?"

I released a breath. She'd provided an excuse for me. "No. Unfortunately, I don't."

"No problem." She grabbed a violin case from her tiny elevated stage next to us. "I happen to have one."

Why did I feel like I was being set up?

She handed it to me. "Go on now." She stepped aside with an odd bow, grinning eerily. "I'll give you room."

Everyone stared at me. There seemed to be no way of getting out of it. I removed the instrument, brought it to my shoulder and chin, and played a note. "This isn't my usual instrument, so..." I let my caveat hang in the air. No one was buying it anyway. Giving my head a faint shake, I inhaled and began playing Evanescence's "My Immortal," which was kind of a go-to of mine. It was the first song I'd played in front of people.

Within a few notes, I found myself relaxing. It's a beautiful piece and it's almost like a lullaby for me as it seems to calm me, which was what I needed at the moment.

"No. No," the director interrupted. "Like you did that night. Really get into it. I want to show people the way you work."

I mentally added, "*you little freak*," to the end of that, which was perhaps not fair. I gave a slight nod and closed my eyes.

Just forget they're there. It's all right. I can do this.

I let the music speak to me and move me. Physically. When I performed, it was half-dancing, half-playing. My actions were small at first, but as per usual, I got lost in the voice of my violin and commenced tramping all around. Drawing the bow across the strings at the very end on this song was so satisfying, in a way I didn't fully understand, but loved.

Ms. Van Hoof clapped. "Isn't that wonderful?" They offered a polite smattering of applause, but for the most part, seemed appalled at my lack of decorum. "Mrs. Prentiss—and I, of course—were quite taken by Elise's performance and, well—" She sighed. "Here we are," she finished without enthusiasm. I was bent over putting the violin back into its case, but I shrugged it off. She continued by telling everyone what we'd be working on, and I slinked away to my seat.

"That was lovely," a girl behind me said as I took my place again.

I twisted my head. "Thank you."

"Uhh, Elise? If we could...just...get started, please?" The director looked at me primly.

"Yes, of course." I hurriedly prepared my violin and bow, finding my sheet music and placing it in the stand in front of me. She had begun without me, and I was left with the awkward task of picking up the tune, which was going at a full gallop. I came in a fraction too late. She brought everything to an abrupt halt.

"Umm...you were late, dear."

I was starting to not like her. "Uhh...yes. I know. I'm sorry."

"No problem," she replied sweetly, and raised her baton to begin the piece again.

I concentrated, determined not to make any more mistakes, and things were going pretty good, until...I fell in love. We were working on the score from the movie *The Prince of Egypt*, as we were playing it while the movie was displayed on a gigantic screen in the background for the audience. I was unreasonably excited by this prospect. I thought it was a cool idea and I couldn't wait to be part of it. It was a very powerful soundtrack, and I was familiar with it but hadn't attempted to play it before. So, it was about a quarter of the way through the song "Let My People Go" when I completely and utterly lost my mind. The genius of the composition, it simply captivated me. Until someone hit an off chord and we stopped. I was secretly happy it wasn't me this time. And on top of that, it was the wench who pointed me to the wrong seat.

"Isabelle, dear? You seem upset."

"I-I can't concentrate with *her* dancing over there," the woman huffed.

My mouth dropped open. I was a half-dozen seats from her.

Ms. Van Hoof looked at the woman, her lips lifting slightly, and cleared her throat. "Elise...I know when you do your little shows, you're used to being very...expressive. And that is great. But it doesn't belong in a symphony orchestra."

I blinked. *Then why did you hire me? You saw me perform. You knew how I play.*

"You need to...tone it down a bit. Do you think you can do that?" Her tone dripped with condescension.

I found my voice. "Of course. I apologize. I must have gotten caught up in the music." I chanced a smile and a small shrug of my shoulders, glancing along the row, hoping to find at least one sympathetic face. But all I saw was horror and disdain.

"Indeed," spouted the woman whose seat I accidentally took. She looked away from me as if it had been lowering herself, and painful, to cast her gaze my way in the first place. Like I was less than a bug squashed underneath her Jimmy Choo's.

Tears threatened, but I refused to let anyone see them. "I'll make sure it doesn't happen again." I would sit in my seat like I'd been hit by a stun gun if I had to, the only things moving would be my eyes across the sheet music, and my bow across the strings, in an orderly, repressed fashion.

But within five minutes the director sighed at the end of a song, setting her baton on her stand. "I think that's enough for today." She rubbed her temples dramatically. "I have a headache. Don't forget tomorrow's practice won't be here. We'll be at the Jerry Garcia Amphitheater while they are working on our stage mechanics and sealing the floor." She stared directly at me. "Nine o'clock sharp."

Got it, Broomhilda. Geesh. I was developing a headache myself.

I collected my stuff and people skirted my area, no one addressing me until I turned to leave. The girl behind me gave me a shy smile. "Hi. My name's Carrie. Carrie Fisher. But not, like, *the* Carrie Fisher. Because she's dead and..."

She trailed off. One corner of my lips lifted. "And you're not."

She laughed. "Yes, exactly." Her gaze darted around, and she leaned in. "I saw Isabelle tell you to sit in that seat." She peeked in the prima donna's direction with a frown. "She's a bitch. Don't worry about her." Gesturing in a vague way, she added, "Most of the people here are...well, they're not mean like Isabelle."

I surveyed her more closely. She wore glasses which sat on her nose loosely, like they were ready to take a leap and escape at any moment. She had on no makeup to speak of and straight hair without any clear style, although there wasn't much to mine either. Still, she was pretty in some undefined and totally downplayed way. I smiled and hefted my case. "Good to know."

Her hand floated to the side. "I can show you the way out, if you'd like?"

"Oh, yeah. That would be great."

"Oh, Carrie?" Ms. Van Hoof called.

She startled. "Uhh...yes?"

"Could you please come here for a moment?"

"Uhh..." She glanced at me.

"I can follow people. You go on."

"Okay." She went to move past me, and I touched her arm.

"Thanks, by the way."

Her face brightened. "No problem. See you tomorrow at the amphitheater. Do you know how to get there?"

"Carrie," the director demanded.

"I'll find it."

"Okay." She headed toward center stage, and I watched. The director wasn't looking at her at all; she was staring at me with an irritated air.

I swung around and walked away.

What the hell have I gotten myself into?

CHAPTER THREE

Scott

I strolled down the hall, tugging on the cuffs of my favorite shirt, an expensive blue button-up, whistling. Elise was due any minute and that had me in such a good mood even Sergei wouldn't be able to get on my nerves. I entered the kitchen, where he was hunched over the long island in the middle of the room, chowing on a burger.

"Well, well. Don't you look dapper. Going out?"

I nodded, unable to keep the smile from my face. "Taking Elise to dinner."

His eyebrows lifted. "Oh."

I spun to get a bottle of water from the fridge. I lived in a large condo with an open floorplan. I could see the front door from where I stood, so I would know when Elise arrived. I wanted to give her a tour of my place and, yes, show off a little. To my right, across the wide living room, the exposed brick of the walls gave way to glass, where a long balcony offered some killer panoramas of the city. Above the fireplace, two hockey sticks were crisscrossed, and under them, on the mantle, was my Conn Smythe trophy. Well, not *the* Conn Smythe, I didn't get to keep that. It was a replica that I still needed to get a display case for. Maybe Elise could help me pick one.

Sergei spoke with food in his mouth. He was such a pig. "So where are you guys going?"

I puffed out my chest. "Delicieuse Danse."

He frowned. "What the hell does that mean?"

"I haven't a clue." *But I hope it means Elise is impressed.*

"Oh." He looked me over. "Nice place, is it?"

"Four hundred dollars a person nice."

He about choked on his burger.

I laughed. The doorbell rang. I put my hands on the island, arms wide, leaning toward him. "My date has arrived."

"Date? I thought it was your sister?"

I smiled smugly. "Date with my sister." But as I went to pass him, I was hit by a stream of yellow. I stared at my mustard-covered shirt. "What the fuck, dude?"

"It was an accident."

"Yeah, right." I grabbed a napkin but hurried to the door as I wiped at it. I didn't want to keep Elise waiting.

When I opened the door, I was focused on my shirt. But when I raised my head and saw her, I froze. She had on this little slip of a black dress, and that's exactly what it resembled, an undergarment or piece of lingerie, very simple. Not in a slutty way, in a classy way. Her hair was curled—the only time I'd seen that was at her mom's wedding—and she was wearing...makeup. Her face was so fresh and beautiful, her eyes dancing in the hall light. I stood like an idiot with my mouth hanging open.

She shifted her gaze from my moronic expression to my shirt. "Oh. Were you in some sort of accident involving Big Bird? Or a giant hot dog?"

So Elise. I grinned at her, leaning in with my hand above me, gripping the door. "Hamburger, actually." I licked my lips, which were suddenly dry. "You look..." *Amazing. Incredible. Sexy as hell. Phenomenal. Good enough to freaking eat.* "...nice. Very nice."

She glanced at her dress. "Oh, thanks." She said it casually. Like a sister would say to a brother. I berated myself.

What the hell? This is Elise I'm thinking of here. Talk about inappropriate. I'm merely surprised to see her...all dolled up. I haven't seen that in a long time. And I've never seen her looking so hot. Shit. There I go again.

She tried to peek around my body. "Uhh...your place seems nice."

"Oh, shit. Come in." I stood back to let her enter. "I'm just...I need to change my shirt really quick. I'm sorry."

"Oh, no. That's fine. Go and change."

Sergei came out of the kitchen and gawked at Elise the way I must have gawked at her. "Hi." He was adopting his fake Russian accent like he always did when hitting on women. The guy was from New York, for God's sake. He was about as Russian as those Made-in-China nesting dolls.

I waved in his direction. "This is my roommate, Sergei. Sergei, this is Elise," I said proudly.

"Hi," she said with a smile, reaching to shake his hand.

He took her hand, turned it, and brought it to his lips to kiss it. "Very nice to have met you."

I smirked. *Yeah, lay it on thick, Sergei. That'll make it even easier for her to see you as the creep you are.*

Elise giggled. "Oh, wow. Very charming." She looked at me and raised her brows. I took it as a polite rolling of her eyes.

"I'll be back in a second."

"Take your time," Sergei said. "I will entertain your friend."

I did roll my eyes. "Great. You do that." I laughed as I walked along the hall, but when I glanced behind, I'm pretty sure they had both stepped closer to each other.

Huh... Well, she'll be wise to him in a few minutes. Still... I quickened my pace, ripping my shirt off and throwing it on the bed before drawing another from my closet. I put it on, checking my hair in the mirror while buttoning it up. I peeked over my shoulder.

If Sergei ruined my shirt, I'll kick his ass. That's a four-hundred-dollar shirt.

I smoothed my hair one more time and hustled out of the room. To my surprise, Sergei and Elise were no longer in the living room, and, upon investigation, not in the kitchen either.

Did he take her down to the game room?

I was on my way there when a flutter of her dress caught my attention. They were on the balcony, both leaning on the railing. Elise was turned toward him, her face bright, the setting sun bathing it in a rosy glow. She was saying something and laughing. The air left me like the hit at the beginning of the year that had given me three broken ribs. They still gave me problems.

What the hell does she have to talk to him about? It was me carrying her home in seventh grade when she had that colossal wipeout and broke her leg. Six blocks. Sergei wasn't there for that. He didn't know she could work magic with a violin. He didn't know her at all.

The breeze was blowing her hair and a strand got caught in her lashes. She tried to shake it loose, but it was stuck. Like it was in slow motion, I watched Sergei reach over and disengage the tendril and push it back. Elise lowered her gaze, then tucked her hair behind her ear herself, before lifting her head to peer at him again. It didn't take a lip reader to see she thanked him. I'd seen her with that expression before. With Hunter. An involuntary growl escaped from my throat.

That's a long-assed balcony, and the two of them are practically cuddling in the corner. Their arms have to be touching.

"Shit." I grabbed my jacket from the top of the couch and rushed across the room, tearing the door open. They both spun around as if guilty of something.

Elise covered her heart with her hand. "Geez! You scared me."

I glared at Sergei and held the door for Elise. "Are you ready?"

"Sure," she said uncertainly, glancing from me to Sergei and back.

I let her pass me in the doorway, stepping onto the balcony for a second. I glowered at him, lowering my voice. "We're talking later."

Sergei grinned, lacing his fingers and leaning on his arm on the railing, his legs stretched in front of him and crossed cockily. "Sure thing, comrade." I wanted to check his ass off the balcony.

Elise tugged on my elbow. "Come on, Scott."

I gave him one last disgusted scowl, then followed her.

She didn't say anything until the door of the condo shut behind us. "What's going on between you two?"

I didn't look at her, my jaw tense. I hunted for an answer, stabbing at the elevator button at the same time. Impatient, I jerked my suit coat on. "I could ask you the same thing."

"What? What do you mean?"

My gaze flicked away. "Never mind. Forget it." The elevator opened and we got on.

"No. No. You put it out there, so let's talk about it."

I knew by her tone what she meant was let's fight about it. She would take shit from anyone else, but me she had to fight with. I exhaled and closed my eyes, then opened them and stared into her ticked off little face. I ran my hands along her arms. "I don't want to fight over this. This is the first time we've seen each other in...forever. Let's not let Sergei ruin our night."

She shifted her jaw, debating, but she couldn't let go of it. "How is Sergei ruining our night?"

I glanced to the side and back. "Listen. I just don't want to see you get involved with someone so soon after your relationship with Hunter ended, okay? You need time to clear your head."

She dropped her gaze, blinking rapidly. "I know that. You think I don't know that?"

Her arms slackened and I felt the fight leave her. This was not the Elise I knew, and that bothered me. A lot. Hunter broke her damn heart, and I wanted to break him into little pieces. She surprised me by slipping her arms around me and laying her cheek on my chest. "I'm sorry, Scott. I've had a bad day, but I shouldn't take it out on you. I mean, you're being nice and taking me to dinner and I—"

Shit! She's going to cry. Elise Scofield is about to fall apart on me. "Elise?"

She sniffed. "What?"

"Hey," I said softly, getting her to look up at me. I brushed the hair from her face, an image of Sergei touching it flitted through my mind, but I checked it aside. I searched her eyes.

"What's wrong, honey? What happened today?" *What happened to you? The tough-as-nails broad who punched the neighbor kid when he was being mean to Tabitha?* Tabitha was my little sister.

As I stared at her, I realized the girl I'd left in Lincoln had become a woman. A stunning woman. Who I wanted to kiss. Badly. But it wasn't necessarily because I was attracted to her. It was because I remember what it felt like. I saw us rolling in her twin bed, while my family and hers were downstairs. I hadn't been with a woman since...the night she'd called and told me Hunter broke up with her. Why was that exactly? My thinking seemed a bit fuzzy. And although I knew I shouldn't, I found myself lowering my head to kiss her.

She jerked away from me. "Let's— let's talk about this at dinner." Her voice was trembling. I had upset her more.

I sighed. "Elise. I'm sorry. I—"

"There's nothing to be sorry for," she said hurriedly, but her tell said differently. I always knew when I'd hurt or angered her because she folded one arm across her chest, and held the other, occasionally drummed her fingers against it. "We've both just had a bad day, is all. We'll feel better after we get something to eat. I'm starving."

Another tell. She always ate when she was stressed. She said she was lucky her metabolism was fired by her constant anxiety and Type-A tendencies, and it never showed on her or, according to her, she'd weigh a thousand pounds. The door opened and she practically flew through them. I needed to watch it around her. She was fragile, and I didn't want to send her any mixed messages.

I followed her, and we crossed the lobby to the glass doors leading to the street. Once outside, the doorman tipped his hat to her. "Ms. Scofield."

"Hi, Jimmy," she said with a steady voice, seeming to have pulled it together for the moment. She took in the car at the curb. "Ooh. Look, Scottie, someone in your building got a limo. Who do you think that would be?"

My lips twitched as I struggled to hide my amusement. I addressed the driver, who was standing next to the door with his spine straight, weight balanced over both feet, holding his opposite wrist in front of him. "Sorry we're a little late, Ben. I had to change my shirt."

He opened the door. "No problem, sir. No one complained about me being parked here."

Elise eyed him, then me. "This is ours?"

"Well, for the night it is."

Ben held his gloved hand out to help her in.

A wicked grin spread across her face. "Nice touch, McCord."

She got in and I went to tip Jimmy. "Very nice young lady, sir," he said quietly.

I beamed, my earlier excitement stirring in me again. "Yes. Yes, she is." I gave him the bill.

"Your sister, you say?" He tilted his head, squinting at me.

"That's right. Why do you ask?"

"Oh, no reason. I was just getting a different vibe."

"Purely platonic," I reassured him, my smile wavering a bit.

"Mmm, too bad. She's a looker." He elbowed me lightly.

"Yeah. I guess so."

He laughed loudly. "You guys have a good night."

I returned to the car and climbed in the back, but by now I was frowning.

I know some people consider me a playboy, but is it really so hard to believe I could spend a night on the town with a beautiful woman and have it not be about sex?

Elise grinned at me when I climbed in beside her. "This is pretty awesome."

I tried to downplay it. "Yeah, it's pretty nice." Coach always said, *You need to act like you've been there before.* In other words, make them believe you are unimpressed when visiting a strong opposing team. It applied here as well. I wanted her to think it was no big deal, and for me, it really wasn't. I took limos a lot. Driving in San Fran could be a pain in the ass, and parking spots were scarce. I found the champagne I'd asked him to bring. "Would you like a glass?"

"Hell, yeah."

I started to feel better. *This* was my Elise. I popped the cork and it fizzed all over. "Oh, shit."

She covered her mouth, her eyes sparkling in the streetlight.

I laughed at myself too, shaking the bubbly off my hands.

"Careful. We don't want a reenactment of the mustard incident." Her gaze followed me as I returned, passing her a flute before I sat next to her. Without thinking, I stretched my arm across her shoulders, then realized it was somewhat inappropriate and waited for an opportunity to remove it politely.

"So, you want to tell me about your day now?

She gave me a strained smile. "Not really."

Tread lightly.

"Okay. Let's see, then..."

I pointed out some sights along the way and described some of the wild rides some of the Fire players had taken in limos, especially last year when we won the cup.

I sighed. "Man, I was the golden child then."

She scrunched her brow. "What do you mean?"

"Well...my first year, they worshiped me. Hot new prospect and all that... And I was on fire that year. Last season, we won the playoffs, and I was awarded the Conn Smythe award. I could do no wrong. This year...different story. I had the flu in February, and it took me a while to fully recover. I was really dragging ass for a long time. Then, just when I was getting my wind back, Paul Frazer gave me that dirty hit that messed up my knee pretty good. I never had to miss a game, but...I haven't quite returned to top form yet. And some fans don't give you a break. In their eyes, there's no reason you can't play better when you're making the kind of money I do. And I agree."

She gave my arm a squeeze. "But that's not fair. You're human too. I'm sure they have days when they're not a hundred percent. Why do they expect more from you?" She was cute when she was irate.

I shrugged. "That's part of the game. You've got to take the good with the bad."

"But...doesn't the criticism hurt sometimes?"

"Nah," I said at first, but I amended myself. "I mean, yeah, sometimes it doesn't feel real good to have people call you a 'flash in the pan,' a loser, or worse." I frowned. "But you deal with it. Like I said, it's part of the game."

"Part of the game, huh?" She sat back in her seat, mulling over that.

Ben slowed and pulled alongside the curb. I glanced through the window. "Oh, we're here." I put my hand on the door.

"Uh-uh-uh," Ben scolded. "*My* job." He hopped out and came around to open our door.

"He gets touchy if I try to open the door for myself. It's like I'm threatening his job security or something." I exited and twisted to help her, appreciating her legs as she got to her feet. "Right, Ben? You don't like it when I open the door."

He smiled. "No, sir."

"And he won't call me Scott either. No matter how many times I tell him to." I looked at her. "So I started to call him sir," I turned back to him. "And he didn't like that either, did you?"

His lips quirked. "No, sir."

I chuckled. "There's no winning with this guy. He's almost as stubborn as you are." I lifted my elbow for her, and she linked her arm with mine and laid her head on my biceps for a second. "I'll text you in a couple of hours," I told Ben.

"I'll be ready."

I led her to the door, proud to have her by my side.

"A couple of hours? Do you really think it'll take that long?"

"At least. You are in for an experience." I opened the door for her. "This is one of those places where they serve you several courses and—"

"Mr. McCord. Welcome back. We have your table ready, sir. Right this way." We followed the maître de, Tony, as he weaved through the restaurant toward the table I requested.

"Hey, you're Scottie McCord," a guy said as we passed him.

I nodded without stopping. "Hi, how are you doing?"

"Go Mavericks."

I paused. "You go to school in Omaha?"

He stood. "No, but my sister did." I recognized him now. It was Nathan Houston. And if I was correct, the woman across the table from him—whose gaze was currently on my ass—was his costar from his latest film, who he was rumored to be having an affair with. It never failed to amaze me how brazen people could be with their cheating. It wouldn't have surprised me at all if his wife, who was a star in her own right, wasn't here in this same restaurant with someone from her set. That wasn't a marriage in my eyes, but I tried not to judge. "I caught a couple of your games before they brought you up to the big leagues. You're quite the player." He openly checked out Elise, making his double-entendre clear, and I reflexively covered her hand on my arm with my own and gave him an over-my-dead-body glare.

"If you'll excuse us," Tony interrupted. "Mr. McCord has a table waiting."

"Oh, yes, of course. Nice to meet you."

We moved away and Elise leaned in and whispered, "Was that—"

"Nathan Houston, yes. Interested?" I said tightly. "Because he sure was interested in you."

She gasped. "Nathan Houston?" She glanced back. "No way. I mean, he's hot and all that, but he's always impressed me as somewhat of a creeper."

Good answer.

When we got to the table, Tony knew me well enough to not pull out Elise's chair and allowed me to do it. Then the waiter arrived and introduced himself and asked what we'd like to drink.

I looked to Elise. "Would you like to continue with champagne or switch to wine, or...?"

"I'm honestly not much of a drinker...but the champagne we had on the way was good..."

"They don't have the same brand here, but what I asked for them to chill for us should be similar. Would you like to try it?"

She tucked her hair behind her ear and her cheeks seemed to redden for some reason. "Umm...that would be nice. Thank you."

The waiter peered at me. "If you could bring the bottle of wine I told Tony about..." He nodded. "And maybe bring an extra glass in case the lady decides to try some."

He left and Elise searched me. "Who are you?"

I blinked. "What?"

"This isn't the little boy from Nebraska I used to know."

"Well, I have grown," I said defensively. "Is there something I'm doing you don't like?"

"No. No." She reached across the table to take my hand, nearly upsetting her water. "No, Scottie." She stared at the table and her voice softened. "I...I didn't expect you to be so thoughtful. I mean, you called ahead to make sure champagne was ready, just in case I wanted that?"

I leaned closer. "Yes. I wanted tonight to be special for you."

Her lip trembled. "That's so—" Her eyes filled with tears. "I'm sorry. Do you know where the restroom is?"

"Elise, what's—?"

She jumped up. "Never mind. I'll find it."

She rushed off and I sat for a moment staring at the table. Then I realized she'd gone in the wrong direction. I put my napkin on the table and rose to follow her. I almost passed the hall she had ducked into. It must have led to the kitchen or a private room. She was pacing like mad, one fist on her chest, one covering her mouth. My stomach dropped. I couldn't stand to see her like this. When she saw me, she froze. She blinked rapidly but couldn't keep a tear from slipping out. She brushed it away quickly then acted like it hadn't happened. "Oh. Umm...I took a wrong turn I guess." She tried to slip past me, but I grabbed her arms.

"Elise. What's troubling you?"

She dropped her gaze to try to hide her tears. "I-I-I— It must be the champagne, or hormones, or...everything, moving here, starting a new job..."

I pinched her chin lightly and raised it. "It's all right, honey. I'm here. I won't let anything hurt you." I had no idea what I was saying, because I had no idea what to say. Words just came tumbling from my mouth. Stupid words, but words meant to comfort. Then, surprising us both, I kissed her. It wasn't the kiss of a lover or a friend. More than a peck, but way less than what I wanted to do. It was simply reflex. I wasn't thinking clearly. I lowered my forehead to hers, leaving my hands behind her neck and closing my eyes. "It's all right, Elise. I've got you." What the hell was I saying?

"Okay," she squeaked. I lifted my head and she kept nodding. "Okay. Okay. I'm fine now. I'm sorry."

"No, don't say that. You have nothing to be sorry for."

Simultaneously, a waiter with a tray of empty dishes at the opening of the hall and a waiter with a tray loaded with food deeper in the hall appeared. They both had the same reaction when they saw us; they reversed direction, ducking out of sight.

"Umm...I think we need to vacate this hall. Do you want to go home?"

"No. No." She inhaled and exhaled deliberately. "I'm fine."

I looked at her doubtfully.

"Really, I'm fine. Let's just go and enjoy our dinner."

I took another second to weigh my options. "Okay. You're sure?"

"I'm sure."

She gave me the fakest smile ever, but what could I do? I led her along the hall. The waiter had held up right beyond the doorway. "Sorry," I told him.

He nodded rapidly, not making full eye contact and appearing uncomfortable. Our waiter was at the table, staring at our spots like he expected us to materialize out of thin air. He had an ice bucket with the champagne. I hurried my strides. "Sorry." I held Elise's chair for her again. "We're back."

"Ahh, yes. I have your champagne, madam."

"Thank you," Elise responded in a much calmer voice than earlier.

He filled her glass and twisted to return the bottle to the ice before pouring my wine. Elise took a long drink, downing three quarters of her flute all at once. The waiter offered me a taste and stepped aside while I sampled it. Glancing at Elise and seeing the level of her champagne, he blinked once, then politely filled her flute again without saying anything.

"It's good. Thank you." He poured the rest of my glass, checked Elise's flute, then left.

Elise leaned forward right away. "Scottie, I'm sorry. You've gone out of your way to make everything nice, and I'm ruining everything."

I took her hand. "Stop apologizing. You're not ruining anything."

"Okay, if you say so." She gave me a squeeze, then let it go, taking another large drink. "Now...I really do want to go to the restroom. Can you point me in the right direction?"

I creased my brow, studying her. "Are you sure you're all right?"

She smiled, seeming much more put together. "I'm fine. I need to freshen my makeup."

"Well, it looks great, but..." I spun. "Go that way and—see where the light is on the left?" She nodded. "Turn there. Or I could escort you...?"

"No. I'm good. Thanks. I'll only be gone a second."

I exhaled and sat back, extending my legs under the table and trying to process what had happened during the course of the evening.

My best friend fell apart for no apparent reason...then I kissed her, and we both acted like that was nothing unusual. Just another night.

I took a big gulp of my wine, then huffed out a breath, shaking my head.

Why did I kiss her like that? I checked the other patrons. *Solely because I wanted to stop her crying. That's all. Perfectly natural thing to do.* I took another drink. *So, why does my blood pressure rise any time a guy makes some comment about her or even so much as glances in her direction?* I drummed my fingers on the table. *Merely a big brother protecting his little sister. Although...we're actually the same age. A brother protecting his sister then. That's it. No big deal.* I was so absorbed in my thoughts, she seemed to reappear far too fast, like it should have taken her more time to walk down and return, let alone mess with her makeup. I scrambled to my feet, but she was seated before I could help her with it. As she draped her napkin in her lap, she noticed someone had brought us bread and butter along the way.

"Whoa. You know you're in a fancy place when even the butter has flowers on it."

I laughed. "You mean to say you don't decorate your butter at home?"

"Only on special occasions."

The waiter arrived with what looked like a tree stump with flowers growing from it and placed it between us.

"Enjoy." He disappeared again.

Elise's eyes were big when she peered over at me. "We're supposed to eat this?"

"Yes. Almost everything they bring is edible, including what appears to be the serving ware."

She removed a piece of paper stuck in the middle and read from it. "What's this?"

"I believe it's your menu. They make it into a poem."

She raised her brows then refocused on the writing before her. She set it aside carefully, folded her hands on the table, and stared at me. "I still have no idea what we're eating."

"I never do either, but it's always good."

She examined it again. "How do you know what is edible and what isn't? What if I bite into something and it's ceramic?"

I remembered being overwhelmed my first time too. I could tell she was playing with me, though. "I'll go first, you big chicken."

"Me? It wasn't me who about jumped out of their skin the day we were hiking and the snake was on the trail."

"It was a *big* snake," I said, defending my manhood.

She laughed. "It was not. It was a baby garter snake. It couldn't have been any longer than six inches."

I plucked a "flower" from our dish. "Bull. It was a python. A bull python, in fact."

She snorted. "It's *ball* python, you idiot."

Oops. "Oh." I suppressed a grin. "And I was only like five years old."

"Liar. We didn't meet until we were ten."

"Oh, yeah." I frowned, trying to come up with some other excuse, and popping the flower-thing into my mouth. I made a face. "Ooh. This isn't edible."

She bit. "Really? Spit it out then. Don't eat it."

I swallowed and pretended to choke.

She almost flew across the table. "Scottie?"

I laughed. "Kidding."

"Oh." She fell into her chair, crossing her arms. "I hate you. Scaring me like that."

"Nuh-uh." I leaned forward with a smirk. "No, you don't. You're crazy about me."

She smiled. "Whatever." Her gaze bounced around. "We need to stop."

I looked too. Apparently my fake choking had drawn some attention.

"We're supposed to be acting like adults. A little easier for me than you."

I held in a chuckle as we stared at each other. An unspoken dare was on the table. It was like I could hear her saying, *Come on. Bring it.* "I always act like an adult."

She rolled her eyes. Then seemed to be focused on something behind me. She angled inward, timing her statement with the arrival of the waiter so I couldn't respond. "Says the man who *plays a game* for a living." She sat back, biting her bottom lip, glowing, no doubt feeling victorious. I'd let her have this one. Evidently she needed it.

I loved watching her every time they brought something new. We had smoking dishes, and others suspended from wires, and our dessert was shaped like a snowman. At one point I guess I kind of got lost, mesmerized by the way the candles lit her face.

"Scott?"

I stirred. "Huh?"

"I asked if you want any more. Are you in a food coma?"

"Yes. I guess. Do you want another drink?" We'd been finished for some time.

"No, I'm at my acting-like-an-adult limit. I just want to go home and get out of this dress."

Really, Elise? You're killing me here.

I signaled for the check and texted our driver. When I was signing the bill, she glanced over and gasped sharply.

"Scottie, did I see four numbers on there?"

"Yeah. So?"

"Scottie!" She was totally floored. "You shouldn't have done that."

I stood. "What are you talking about? Come on. Let's go." I pulled her chair away from the table, and she stood.

"But that's like, my grocery bill for two months."

I put my hand on the small of her back and bent in to speak into her ear. "Don't start an argument. Let me do this for you."

She pressed her lips together and hesitated. "Thank you."

I squeezed her shoulders. "You're welcome."

When we stepped out on the sidewalk, a stiff breeze was blowing in off the water. She shivered. "I should have brought a wrap or something."

"Yeah, it can get pretty cold here at night." I rubbed her arms to try to get some heat going. When we climbed in the limo, I asked her if she wanted any more champagne. Ben had a fresh bottle in the bucket.

She moaned. "No. No more champagne. I think I've had too much as it is." She lay against the seat and closed her eyes.

I chuckled and sat beside her. As if it was the most natural thing in the world, I put my arm around her, and she snuggled into my side. "Why, Miss Elise Scofield, are you buzzed?"

"I am."

I kissed her hair above her temple. "Did you enjoy it?"

"Are you kidding? It was awesome. I just wish I could have finished that snowman. It was amazing."

"It all was."

She opened her eyes and lifted her head. "But Scottie...you know you don't have to impress me, don't you?" She put a hand on my cheek. "I already think you're the bomb."

I grinned down at her. "Is that you speaking, or the champagne?"

She smiled loosely. "Both of us."

"Ahh. I see."

"No, I'm kidding. It's me speaking." She patted my knee. "And besides, it's hard to impress a girl who's seen you wipe out on your bike, scab your knee, and cry like a baby."

I rolled my eyes. "Here we go again."

"And I was present when you actually told the teacher the dog ate your homework and—"

"That one's not so bad."

"*And* the teacher was your *neighbor* and knew you didn't own a dog. Have, in fact, never owned a dog."

I laughed. "Okay. You can stop now."

"Not to mention that historic moment when I was privileged to witness the hot dog incident."

I paused with my lips puckered, ready with a comeback, but I was curious, despite myself. "Hot dog incident? What the hell are you talking about?"

She sat more square to me. "You ate a Play-Doh hot dog, Scott. How can you not remember eating a Play-Doh hot dog?"

"No, I remember." I patted my stomach. "I think I'm still digesting it. But Zack dared me."

"Well, then, it made all the sense in the world for you to chow down on what was essentially modeling clay."

I sat straighter. "*You* forget I witnessed you trying to blow a bubble and spitting your gum into Mr. McAfee's hair."

"But you were my teacher. You were the one who taught me how to blow a bubble. Did you forget that too?"

I was suddenly awash in memories.

No, I remember it all, Elise. The way your lips feel. The first time I watched you play violin and was totally captivated by you. The millions of times when you were the only one in my corner, the only one who understood me...

"Scott?"

I resurfaced. "What?"

"What? You can't think of anything more than the incident where I had to suffer because of your lack of teaching ability?"

I stuck my finger in her chest. "You are not telling anyone on the team about this."

She closed her eyes and sank into the seat cushions again. "I don't know...that may require some hush money."

"Hush money? I just dropped a grand on you."

"I know. And that's crazy." She straightened, finding a burst of energy. "That's insane, Scott."

"Come on," I wheedled. "Please don't tell the guys. I'll never hear the end of it." I could hear them now.

"Fine, I won't tell the guys." She squeezed my face. "I'll keep all of your horrible little secrets." She slapped my cheek and released me.

I pretended to be injured, moving my jaw around and rubbing it gingerly.

"Stop, I didn't hurt you."

I took her hand and brought it to my lips to kiss it. "Thank you."

"You're welcome."

I checked out the window to see how near we were to Elise's. She didn't live far from me, so she'd walked over during the day—although I don't know how in those heels of hers—but it was too dangerous for her to walk home alone at night.

"Scott?" I turned back to her. "I've been thinking about something you said earlier."

My lips lifted. "When did you do that? It seems like we've been talking all night."

"When I went to the bathroom," she said matter-of-factly.

"Was it something in particular...?"

She slapped my leg. "I'm getting to that."

"Ouch! I think you've inherited Kyle's leaning toward violence." It was a running joke that her stepfather, who had been an NHL referee, was "prone to violence."

"No, that would be you. Ha. I just thought of something. I am a violinist, and you are a *violentist*. See what I did there? Because of all the fights you get in."

"Yeah, I see, you little goofball." I stroked her hair. "And I don't get in that many fights."

"Eight last year."

"Really? Eight? Wait. How do you know that?" She was keeping track of me?

"Anyway," she bulldozed right through that. "You said taking criticism was part of the game."

"Ah-huh," I said slowly. "Did someone criticize you?"

"Not exactly." She stared off for a moment. "This is what happened." I realized we'd come to a stop, and we were probably in front of Elise's building. I caught Ben's eye in the mirror and made a circular motion without her seeing it and he nodded. "I got to practice. I was waiting for everyone to sit so I knew which seat was mine."

"Sounds like a good plan." I glanced through the window. Ben had pulled back into traffic and was circling the block to give us more time.

"Then this woman smiled at me and patted the seat next to her as if indicating that was my seat, so I thanked her and sat."

"But it wasn't your seat."

"No. It was the first violinist's chair, and she wasn't happy at all I was sitting in it."

"Well...that doesn't seem like too big a deal."

"Yeah, but...the director was all over me. Pointing out every mistake I made."

"Could it be she was just trying to help you to improve? I mean, Coach is all over my ass sometimes when he thinks I can do a better job."

"Maybe..." she said doubtfully. "But...I kept getting the sense that...I don't know. Something wasn't right. They seemed to be making fun of how I played."

I bristled. "Why? What's wrong with the way you play?"

"Well, it's not really up to their standards." She looked me in the face. "To tell you the truth, Scott...I'm not qualified for this job."

"Don't say that."

"No, really. Why would they hire some girl from the backwoods to come and play in a symphony the size of this one?"

"First of all, Lincoln is not the backwoods. And second of all, because you're extremely talented."

"Well, you're a bit biased, don't you think?"

"No. I'm serious, Elise. I've never seen anyone...give life to music the way you do."

She became teary again. "That's the sweetest thing you've ever said. Oh, wait." She was peering out the window. "That's my building."

"I'm sorry, what was that, miss?"

"Uhh...we passed my building, but you can just pull over anywhere."

"Oh, no. Wouldn't be doing my job. I'll circle around and we'll catch it again."

His eyes twinkled in the mirror. He was getting a big-assed tip. He bought me more time, but only a little. "Listen, Elise, I need a favor."

"Yes. Whatever it is I'll do it. I owe you for that expensive dinner."

I frowned. "Okay, one, you don't owe me anything. Two, you don't even know what I'm even asking you."

She gasped. "Are you asking me to off someone?" She paused with a finger on her chin. "I don't care. I'll do it."

"Well, nice to know you'd do time for me, but I don't think this'll be that hard. I mean, I guess it could be..."

"Ooh. Now I'm getting a tad nervous."

"There's this thing. It's a fundraiser we do with the fire department every year. You know, the "Fire and Ice" fundraisers. One part of the weekend is a game where we split fire fighters and Fire players up into two teams and pit them against each other. The other, equally grueling and perhaps demeaning is..." I grimaced. "One of those auction deals where you purchase an evening with a player."

"Oh." It was clear she wasn't expecting that.

"And here's the problem with that... Sometimes women feel—even though they make it clear the players are not expected to—sometimes women feel they deserve more than just a meal for their money. If you get what I mean."

She made a face. "Eww."

"Yeah. Eww is right. I'm not saying I would ever let someone influence me to do anything I wasn't down for, but it can be awkward."

"Okay, where do I come into play?"

"Well..." I hesitated. Should I really ask her to do this? "I need a shill. Someone to come in and outbid all other comers so I can escape from this 'date' with someone who may be...less than desirable."

"Oh. I see." She wasn't hopping on board.

"I will give you the money to cover it. I just need you to bid."

"I can do that. What's the attire?"

"Black tie and...it's Friday."

"Like...the day after tomorrow Friday?"

"Yeah, but you don't have to get anything new. You could wear this."

She wrinkled her nose. "What I have on now?"

"Or, if you'd like to get something new, I'd be happy to reimburse you for it. Shoes, jewelry, whatever you want."

She rubbed her palms together. "Ooh, you're very trusting."

I grinned. "No, I know you. You won't take advantage of me, even if I were okay with that."

"Yeah," she sighed, "those damn scruples of mine are always getting in the way of me having a good time."

Ben glided to a stop. He wouldn't be able to circle the block again without her getting suspicious.

"Oh, here we are," she chirped.

I reached for the door handle.

"Uh-uh-uh." Ben shook his finger.

I rolled my eyes and he laughed, then exited the vehicle and came over to open the door for us.

We stepped out and Elise took my hands, stretching to give me a kiss on the cheek. "Thank you so much for everything. It was a really nice—"

I put my arm around her and began to lead her down the sidewalk, but she drew up short.

"What are you doing?"

I blinked. "Walking you to the door."

"That's not necessary."

"Uhh...yeah, it is. It's dark. You're alone..." The neighborhood, while not exactly sketchy, still concerned me, but I didn't want to make her nervous. Her building was a historical one, set back a distance from the curb with a wide patch of green space on either side of the path leading to the door.

She scanned the area. "It's not like you'll be here every time, Scottie."

Yeah. And the idea doesn't thrill me.

"I know, but I'm here now. And besides, I'd like to. It'll give us a little more time together."

"Okay." She was quiet. Did she not want me to come along with her?

When we got to the door, I was glad to see her produce a keycard. At least there was some level of security, and the stoop was well-lit. But the place itself was kind of run-down.

How much does a violinist make? Is this all she can afford? Although real estate in San Francisco does come at a premium...

"Thanks again for everything."

"I'd like to see you all the way in, if you don't mind."

"Oh, well, I mean...sure." She opened the door, then took a peek at the street. "What about Ben?"

I reached above her to hold the door open. "He'll wait."

When we got in the elevator, I began to recognize a shift in her behavior. She put a lot of distance between us and took that stance, one arm over chest, holding the opposite arm, and tapping. She focused on the numbers above the door.

I cleared my throat. "So...what are you doing tomorrow?"

"Umm...tomorrow?" It was like I'd interrupted her mentally hurrying the elevator up the shaft. "I've got practice."

"And after that?"

"I'm not sure. Why?"

I rolled a shoulder. "'Cause I thought it might be fun to take you down to the rink and...I don't know. Show you a few things."

She got a huge smile on her face, finally looking at me fully. "I'd like that."

I exhaled. "Good. I'll have to ask the trainer if he can get his hands on any women's skates..."

"Oh, that's not a problem. I brought mine."

Well, I guess figure skates would work. I'm not sure what the difference is between them and hockey skates...

The door slid open. When we got to her apartment, she turned and said brightly, "Well, here we are. Thank you for walking me up."

"You're not going to show me your place?"

"Oh. Well...it's not like yours, Scottie. In fact, the whole place could fit into one of your bathrooms."

"That's okay." I took her arms, rubbing my thumbs across her satiny skin. It's like I couldn't stop touching her. Like I needed to know she was really here after all this time. "I want to be able to imagine where you are when we talk on the phone."

Her gazed roamed over my face. "I—I don't think that's a good idea."

Not a good idea? What does she mean by that? I tilted my head. "Why?"

"I..." She continued to search me, as if the answer lay hidden in my features somehow. "It's not clean," she said suddenly. "Yeah, I'd rather you see it when, you know...I've had time to fix things up a little." She tucked her hair behind her ear.

I don't care what it's like. Does she think I care what it's like? Does she think I'd look down on her now that I'm in such a nice place? I don't give a shit. I was torn. I didn't want to say goodnight to her...but I didn't want her to be uncomfortable either.

"You know," I said softly, "I don't care what your place is like. I mean...I get that you haven't had time to decorate it yet." She still hesitated. "But if you'd rather wait, that's fine."

She let out a big breath. "Thanks for understanding."

I didn't understand, but I wouldn't pressure her, for God's sake. I mean, if she didn't want to let me into her place, she didn't want to let me into her place.

She took my hands, leaning against her door. "Tonight was...really nice, Scott. I needed to be with you. I don't know why, but, when I'm with you, I feel safe. Stronger, I mean...I've really missed you."

"I'm glad you feel that way. I've been so excited to see you too, ever since you called." We stared at each other. Her gaze was still moving back and forth across my face.

"I wish..." she said dreamily, but she stopped.

"What?" I tried to read her too. "What do you wish, Elise?"

Her expression shifted from thoughtful musing to more of a 'kid-caught-in-a-lie' kind of alarm. She pushed off the door abruptly, looking down and releasing my hands. "I...uhh...wish I hadn't eaten so much, or I'd make you take me to Ghirardelli Square."

"We could still go..."

"No, it can't be open this late."

I checked my phone. "You're right. It closed at ten." I couldn't keep the disappointment out of my voice. "We could go for a nightcap somewhere. Or to my place?" *Or in your place?*

I thought for a moment she might agree. "No, I have practice tomorrow so I...should probably get some sleep."

"But after that, you're coming to the rink with me, right?"

The smile made another appearance. "Yeah, that'll be great."

"Okay." *At least there's that.* "I can pick you up at the performing arts center."

"Okay." She put her key in the lock, then spun around again. "No, wait. We're at the Jerry Garcia Amphitheater tomorrow. They're doing some work at the symphony hall. I'll just text you because I have no idea how long practice will take. Today was a little over an hour, but I don't know if that's typical..."

"Okay, text me then." I leaned in and kissed her cheek, pulling away slowly, for some reason. "Yeah, okay." I patted her arms. "Make sure you lock your door behind you."

"Okay, goodnight."

When I turned at the elevator, I was sorry to see she had disappeared. But when I heard the deadbolt click into place, my spirits lifted. My Elise was safe and living in San Francisco. That made me happy.

CHAPTER FOUR

Elise

I shut the door behind me, then whirled to lay my forehead on the worn wood as I locked it. "Oh my God!" I closed my eyes, clenched my fists, and laid them near my temples. I'd almost said, "I wish I stood a chance with you, because you're a great guy." It was screaming in my mind. Dancing on my lips. I was on the verge of saying it. That would have been disastrous. He would have then been forced to put distance between us, and I would have been all alone. I don't think I could take that.

How will I ever deal with this? A tear leaked out.

I made my way to my Murphy bed, which is to say, I took two steps. My place was tiny. It had basically a hot plate and a bar fridge for a kitchen, although there was a sink and the bed, which I kept extended. The bathroom was through a pocket door to the left of the entrance as I came in, and the rest was all one room. I'm pretty sure my dorm room had been bigger. But I really didn't need much, and the prices in San Fran were exorbitant.

Moving here was such a bad, bad idea.

I fell flat onto the bed. Tonight had been wonderful and torturous.

He's so damned clueless about what he does to me.

The way he was always casually touching me sent my pulse into orbit. The way he looked at me sometimes sent shivers along my spine. I was constantly fighting to keep myself from hopping into his arms and wrapping my legs around him and freaking begging him to kiss me again. Even that kiss at the restaurant. It meant nothing to him, but it made me weak in the knees. And besides the fact that his nearness set me off like vinegar does baking soda, making me equally fizzy inside, he was just so much fun to be with. So, on top of the fact that I was convinced the people at work hated me, the guy I had been in love with since I first understood what that meant, was indifferent to me. I mean, loved me like a sister, sure. But anything more was simply Scott on the hunt for a good time. I'd learned that lesson. We'd made out a couple of times when we were in junior high, and I made the mistake of thinking it meant something, only to discover later he was merely experimenting with kissing. Although he had nothing to learn in that category. His kisses were both searing and addicting. That's why I wouldn't let him into my place. That close to a bed and we might ignite it.

I flopped onto my back with a groan, letting my mind think of him so it would hopefully get it over with and I could settle down for the night. He had the handsomest, most expressive face. A face I knew well. I knew the way his eyes fired when he was mad, and how they twinkled when he was amused. Sad I hadn't seen much of. It was like Scott didn't do sad. I think that was one of the things I found attractive about him. That confidence that was border-line cockiness...how I wished some of that would rub off on me. The insecure thoughts that bombarded my mind at all times would be laughable to him. If even a whiff of self-doubt crept in, he would bat it away. He'd been like that since we met at ten, and it had obviously gotten stronger the more capable he had become.

I pictured him again. My fingers had itched to trace that tiny white scar by his lips he'd gotten in a fight with Robert Taninni of the Dallas Stars, one of the few he'd lost. I loved that little twitch in his dimple when he would joke around, or when he tried to hide his amusement. When he enclosed me within those well-muscled arms, those arms that could slap a shot at more than a hundred-three miles an hour at the All-Star Skill competition, it was like he kept the world from harming me. Those cute freckles that had been sprinkled across the bridge of his nose when we first met had left and been re-placed by a square jaw. His strawberry-blond hair was now more beach-boy-blond, and long enough to fall into his eyes, causing him to either shake it back, or rake it back, both options sexy as hell.

"Ugh!" I screamed, staring at the dirty blades on my ceiling fan. I flipped onto my side, punched my pillow and both laid on it and clutched the corner. "This is useless," I whispered in frustration. I had convinced myself I was over him when Hunter came into the picture. Then when Hunter proposed to me one night, underneath a starry sky on a camping trip, I was ready to yell "*yes!*" but "*I'm sorry,*" came out instead. I told myself it was because we wanted different things. He wanted to settle down and raise a family. I wasn't ready for that yet. But after tonight I knew that wasn't the truth. I'd never gotten over Scott. If he had proposed to me tonight, I would have said yes in a heartbeat. But that would never happen, and I needed to once and for all come to terms with that.

Maybe I should go home.

I couldn't turn tail and run home to Mommy and Daddy...and Stepdaddy. I wasn't a quitter. Mostly because I was super stubborn and hated to admit defeat. I sighed. I couldn't give up after one day. I needed to stick it out for a bit before I made a decision. I switched off the light, lying in my dress on top of the covers.

It took me forever to get to sleep, and it seemed like only a few minutes had passed before my alarm rang. Day two would be a better day. It had to be.

I saw him during a break between songs. He was at the top of the hill, sitting cross-legged in the grass. I couldn't help the little *blip* my heart did. It was involuntary and therefore couldn't be used against me.

What's he doing here? I told him I'd text him.

"Elise?" The director glanced over her shoulder, spotting Scott. "Do you have a friend here today?"

"Uhh..." Would I get in trouble for that? "I told him I'd text him after practice. I don't know why he's here."

She raised her eyebrows but all she said was, "Hmm." Looking over her shoulder again, she did a double take. "Ophelia!"

I took a gander myself. A lady wearing a tight, canary-yellow dress with a short, matching cape wrapped snuggly around her, had paused beside Scott. She stared at him for a moment, then lowered her sunglasses to say something to him. He responded and she smiled, returned the sunglasses to their former position, and sashayed along the aisle like she was on a runway in Paris.

Ms. Van Hoof rushed to the edge of the stage. "How nice of you to come."

"Oh, please, go on with your practice. Just act like I'm not here," she said regally, which was the exact opposite of what she wanted. She definitely wanted everyone to know she was present.

Ms. Van Hoof suddenly seemed to be all smiles. She pivoted to address us, clearing her throat. "Let's work on 'All I Ever Wanted.'" She lifted her baton, but we'd barely gotten started when it was clear to everyone I was off. Frowning at me, she brought the song to a halt. "Is there a problem, Elise?"

"Uhh...no. I don't understand."

"Clearly," the first chair violinist said underneath her breath, and everyone snickered.

"No. I mean, I'm playing the piece correctly."

Isabelle looked down her classical Greek nose at me. "So, I suppose it's the rest of us who are off then?" Once more, their laughter was at my expense.

"Let's give it another try, shall we?" the director bubbled.

Despite the fact I was following the sheet music set before me, the same scenario repeated, the music coming out all wrong. Ms. Van Hoof waved us quiet. Someone in the horn section thought it funny to leave one withering note hanging in the air, a noise of disappointment and complaint that shouted, "She's done it *again*." And it had to be the first time we had an audience.

In front of Mrs. Prentiss. And Scott. So not cool.

"I think we've all had enough for today," she glared at me pointedly. "Wouldn't you agree?" She slapped her baton on her stand and twirled to descend, via a ramp, and talk to Mrs. Prentiss.

I chanced a peek at Scott. He was sitting, back straight, surveying the stage with narrowed eyes. I sighed and my shoulders drooped; the tension I'd had since practice began washing away in a wave of failure.

"Elise," Carrie was leaning forward behind me with her hand extended, "let me see your sheet music." She held it beside her music, her gaze darting left to right and growing larger. "These aren't the same." She stared at me. "You have the wrong sheet music." She rubbed the paper between her fingers. "This isn't even the same kind of paper."

"What?" She angled sideways so we could both see the pages. "But Dalia played correctly." I spun to question my sheet music partner, who was hurriedly packing her instrument. She would turn the page for us, and I would keep the tune going while she did it. "Were you following our music?"

"Uhh, no. I thought something seemed off, so I didn't play."

She sat there while I made a fool out of myself without speaking up? "Why didn't you say something?"

She shrugged and seemed to glance at something over my shoulder, so I twisted to see what she was looking at and saw nothing noteworthy. "I wasn't sure if something was wrong or not, so I didn't want to say anything."

"When I was making a mess of things, wasn't that confirmation something was wrong?"

She snapped her case shut and lifted it. "No offense, Elise, but you've been making so many mistakes, I just assumed that's what was going on." She swung around to leave.

"Wait. Aren't you staying to help me determine what's wrong with our sheet music?"

"No, I'm sure you can handle it. I have an appointment," she added as she spun to leave.

I stood gaping for a moment then returned to the crisis du jour. But I couldn't shake her strange behavior. "Was that...somewhat odd?"

"What do you mean? The fact she wouldn't stay to help you uncover what's wrong with your sheet music, or the fact she didn't say something in the first place? Both are odd."

Someone cleared their throat behind me.

Carrie's eyes brightened. "*Who's* that?"

I spun to find Scottie right by the stage. "You ready to get the snot beaten out of you?"

I grinned. "Sure, big boy. Why don't you show me what you've got?"

He backed away, spreading his arms wide with a cocky smile. "Game on."

I'd forgotten Carrie for a second. "Oh, Scottie, this is Carrie Fisher. The live one." He looked appalled. "Inside joke. You wouldn't get it."

"Well, hello, Carrie Fisher. Nice to meet you."

She pushed her glasses up. "Nice to meet you."

"I'm afraid the next time you see Elise she will be bruised and humbled."

"Because you, the professional athlete, the guy with...what? A hundred fifty pounds on me?"

He scoffed. "More than that."

"All right. More than that. You're going to school me in the fine art of hockey?"

"That's right. Now hustle."

I couldn't help but be excited. I mean, I was getting to skate on a professional hockey rink; anybody would be excited over that. But on top of that, I had a little surprise for the great Scottie McCord.

Scott

"Whoa! This is so cool."

We were in our locker room and Elise's eyes were shining as she scoped out the digs. She spotted something and rushed forward.

"Sweet! I love this picture of you."

My chest puffed up.

She gave me a wry expression. "But don't get a swollen head about it."

I frowned. "Oh, no. That's why I have you here. To keep that from happening."

She smiled innocently. "You're welcome."

One side of my mouth lifted. "Come on. Let's get on the ice so I can return the favor."

She checked the surroundings. "Oh, umm...do you think it'd be all right if I changed? I brought an outfit to wear."

I rolled my eyes. Probably was some cute little getup like a tennis dress that she would freeze her ass off in. Then I imagined what she'd look like in that kind of ensemble and almost fell over myself to vacate so she could put it on.

When I first walked into the arena, it was very dark. Lights were on behind some of the box seats and exit signs shone in every section, but for the most part, it was bathed in black. I found the bank of switches I needed and flipped them with a series of satisfyingly loud *clicks*. It took a few seconds for the lights to warm up, then the ice was lit. I absolutely loved coming to the arena by myself and hitting the puck around. I could really practice on my form, and strategies, without being distracted. I could do drills again and again to establish muscle memory and improve my hand-eye coordination. I could strengthen injuries or chase away the ghosts of a bad play haunting me. The coaches had seen how it helped me and given me free rein. Would they be happy that right now a woman was changing into an "outfit" in the men's locker room? Probably not. But I could sweet-talk my way back into their good graces if I had to.

I got pucks and practiced slap shots. It took Elise longer than expected.

Probably working on her hair. Although Elise's hair style is pretty simple. Who knows what girls do when they're getting ready?

I rifled puck after puck into the net, creating different scenarios in my mind. I heard a noise and lifted my head to see if she was coming, still bent over the puck. Then I straightened.

"Where did you get that?" She was wearing a UNL jersey with matching pants, helmet, and gloves.

She skated onto the ice gracefully, shrugging. "From a friend."

I grasped the knob of my stick. "Uh-huh. What friend?"

"Coach Hess." She gave me a wicked smile that I caught through the grid work of her helmet. College players had to have the full monty, while we pros got to wear the slick visors.

"You play?"

She lined up a shot then zinged it into the net. "Yeah, I play."

The little shit. "What position do you play?"

She took another shot and hit the post with a ding. "Right wing, mostly. Sometimes center."

I huffed. "You? You're tiny."

"Yeah." She winked at me. "But I'm tough."

"What—?" I was flabbergasted. "And Aunt Sam lets you play?"

She snorted. "*Lets* me play? I am an adult now, Scottie." She skated to a puck that had slid across the ice a couple of feet when I dumped them and charged the net with it on her stick. She switched to backhand and put it in, high in the corner. She circled the net and returned, using both skate edges to stop, spraying me with ice. She laughed. "I wish you could see your face."

I frowned, tilting my head.

"Come on. You didn't think I'd learn a thing or two from Kyle?"

I guess having a stepfather who was an NHL ref had its advantages.

"It never crossed my mind, to be honest."

She took the puck from my stick and skated backward with it. "You always underestimate me."

That's not because I don't believe in you. It's because you're amazing.

I'd gotten her one of Lucas' sticks as our centerman was the shortest on the team. I stretched to corral another puck and acted like I was taking a shot but knocked the puck off her stick instead. "I'm shocked you didn't bring your own stick."

"I did. I left it in the car. Would have given away the surprise." She was glowing.

"You're loving this, aren't you?"

She skated over to me again, stopping within inches of me. "Yeah, I am."

I swallowed, staring down at her, my heart suddenly pounding. I found my voice finally. "Let's see how good your defense is. Let's play a little one on one."

"You're on."

We collected the pucks, leaving just the one to play with, and went at it. We brought the puck to center ice, put our sticks on either side, tapped the ice, then each other's sticks three times, mimicking a faceoff situation. Her reflexes were remarkably quick, but I beat her by a fraction of a second, poking it through her legs. She tried to back up on it and made a laughable attempt of checking me off the puck, but I didn't give at all. The blade of my stick battled between the cage of her skates and this time was able to get the puck some distance from her, enough that I could get around her and score easily.

"All right," she said to herself, looking determined. We returned to the middle circle and repeated our stick tapping, but this time she leaned into me at the end—an illegal move for a faceoff—and actually got her stick in a position to take the puck. I shifted but she quickly banged it into the boards and beat me to the spot it ricocheted to. Luckily, I was able to tip it when she shot, sending it wide of the goal. I skirted the net, getting behind it to retrieve the puck. She waited in front for me, waving her stick left and right and swaying to try to block me. I began to take it up ice and she again bumped me, elbowing me without results, but able to knock the puck away. This would have been the point when I would have creamed my opponent against the boards, but obviously I wouldn't do that to Elise. She faked to the left and I bit. She adjusted to the right, getting some room and made a nice little shot from the slot, putting it in and doing a brief celly—or celebratory move—before we went at it again at center.

We traded goals for the most part, but she gained the advantage at one point when I tried to go top shelf and the puck soared over the net. I got it back pretty quickly with a dirty deke that left her out of position. I came to center ice and stood opposite her, dropping the puck between us, but breathing hard. She readied herself for the preliminary steps of stick tapping, but I remained bent in half, my stick held across my knees, trying to fill my lungs with the cold air rising from the ice.

"You're taking it easy on me."

I glanced at her. Even with her lid on I could see her features were tight. I continued to gulp in air. "Are you...kidding? You...know me...better than that." Sure, there'd been plenty of times when we were growing up I'd wanted to toss her a bone while playing hoops on my driveway, but something inside me wouldn't let me do it. Even when she'd plod off the "court" without a word, dirt on her face, a skinned knee, and tears in her eyes. That elation I got from beating her would be totally obliterated by the guilt that swamped me as I watched her leave, my heart in a vise. Even then she could move me like no one else.

Her eyes lifted and became squinty like they did when she smiled. "Okay, then."

My lip curled on one side, and I huffed as I tried to catch my breath. "We have to stop, or I'll have nothing left for the game tonight."

She nodded, looking serious again.

"One more, for the whole ball of wax. Whoever scores here is taking home The Cup."

She groaned, realizing that there was no way that I would let that happen. Some things never change. "Fine, let's go."

I put the puck on the ice between us and hoped to catch her gaze, but she was focused. Her lips were in motion; she was strategizing. I chortled. "You're so cute when you think you have a chance of winning."

"Shut up and play."

I raised my brows. *Ooh, touchy.*

We tapped ice, then stick, ice, then stick, ice, then stick, and then with lightning speed she got the puck. In her excitement, though, she let the puck get away from her. Rookie mistake. She had to go deep into the corner to regain control, which gave me the opportunity to get in position in front of the net. Our eyes met. She knew it was over. If she took a shot, I wouldn't let it go in, and I'd take it to the other end before she'd finished her follow-through. She skated warily to the blue line, giving herself time to think, then poured it on, weaving across the ice, going backhand to forehand and back, honed in on me, hoping I'd commit one way or another. I opened my legs to give her a glimpse of the five-hole and she bought it, taking her shot. I didn't have goalie's pillows to seal it off, but I still managed to block it. Elise lost an edge and went sliding into the boards with a loud *thud*. She moaned, lying face down on the ice.

"Shit! Elise!" Forgetting everything else I sprinted to her side. "Are you okay?"

"Oh." She lifted her head, grimacing. "What happened?" she said shakily. She got on all fours.

I tried to assess the level of damage. "Where does it hurt?"

"Umm..." She lunged to her right, hooking the puck with the blade of her stick and swung it into the net. "Yes!"

It took me a second to realize I'd been had. "Wait. That didn't count."

"I didn't hear any whistle, so the play was not dead. I won." She rolled onto her butt and extended her arm for me to help her up.

I jerked her to her feet and again her closeness made my throat tighten. "I should have dumped you on your ass."

She removed her bucket, shaking free all of that gorgeous hair and grinning at me. "Yes. You should have." She tapped my lips with her finger. "But you didn't."

I really, really wanted to kiss her. Like, knock her onto the ice and rip off her pads. And rip off my pads. And touch her smooth skin. And feel her lips under mine. And—

"Are you coming?"

She had glided about halfway across the ice and had pivoted, looking at me with a little cocky lift of her chin. I let out a scream that was partially a deep-throated yowl, partially an unidentifiable shout and rushed her. She shrieked and jumped then tried to race away from me, but I caught her at the boards where she had been hindered by opening the gate, trapping her in my arms, my mouth at her ear.

"You, my dear, are a cheat."

She squirmed, and I had to adjust my stance so she wasn't coming in contact with my lower regions. A painful zip of electricity rocketed through me. Every fiber in my body was on edge, begging her to spin around.

"Scottie, stop." Her voice was shaky.

I released my grip on the boards finger by finger and moved back, flush with disappointment.

Clearly it's been too long since I've gotten laid if being this close to my friend, who happens to be a girl, is turning me on.

She jerked the gate open and practically sprinted down the tunnel. When she slowed to round the corner into the locker room, she twisted her ankle and fell off her skate. She caught herself on the wall, then kept going.

I followed her unhurriedly, pinching my bottom lip as I thought over our little "game."

I'm supposed to be an elite athlete, and I could barely hold my own against Elise? And I thought I was nearing my former level of play. I shook my head with a sigh. Obviously, I had a long way to go still. When I entered the locker room, she was nowhere in sight. I was about to call her name when I heard a noise to my left. I could see her feet in one of the bathroom stalls. She'd wrestled one skate off and was working on the other. "Do you need to take a shower? I could stand watch and make sure no one interrupted you, if anyone is in the building, which I doubt."

She waited so long to answer I began to wonder if she'd heard me. But her movements had stilled. She heard me all right.

"No, I'm good. I'll just take one when I get home."

"Are you sure? It's not a problem."

"Yeah, yeah, I'm sure." Her voice pitched. I observed her feet and heard her muttering to herself as she dropped first her skates, then her sweater and pads. She must have taken her clothes in with her, or maybe she left them when she changed into her gear.

I spun slowly, peeling my own jersey off and strolling to my locker. I was arrested by a fantasy of her in the shower, the water running over her body...then I was joining her in the shower...and on the bench...and—

"Holy fucking shit!"

I whirled around and she was staring at me with her mouth hanging open.

"What?" I glanced down, half expecting my skin to be the red, orange, and yellow from my practice jersey or something. I brushed at my chest. I was sweaty, but the material hadn't bled. I looked to her again for an explanation. When she tore her gaze from my chest and met mine, a wave of color rose on her cheeks.

"Good Lord, Scott. Put that-that shit away."

"Put what shit—" I examined the jersey in my hand, confused by her re-action.

"I-I'll wait for you in the hall."

"No, wait. Hold on. It'll just take a second..."

I was speaking to empty lockers because she was gone.

CHAPTER FIVE

Elise

I paced in the hall trying to release all of the energy pent up in my body. *Holy shit, he was hot!*

I stood still, closing my eyes and sucking in deep breaths, but it didn't help. With my eyes closed it was easier to picture him again...broad shoulders, chiseled pecs, popping veins, and that "V" thing. My God, the "V" thing. It was making me weak as I thought about it.

I so did not need that. I mean... I rubbed my lips together. *Just holy shit.*

I'd imagined what he looked like. Of course I'd imagined what he looked like. My gaze skimming over that body straining against his shirt and picturing what he was like underneath...I mean, he was an athlete. Of course he was built. But I never imagined...*that*. So unbelievably flawless. Like the exact definition of my perfect guy.

Before today, I thought Hunter's body was the bomb, and it was. But Scott...Scott edged him out in every category. Not by a great deal. He was infinitesimally more toned, bigger, yet more svelte at the same time...like the sculptor had taken a few more minutes, tightened the lines one more time, chipped away at the image with a finer stroke.

It was suddenly like the air was sharp and I needed water to soothe my throat. I rushed to a drinking fountain down the hall and took a long drink.

"Is something wrong?"

I jumped, then wiped my mouth with the back of my hand. "Nope, all good here," I said a little too brightly, the tone coming off as forced.

"Did you have fun?"

It was like his words didn't compute. Fun? What was fun?

"Huh? Oh. Yeah. It was great. But we should get going," I said rapidly.

"Oh? You in a hurry?" He fell in step with me.

"Yes. I mean, no. Actually, yes. I need to...practice. I mean, you saw how things went today."

"Yeah." He was quiet for a moment. "I was thinking about that earlier...do you remember a lady with a red scarf tied around her neck?"

My brow furrowed as I tried to remember what people were wearing. Then it dawned on me. "With long dark hair?"

He nodded.

"Her name is Isabelle."

He didn't say anything but pinched his lips like he often did.

"She was actually the one who pointed to the seat for me yesterday."

He made a humming noise in his throat. "I saw her talking to the conductor lady, and the other chick in the yellow dress."

"Mrs. Prentiss?"

"All three of them were looking at you as they talked. It seemed kind of weird."

"Hmm..." I'd gotten a feeling something was up.

"Just...keep your eye on them."

Interesting. He sees something too. Hmm...

"Thanks."

Scott

I timed my arrival in the corner to the defenseman's, Alex Goodrow. I hated that prick. And I hated the team he played for, the Las Vegas Golden Knights. Along with us, they were one of the newer teams in the league, and therefore a natural rival, as we both had something to prove. During warmups, Goodrow had passed the bench and spouted. "Oh, yeah. We'll be extinguishing the Fire tonight."

To which I countered, "You don't have a long enough hose."

Sergei laughed, spitting out his water, and the others joined in.

Goodrow glowered. He'd obviously prepared that ahead of time and didn't like the way I turned it around on him. But his next chirp crossed a line. "Mansford, the only hit you'll get tonight is from your dealer." Blane about went over the boards at him. He'd spent a stint in rehab during the off-season when he continued taking painkillers for an injury. The kind the doctor doesn't prescribe.

"Yeah? Your mom roots for the other team," Sergei retorted.

I frowned at my roomie. "That was weak."

"I couldn't think of anything fast enough."

"That may be, but I've heard better chirps from a dead bird. You need to work on that."

He got his chance because Goodrow wasn't done being an asshole. At the end of his next shift, he took a jab at Rosetti, who was a healthy scratch for the night. Tommy'd spent his own time in detox for his issues with alcohol. "Rosetti, the only ice you're seeing tonight is in your glass of scotch."

Another Knight skated up to his side. "Yeah, you've been scratched more than a lotto ticket."

This time Sergei's comeback was marginally stronger, "Well, you guys will blow this game tonight the way your momma blew me last night."

I shook my head. He got some yucks from that, but I knew he could do better. "Too easy." I timed my next statement right before we started a shift. "Besides, the best revenge is a W."

And to that end I proceeded to check Goodrow off the puck. I saw someone driving toward the net from the corners of my eyes and instinctively shoveled an outlet pass to the point where he would be when it reached him. A second later the horn blasted, and the light flashed, indicating we'd made a goal.

Sergei pointed at me, then glided across the ice to put his arm around me and gave a celebratory shout along with Lucas Barbeau, who had just joined us. The defensemen, Joey Hoskins and Jacob Tremblay, arrived last, and then Sergei coasted in front of the bench, knuckling people as he went by. I followed, searching the audience behind the bench for Elise. It didn't take much effort to find her because she was the one high-fiving the complete strangers sitting near her. Then, as I approached, she banged on the glass. It was not so much lip reading as it was knowing what she would say that told me she was yelling, "Nice!" I was filled with a warmth that had been lacking in my life. But I didn't have much time to think about it as Coach was keeping our line on, and they were setting up for the faceoff.

In the third period, things were getting chippy. The score was 1-1. Ctirad had been standing on his head in goal, but at the end of the first, a lucky shot ricocheted off Tremblay's skate and into the net. Shit-turd couldn't adjust in time for the puck's redirection and, on top of that, he was partially screened by Joey, so he didn't have a clear look at it.

"Hey, goalie. Maybe you should switch to Geico. You'll save more," a Knight shouted as he passed the net.

"Yeah, I've seen more saves from a coupon," his friend added.

"Whatever," I jeered. "Franklin, you're the human equivalent of a participation award."

He started to skate over to me, but his friend pulled him back.

"Yeah, keep skating," I muttered.

After we killed a five-on-three power play for the Knights, the momentum shifted our way. But when they scored less than five seconds later, the story was reversed. I wanted to be out on the ice, but I'd just come off the power kill and was winded. While I waited for Coach to put me in, I tried to encourage the team. As the captain, that was my responsibility.

"That's it there, boys. Wheel! Wheel! Wheel!"

"Nice hit, Jaky."

Jacob Tremblay had nailed someone in the corner creating a break away for Noah "Boat" Martin, a right winger on the second line, and Liam Bouchard, who played center. The story on Noah's nickname differed depending on who was asked. Some said it was because of the whole Noah's ark thing; some said it was because of his love for speed boats, and the guy was crazy for them. But those of us who had been around the longest knew it was because he always wanted to motorboat chicks at the bars, as in, bury his face in their chest while they shook it like a pit bull.

"Come on, dig, dig, dig. You've got this."

They did a little give and go. The Boater had saucy hands and could put the puck right on the tape, which he did, but a *ding* meant Bouchard, or Sharty, as we liked to call him, posted it. He followed his shot, though, and got the rebound in the corner, passing it back to the point where Joey-boy tried to one-time it but whiffed. The puck left the zone, and he decided to take a walk with it so we could change lines.

I flew over the boards and Sergei followed, almost a bit too quickly. We were lucky we didn't get called for too many men on the ice. A few seconds into our shift, Cameron Barrett, on the Knights, was standing like a pylon waiting for a line change and not paying attention. I swept in and stole the puck and Sergei, anticipating what I would do, charged the net. Their defenders skated backward, but I was able to get a saucer pass right to the Douche, and he buried the biscuit in the basket, tying things up. We didn't waste time on the celly because he and I were alike; we wanted to get on with winning the game.

As I skated passed Barrett on the way to the bench, I remarked, "You know if you'd wanted to watch the game you could have just gotten a ticket."

He replied, "Yeah, sure, McCord. Get out of here. Figure skating was over an hour ago."

After our next shift, as we were headed for the bench, Goodrow came crashing in, and checked Sergei, bending him on top of the board. It was exactly like the play that broke my ribs, a cheap shot, as Sergei was blindsided.

I shoved Goodrow. "What the fuck, man?"

He smiled, chewing on his mouth guard rather than wearing it. "It's called hockey, Pretty Boy."

A ref slid between us, but I was able to give him a little face wash across the striper's shoulder. The smell of my gloves was enough to kill a horse. "You'll pay for that," I added. Sergei might be an asshole, but he was our asshole, and if Goodrow messed with one of us, he'd have the whole lot skating up his back.

"Huh." He laughed. "You ain't doing anything. You don't want to have your face rearranged before the big Fire and Ice thing. You won't bring in any money." He'd obviously done some reading on the team.

Another ref got between us and pushed Goodrow away.

"Oh, I'm not worried about my face, 'cause all it'll take is one punch, and you'll be on the ice." The guy had probably intentionally picked one of my pet peeves to incite me. When I first came to the show, opponents called me Pretty Boy. But once I proved I wasn't afraid to fight, I'd earned the respect of most players.

I don't think this clown has respect for anyone besides himself.

"Come on. Come on. Let's play some hockey," the liney interjected.

Goodrow and I looked at each other and came to an unspoken agreement. "Fine," I spat then backed down. Out of politeness to the refs, we wouldn't throw down right now, but it was coming.

And it didn't take long. The very next faceoff we lined up next to each other with one goal in mind. From the side of my mouth I said, "The only hard hits we'll get in Vegas are at the blackjack tables."

"Fucker," was his pithy return.

When the puck dropped, so did our sticks and gloves. We raised our fists and circled, and players gave us room, while pairing up with someone

from the opposite team, in case something was done that required retaliation. The referees drew closer to be ready to put an end to the fight, if need
be. Goodrow took a weak jab at me, not intending to land it, but to either
judge distance better, or bait me into making a mistake.

I snarled at him. "Come on, you pussy. Let's go."

At the same time, we lunged and grabbed hold of each other's sweaters.
This acted as a sort of counter-balance to keep us on our feet. It also gave the
fighter the advantage of being able to use a little bit of their hips, and that's
where the power for a punch comes from. We exchanged a few haymakers,
not landing much with our pads and buckets still on. I dragged him toward
the boards. Bracing myself against them was another way to stay on my feet
and get more behind my punches. Goodrow's haymakers were glancing off
my helmet as I dodged them, but I was waiting for the right moment. It was
something I would feel more than determine. It came when one of my wild
swings dislodged his lid. When I got my shot, I had to purposely not dodge
a blow in order to keep my gaze on him and make sure I landed my punch. I
might lose some Chiclets, but I had a good dentist. I clocked him good and
followed with an uppercut. I let him go and he crumpled to the ice.

"You just got the shit beat out of you by a pretty boy," I commented as
the refs stepped in. The crowd went wild, and my boys tapped their sticks on
the ice or on the boards in front of the bench, cheering for me while also rib-
bing me. Most of it was unintelligible, but I picked up on Sergei's, "Good job,
champ."

Elise, however, was not cheering. She had moved into the aisle and down
to the glass, covering her heart. "Are you okay?" she mouthed.

I nodded and she inhaled, but her brow remained furrowed.

"Are you sure?"

Again, I bobbed my head and shot her a grin to reassure her.

Her shoulders relaxed and her expression brightened, a smile slowly blos-
soming on her face.

As I was being escorted to the penalty box, I took my helmet off to check
it. It seemed undamaged. I shook the hair out of my eyes, and when that
didn't work, used my hand to push it back. I could taste the salt that was
either perspiration or blood, and the metallic flavor, which was assuredly
blood. The one punch I let him land had cost me, but it was worth it. He had

to pay for taking a cheap shot at my teammate. It was the unwritten law of hockey.

The ref and I shuffled through our sticks, gloves, his helmet, and his mouthpiece. It was a real yard sale. Across from me, Goodrow was being led to his booth. He still looked slightly dazed. I doubted he'd try that shit again anytime soon. What I hated worse than getting punched, though, was spending five minutes in the box. It seemed like an eternity, especially if we were losing. I ran my tongue over my teeth finding a few loose, but not too bad. I grabbed a towel to wipe the sweat from my forehead then watched tensely, hoping the fight would do what I had intended for it to do. Fire up my teammates.

"Come on, guys."

The Knights got a breakaway, but Ctirad made a kickass save and Bouchard won the faceoff after it. Douche sped toward the o-zone and Nick Skavins, who was in on my line, taking my place at right wing, made a sweet little deke on the Knights' Paul Crownhard and broke free. Sergei was in front of him, so Nick had to get the puck into the zone to prevent an offsides call. Skavy rocketed it off the back board at a perfect angle so the ricochet hit Sergei in the slot, and he went topshelf with it and scored. My cheers in my Plexiglas cage.

"Yeah! That's it, boys."

We had the go-ahead goal, but a one-goal lead wasn't enough against this club. Not with their Finnish rookie, Marko Hietala, leading the league in both goals and assists. And Shit-turd wasn't strong in the third. It was like he only had a forty-minute attention span. The first two periods he was usually razor-sharp, but after that, he had the worst record in our division. So, the best power forward against the worst goalie, with one of the team's leading power kill players in the box, could equal the perfect storm. And sure enough, twenty-six seconds later, the refs hand went up.

"What?" I hadn't seen anything meriting a penalty. I hoped it was on them. Everyone else was looking around too. I waited for the ref's announcement.

"San Francisco, number twenty-three, hooking." He made the motion like a shepherd pulling in Baa Baa's black sheep.

Sergei wasn't even paying attention until someone pointed out he was be-ing called for a penalty. He checked the board and saw the minutes next to his number. He shifted his gaze to the ref who had made the call, who was eyeballing him.

The Douche pointed to himself. "Me?"

The fans booed. Sergie skated slowly over, wearing a quizzical expression.

"What the fuck?" he said as he entered the box next to me. We both watched the replay on the scoreboard.

He frowned. "Are you kidding me?"

"That wasn't even close to a hook," I said at the same time.

"What the fuck?" Serg said again, still in disbelief. "Hey, ref," he called. "You better switch your ringer on. You're missing some calls."

"I've seen better refs at Foot Locker," I added.

We followed the play silently for a moment. We knew killing two five-on-threes in a game wasn't likely to happen.

"Nice fight, by the way," he said without taking his gaze from the action on the ice.

"Thanks," I returned. Nick Skavins, one of our best on the penalty kill, dove and poke checked the puck out of the zone. "Nice. Nick's having a great game."

Sergei grunted in agreement.

The Knights had to waste time getting everyone to leave the o-zone and then reenter. They passed around the perimeter and our boys kept it tight in the center, shifting to confront each puck handler. The Knights tried to redirect from high to low and left and right, but Ctirad realigned himself each time, staying square to the shooter. They made a centering attempt, but Hoskins was able to deflect it, though the Knights remained in control of the puck. Mr. Wonderful, Marko Hietala seemed to recognize their time was passing away and he needed to take a shot. He fired a clapper that broke his twig, and our boy Joey didn't have much time to react. He flamingoed and that vulcanized rubber disc hit him right in the jewels at about ninety miles per hour. Sergei and I both hissed in a sympathetic breath. I don't care how much protection a player is wearing, that shit hurts.

"That'll leave a mark," my roommate deadpanned.

There was a brief stoppage in play while they removed the remains of Hoskins and subbed in Mansford, who wasn't normally on the kill. I watched the clock. In eleven seconds, I would be back in. Blane won the faceoff, but they weren't able to clear the puck as a diving Knight kept it in. When time had expired on our penalties, Goodrow and I hit the ice at the same time, but he was in my rearview mirror. I was totally focused on keeping his team from scoring. Catching Hietala by surprise, I was able to send the puck to the other end and kill some more time until Sergei could join us. After another flurry of shots, which Ctirad was able to make saves on, we banged the puck around the boards and out. I could tell Shit-turd was tiring fast, and quite frankly, I couldn't blame him. A goalie shouldn't have to deal with five-on-three twice in a game. Coach would rip us a new one for sure.

Right as Sergei's time in the box ended, Mansford (Manny) won a puck fight against the boards and the biscuit squirted over to me. My stretch pass hit Sergei in stride and since his exit from the sin bin put him behind the defense, it was one-on-one. Shooter against goalie. With two goals on his scorecard, the guys had been trying to get Sergei the hat trick earlier and nothing he shot got through. Their goalie was pretty strong stick and glove side, so I would have shot high and gone bardown on him, but Sergei must have seen something and he went five-hole. The goalie collapsed his pads and seemed to close it up, but where was the puck? He twisted to find it right as the goal judge lit the lamp. Having earned his hat trick, SF Fire hats hit the ice along with some bearing the 49ers and Giants emblems, even a Knights cap was thrown in, although perhaps not voluntarily. And our fans had invented a tradition of throwing a myriad of fire department caps, some with insignias, some with letters, and some simply the number of the station house. We had a special display case for those. But the best was a top hat. Who brings a top hat to a game?

Sergei's celly was a thing of beauty, and I was riding a little high with the prospect of winning until I noticed my roomie searching the stands and followed his line of sight to Elise. She grinned and nodded in an exaggerated fashion, her lips forming the word "nice" again.

What the hell? Did she just give The Douche one of my "nices?"

She wasn't even looking at me. Without my apple he couldn't have scored. Shouldn't I be getting a "nice" for that? Then I remembered it was actually two assists I'd given him on the way to his hattie, and my indignation grew stronger. I played the remainder of the game pissed off, which led to my giving up the puck and a Knight's goal.

Another of my least favorite Knights, Mark Gamison, skated by our bench.

"How do you guys like getting whipped by your own McCord?" he cracked.

Sergei was quicker than I. "Hey man, does your coach know you're out there?"

He smirked and went to his bench.

Luckily, time expired before I did it again, and we got the win despite my misstep. I tried to shake it off as I went through my postgame ritual, knuckling all the players as they left the ice and went down the tunnel to the dressing room. But when I rotated to head there myself, Elise was bending over the railing to have a conversation with Sergei. He was peering at her with a huge grin. Swallowing the shock of seeing that, I walked by them.

"Good game, Scott," Elise called after me.

Not as good as Sergei's though.

"Thanks," I responded without turning, but I couldn't help but peek back when I rounded the corner, and they were in the same position.

Sergei's freaking neck has to have a crimp in it from looking up at her for so long.

I showered and got dressed without much talking to anyone. I slipped away before everyone else. When I got outside, someone was lurking in the shadows.

"Hey, McCord. You wanna take a run at me without your pads to cushion you?"

Surprise, surprise. It was Goodrow. "No need to," I said without slowing. "I already beat you twice tonight."

"Oh, yeah." He spat. "Well, you're such a pussy even your mom didn't love you."

I stopped dead in my tracks. It probably didn't take much searching to discover my mom signed over rights to me the day I was born, giving me to her husband, my dad. With all the cuts and bruises I'd gotten, this was the one wound that never healed. Whose mom does that to him with such callousness? I dropped the bag with my gear in it and whirled around, but Goodrow had snuck behind me and landed a punch before I even knew one was coming.

He thinks he's some kind of badass coming for me by himself. His keister should be on the bus headed home.

We scuffled for a bit, but I was the only one scoring. Elise's stepdad, Kyle, had taught me a thing or two about fighting after I graduated from college and was drafted. Taking hold of my jacket, he spun me so my back was toward the building, I guess thinking he would have me cornered then. I knocked him away, breathing heavy, fists still raised. "Had enough?"

The door opened and a couple Fire players exited the building. They read the situation pretty quickly and dropped their stuff.

I threw my hand up. "I've got this."

"Okay. But if you get tired, tag me in," Mansford said.

While I was distracted, Goodrow tried to sucker punch me again, but I saw it out of the corner of my eye, and my natural instinct was to duck. Goodrow connected with the concrete wall of the building. He howled in pain. "Fuck!"

Even though he was in the shadow of the building, I could see his face was a funky gray color. "Let me see it." He may be an ass, but I didn't want his career to be over because he picked a fight with me.

He did a combination of bouncing and swinging from side to side while clutching his right forearm. Unintelligible noises came from his mouth, interspersed with cuss words.

"Come on. Let me see it."

"What the fuck can you do about it?" he wailed.

I grabbed his elbow and dragged him into the light. His hand was swollen like a cartoon character's. I glanced at my teammates. "Get some ice from the training room." Rosetti took off. "Can you move your fingers?"

He wiggled his fingers, which were stiff from the swelling. "Not very much."

"But you can move them. That's good." I stared at him. "What the hell were you thinking? Concrete wall beats flesh and bone every time."

"I wasn't thinking, okay?" I could see in his expression now he was scared. Add to that the fact his team was probably searching for him, and his coach would be royally pissed when he discovered what his all-star defense-man had done.

Blane added his two cents' worth. "That doesn't look good."

We both glared at Mansford.

"What? It doesn't."

Rosetti came tearing out of the building with one of those cold pack things. He laid it across Goodrow's blown-up knuckles. "Trainer's on the way."

"I don't need your damn trainer," he snarled.

"Are you sure, man? You should probably have that checked." Rosetti glanced over his shoulder as if expecting the trainer to be there.

Goodrow spun and started to walk away. "We have our own freaking trainers, you moron."

"Yeah, but ours are closer," Tommy said under his breath.

Goodrow whirled to face us, walking backward. "I'm filing a report with the league and the cops."

Seriously? "Yeah, you do that," I muttered. We watched him leave. He had a long way to go to get around the building to where his team's bus would be parked. "You could go through the building you know," I yelled after him. He didn't answer, although he had to have heard me.

I bent to pick up my bag, holding a groan in.

"I take it he jumped you, seeing as it was outside our door?" Mansford questioned.

"Uh-huh." They gathered their stuff and we walked toward the cars.

"Ya think he would've had enough of you on the ice," Rosetti comment-ed.

The door crashed open, and we half turned to see who it was. Stan Smith, one of our trainers, was standing and gawking. "I thought you said someone punched the wall?"

"They did," I gestured to his left, where Goodrow was still walking. "But they took off."

He gawked at the retreating figure. "What the hell? He probably broke his hand."

Rosetti shrugged. "I told him you were coming."

After a moment of contemplative silence, the trainer did an about-face, heading inside. "Well, I can't help the dumb fuck if he doesn't stick around."

Some other players passed him on the threshold. "What's going on?"

"Ask them," Stan muttered, disappearing into the building.

"Goodrow jumped Scottie," Mansford explained.

One of the guys was Nick. "You're kidding?"

"Nope. Then he punched the wall."

Sergei, who was behind Nick gestured to the building. "*This* wall?"

Mansford rocked onto his heels, grinning. "Yup."

Sergei stared at the concrete stadium. "He probably broke his fucking hand."

"Pretty sure he did," Manny said matter-of-factly.

Now the players were walking toward us again. Sergei huffed. "Didn't he get enough of you on the ice?"

We laughed. "That's exactly what I said," Tommy explained.

My car soon became a gathering place as other Fire players exited and had to be regaled with the story. I opened the door and threw my bag in. I actually wanted to get back home myself so I could ice my own hand, but I wouldn't let them know that.

My phone vibrated. I retrieved it from my pocket gingerly. Elise.

IS SOMETHING WRONG? YOU DIDN'T STOP TO SAY HI. YOU WEREN'T

HURT IN THAT FIGHT, WERE YOU?

Which fight? I sighed and the thought came out of the blue. *The only thing I was really hurt by tonight was you.*

As soon as the thought crossed my mind, I knew it was ridiculous. Elise could be friends with whoever she wanted to be friends with. I should be happy if she'd struck up a friendship with someone when she was new in town and probably lonely...but did it have to be Sergei?

SORRY. GUESS I WAS IN A MOOD. DO YOU WANT TO MEET SOMEWHERE

AND I CAN BUY YOU AN APOLOGY DRINK?

I waited for a reply, answering questions from my crew.

"Are you worried he'll get the cops after you?"

"Nah, Goodrow's just a blowhard. Besides, he's gonna have enough on his plate when his coach gets hold of him."

They chuckled.

"His ass is grass, eh?" Lucas commented.

Talk shifted to some woman in the stands with big boobs. Meanwhile, my mind drifted to the image of Elise bending over the railing.

Sergei probably got a clear view of her assets too. Oh my God. What the hell am I thinking? That's Elise I'm talking about. What's wrong with me?

"Scott?" Sharty was staring at me.

"Huh?"

"I was asking you how you thought Lambert played?" The Knight's highly touted rookie. "Where were you, man? Dreaming of a dirty hit on that bastard Goodrow?"

Everyone chuckled.

"Yeah," I responded, forcing a laugh of my own.

Luckily, a few minutes later the car party broke up. I yelled at Nick as he was leaving. "Hey. Nice game, dude. That was a sick deke you put on Crownhard."

He spun around, grinning as he walked backward. "Thanks. Ya want to get something to eat?"

"No, man. I'm beat. I'm just going home to bed." *After icing my hand.*

"I bet you are, Muhammad." He began to walk away, and I opened my front door. He turned again. "Hey. Do you know what time we're supposed to be there tomorrow?"

"Five-thirty."

"Five-thirty? Doesn't it start at seven?"

"Yeah."

"So why do we have to be there that early?"

I shrugged. "To practice being pieces of meat? I don't know, man. But I plan to sneak off and get a drink from the bar."

He waved when someone honked as they were leaving. "I'll be right on your tail, my brotha. Have a good night."

I got in the car and inhaled slowly. I held my hand out to the side and stretched it, sucking air in.

Fuck, that hurts. What a freaking crazy night. I can't believe Goodrow freaking jumped me.

I glanced at my phone on the console.

What's taking her so long? It only requires a yes or no answer.

Why was I suddenly being so impatient with her? I mean, we had a great day playing hockey together, why was my stomach gnawing at me now? Laying my head on the seat rest I released a big breath, trying to determine what was bugging me.

I tried to put the image of her bending over that rail far from my mind. But like a light switch for a lamp minus a bulb, I kept coming back to it, although I knew full well it was useless.

I was suddenly struck by a memory. I don't know if it was seeing her by the railing, or what caused this particular scene to pop up, but...we were probably twelve or thirteen. Elise was nearly hysterical because a small bird had gotten frozen to a railing at school. I just happened upon her as I was changing classes, moving from one building to the next.

"We've got to do something, Scott." The little guy was stuck fast.

"No. It's fine. It'll work itself free," I said with more conviction than I had.

"No. Listen to him. He's in pain."

He did seem to be pretty distressed. The bird fluttered its wings, banging them against the railing.

"He's trying to rip himself off," Elise screamed. "He's going to hurt himself more."

"It's okay." Without thinking, I leaned forward and began to breathe on the bird's feet. It was probably a pretty stupid thing to do as the bird could have pecked my eyes out, but he seemed to know I was trying to help him. The railing turned from its frosted white to black, but when I stopped, became white again.

"It's working!" Elise's face was bright. "Keep doing it."

A few seconds later, the bird flew away. He landed on a snow-covered bush not far from us and chirped happily.

Elise threw her arms around me. "You did it."

The memory warmed me. And as I recall, within a week she'd taken a paper route. She saved her money to buy a heated birdbath for her backyard. Her "bird Jacuzzi," as I called it.

She was always doing that kind of thing in school. Always looking out for others. A bleeding heart.

That's why I'm worried about her and Sergei. She's so easy to sucker in.

But was it that? Or was there more making my emotions soar? I shook my head.

You know what? I've made it this far in life without examining my feelings, why begin now?

I slid my key into the ignition and started my car, determined to free myself from whatever it was I was in the grips of at the moment. The screen lit up on my phone and I grabbed it.

THANKS FOR ASKING, BUT I REALLY NEED TO GET SOME PRACTICE IN. ARE YOU SURE NOTHING'S BOTHERING YOU?

Great. She was worried. And much like her mom, Elise would hold on to something with the tenacity of a bulldog until she was satisfied she had the truth. And what was I supposed to say? I'm upset because you congratulated Sergei on his goal? It sounded so childish. "You can't be his friend because you're mine." I snatched my phone and texted without even putting much thought into it.

I THINK I'M JUST TIRED.

Then I had to laugh.

YOU REALLY KICKED MY BUTT TODAY. I CAN'T BELIEVE THE SKITTLES YOU HAVE!

She responded right away.

WHAT DID YOU EXPECT FROM KYLE'S DAUGHTER? IF I HAVE ANY SKITTLES, IT'S BECAUSE OF HIM.

I shook my head. I still was amazed by her. I knew Jake had gotten into hockey but had no idea she was into it too.

I'M GOING HOME TO SOAK MY BRUISED EGO. PREFERABLY IN A GOOD I.P.A.

I hesitated before adding more. She already said no, once, but it wouldn't hurt to ask her again.

WANNA COME OVER AND COMFORT ME?

Quick as a slap shot she texted back.

YEAH, THAT'S A HARD PASS, BIG BOY.

She added an eye roll emoji. I grinned, suddenly feeling better. The blinking dots told me she was still texting, so I waited, turning on the ignition.

SEE YOU TOMORROW AT 7?

I texted Elise again.

SEVEN O'CLOCK SHARP. SLOVENIAN HALL. BE THERE OR BE SQUARE.

She responded:

OH, I'LL BE THERE ALL RIGHT. READY TO DROP YOUR $500 SO YOU CAN TAKE ME ON A "DATE."

Even though it had been my idea for her to outbid everyone on the pretense of buying a date with a Fire player, the quotation marks bothered me for some reason.

Ahh, whatever. I need to get home and get some sleep. I've got a big day tomorrow.

And I was ready to spend some more time with my best friend.

CHAPTER SIX

Scott

The makeup artist, or whatever they called them, was trying to cover the bruises from my fight, so my ass could get a good price for charity. The girl was flirting big time. With no subtlety whatsoever.

She ran a finger around my lips. "Oops, got some on your lips." She gave me a come-fuck-me smile. "We've gotta have ya lookin' good for the ladies."

"Yeah." Whatever. I needed to dangle myself out there in front of a room full of half-drunk women screaming suggestive comments at me, for sick kids. Nothing wrong with that.

She was pretty. Long, dark, curly hair, chocolate-brown eyes. Normally I would have been getting her digits, but I wasn't in the mood for some reason. Maybe it was because she was coming on so hard. Her blouse was low-cut, and although I didn't see her do it, I was pretty sure she'd unbuttoned it more since the beginning of our session. She kept shoving her breasts in my face.

"You've got a hair sticking up." She reached over me, and she was so close my lips inadvertently touched her skin. I tipped my chin back, shaking my head and laughing a little. "Oh, sorry," she said, clearly not sorry.

"Uhh...are we almost done here? I have someone meeting me here, and I want to see if she got here."

She remained undaunted. "Sure. I've just got to cover this one by your temple. You get in a fight last night?"

"A couple," I said ruefully.

"Oh?" She bit her bottom lip. "You one of those..." She wet her lips. "...bad boys?"

"Uhh..." How does one answer that? "Not really."

She rubbed some shit on my temple. But I didn't remember having a bruise on my temple. "Tell me something. We're all alone here...you can tell me the truth...when those women buy a night with you...do you give them their money's worth?"

My jaw tightened. "I guess you'd have to ask them." I stood, forcing her to back away. "I think we're done here."

"Rude!" she exclaimed once she thought I was beyond earshot. I couldn't exactly blame her. She was gorgeous. She probably wasn't used to being turned down.

I crept to the yellow velvet curtain separating the backstage from the ballroom and pulled it aside a fraction. I didn't see her at first, but the guys' cackling drew my attention, and there she was. In the middle of them. Even a couple of firemen had joined the ranks. She was wearing a long, jade green dress with slits on both sides rising above her knees. The top Veed down to a wide band above the waist. Sexy, but not overdone. She had her hair up and wore flashing, dangling earrings. Her arm was draped on top of the seat to her right, and Lucas Barbeau, of all people, had his foot on the chair and was leaning forward with his arms crossed and resting on his thighs. Lucas generally became a plastic bag of jelly around women. In fact, he rarely did interviews because it gave him too much anxiety. He seemed to be listening to her attentively, as in fact, the rest were. They stood behind her and would occasionally say something and she'd twist her neck to respond. It looked like something from a frigging music video, where she would be the singer and they, the male dancers. Sergei approached from the left holding two flutes and passing one to Elise.

I was about to slip through the curtain when I was startled by a voice.

"Oh, there you are, Mr. McCord." It was the MC. "Where are the rest of the players?"

"In front. I can get them."

But before I could move, she replied, "Don't bother. I've got it." She slid a microphone from a stand and in a super cheesy voice said, "Attention, please, ladies and gentlemen...if any of you out there remain gentlemen. The auction is beginning shortly. Firemen and Fire players in Group A, please report backstage. Thank you."

I rotated to peek at what was going on in the front again and almost dropped dead when I saw Lucas kissing Elise's hand.

What's gotten into him?

The answer came as soon as the question was thought.

She did. She got into him.

My best friend was pretty much the bomb. My swelling of pride was burst when Sergei leaned in and kissed her on the cheek, then pulled away, blocking my view of her face so I was not able to get her reaction. I ground my teeth. Sergei shot the rest of his drink, and he and a fistful of others began to filter backstage. I continued to peer from my hidden spot. Fire players in later groups filled in the vacancies of those who had left, but at the moment no one was hitting on Elise. Left alone for a moment, she drank from her flute and messed with her phone. I couldn't seem to take my eyes off her. My friend was a knockout. Absolutely stunning. It was solely this revelation that made it impossible to turn around. The girl I threw a toad on had come into her own. Like me, she had always been a bit nerdy and awkward.

Maybe it took a guy like Hunter falling in love with her to make her realize she had more to offer than the bullies who had hassled her believed.

I'd known it all along. And I was happy she no longer had to slink in the shadows like she did in school, only coming alive like she was tonight when we were alone together. When she didn't have to check over her shoulder worrying whether someone would jump her and beat the crap out of her.

"Who are you looking at?" Sergei's voice came from so near that I jumped, much to the amusement of my fellow players.

I ignored them. "I was searching for you, asshole. This thing is almost starting."

"Yeah, I heard the announcement." He stretched his neck to see behind me. "Are you certain you're not staring at a certain beautiful blonde in a green dress?" He smirked and walked away.

The MC, wrapped tightly in a swath of sequined material, approached and stepped through the curtain. The audience applauded and the spectacle began. I was in the middle of the pack, which was an enviable position. Too early, and people were saving their money because they didn't know whether or not something better was coming down the pike. Too late, and many of the women would be short on funds. And nothing was worse than strolling along that catwalk thing they made without anyone bidding on your sorry ass. I hadn't had that problem yet, but the fear of it still existed, that being the reason I'd given Elise five hundred dollars in cash to bid on me.

When my turn came, I took a deep breath, accessorized with a smile, and headed on stage.

"Ooh, it's a good thing the fire department is here because Scott McCord is one hot forward for our San Francisco Fire. I wouldn't mind if he got a tad forward with me. How about you, ladies?"

I fought to keep my facial expression neutral. Strutting around on the stage was one of the most awkward things ever, and I hated it a little more each year. Various cliché remarks were being thrown my way.

"I'd like for you to take your best shot with me, handsome."

"You can score on me anytime."

Yada, yada, yada.

I recognized a voice sliding through all the others, shouting. "Work it, baby!"

I glanced at her. She gave me a sexy smile. "Knock it off," I said out of the corner of my mouth on my next pass by her, but I was having a hard time not laughing.

She sat forward, running her gaze over me. "Give us your pouty look, McCord."

I could see several guys peeking from behind the curtains and laughing. I was so gonna kick her butt for this later.

"Let's start the bidding at a hundred dollars for this *fine* gentleman. Can I get a hundred?"

An attractive, middle-aged woman at the end of the runway raised her hand.

"One hundred. Can I get one-fifty?"

Someone in front of the first lady gestured.

"Two hundred," someone yelled on my right. I peered in her direction. She was close to my age, with long, black hair drawn up into some elaborate 'do.' The fire-engine red dress she was wearing hugged the curves nicely and a lengthy slit revealed legs that seemed to go on forever. I gave her a grin.

"Two-fifty," the first lady who bid countered.

"Four hundred dollars," the lady in red interjected, skipping a few levels.

Wow, nice.

"Well, we've got one determined bidder here. Anyone for four-fifty?"

The lady at the end shook her head with a sigh, shooting the other bidder a glare.

"Four hundred dollars going once, tw—"

"Five hundred," Elise said clearly. A murmur of surprise ran through the room.

"Six hundred," Red said. I threw her a wink.

This is actually kind of fun having two women in a bidding war, even if one of them was backed with my own money.

"Six-fifty," Elise bid, her voice wavering a little.

The lady in red leveled a stare at Elise. "Eight hundred dollars."

Well, all right. Now we're talking.

Elise blinked but didn't give ground. "Eight-fifty."

Getting tired of walking, and hot under the lights, I removed my jacket and posed with it slung over my shoulder, which incited the crowd to more yelling and whistling.

Her opponent didn't hesitate. "Two thousand dollars."

Elise's mouth fell open.

"The highest bid is two thousand dollars." The MC looked at Elise, but she stood frozen. "Can I get two thousand fifty dollars?"

Why is she hesitating? It's not her money. I dropped a grand on dinner the other night, surely she knows I can cover a couple thousand.

Elise fluttered a hand.

The auctioneer raised a brow. "Is that two thousand fifty dollars?"

"Yes," Elise said weakly. She cleared her throat, then reiterated more strongly, "Yes."

Her competition gave Elise a catty grin as she leaned forward. "Four thousand dollars."

People gasped.

Really? You're willing to pay four thousand dollars for a date with me? It's not like you're homely and can't get people to date you.

I smiled at her, amazed she would go this far.

Elise's shoulders slumped and her face drained. "I can't do that."

What? I tried to catch her eye to tell her it was okay; I didn't mind giving that much to the hospital.

"Going once, going twice, sold to the lady in red."

Everyone applauded. As others had, I descended the stairs to thank the woman who won an evening with me. Other players had kissed their "dates" hands, but I thought having put $4000 on the line, she deserved at least a peck on the cheek, which I gave her. When I turned to head backstage, I searched for Elise. Her seat was vacant. I located her as she was threading through people at a rapid pace, rushing to the far side of the room. I thought she was on her way to the bar for a refill, so was surprised when she whirled instead and escaped out the door.

I guess she figured her job was finished and she wanted to leave.

I was disappointed, but I now had a date with this woman anyway, so I wouldn't be available. Still, I'd hoped she'd stick around so I could at least talk to her before my "date" and I went to dinner.

An hour later we were down to our last bachelor, Sergei. I felt a little bad for him. No bidding war would erupt over him. He'd be lucky if anyone had saved enough money to bid anything at all. I was happy for him when I heard a couple of bids being exchanged.

Then I heard a familiar voice. "Five hundred dollars."

Elise? She better not have wasted my five hundred dollars to win a date with the Douche.

As if on cue, Lucas tapped me on the shoulder. "Elise said to give this to you." It was the plain white envelope I'd given her with my $500 still inside.

CHAPTER SEVEN

Elise

It wasn't so much the humiliation of being outbid. It wasn't even the disappointment over not getting to go spend the evening with Scott. It was the fact that, despite giving me money to bid on him, he seemed quite happy to have me bested. That's what stung so much I almost forgot I needed to bid on Sergei. When I had told him earlier that Scott had given me money to avoid a potential purchased date, Sergei begged me to do it for him. So, I returned to the scene of my defeat to bid again. At least this time I won the bidding on top. I wrote a check at the appropriate table and hurried to leave. I just wanted to get home and remove the dress I had so carefully chosen and put on sweats. I was startled to hear him shouting my name as I was leaving the building.

"Wait." Sergei caught up with me, a bit winded. "Where are you going?"

"Uhh...home, I guess."

"But...you won a date with me."

I laughed. "Yeah, with your money."

He looked hurt. "You don't want to go to dinner with me?"

"Wh— I— I thought that was, you know, for show."

"Well, it was. But I still wanted to take you for dinner to thank you."

"Oh, that's not necessary."

"Oh, but it is." I was surprised when he took my hand. "And I would very much like taking you to dinner."

"Oh. Well..." I knew I wasn't ready to date anyone, but this was only dinner. And I couldn't hurt his feelings. That would be awful.

He tilted his head, his eyes dancing. "Come on. You have to eat dinner." He wriggled his brows. "You might even have fun."

I sighed with a smile. "Okay. Thank you."

We hopped into a slick sliver Porsche and zipped through the streets of San Francisco to Ghirardelli Square. On the way, Sergei had me cracking up and feeling a million times better than when that wench across the room outbid me. He was a good conversationalist and there wasn't any of the usual fake date awkwardness, although this was actually my first fake date, so I was merely guessing it would be uncomfortable. But the stories he told about Scott were hilarious.

"One night we beat the Sharks 5-1, and Scott scored *all* the goals. All five of them! When they announced him as the third star of the game, naturally all of the fans booed. Then they announced him as the second star and the crowd caught on. By the time they gave him the number one title, the crowd was on their feet."

As he finished his story, Sergei pulled to the curb. A young man in black pants and a tie, a dress shirt, and dress shoes opened my door as my "date" exited and came around to my side, extending his hand to help me out. He dangled his car keys.

"No joy riding this time."

"Yes, sir."

He dropped the keys into the kid's waiting palm.

An older couple approached us. "I didn't know McCormick and Schmick's had valet service."

"They don't," Sergei said. "Charles is from the Argonaut Hotel."

The man arched his brows. "What's he doing here then?"

"We had an arrangement," Sergei said with a twinkle in his eye.

He offered me his elbow and escorted me into the restaurant, which had a beautiful view of the bay. When we'd been seated and our wine arrived, Sergei spun his glass by the stem, watching its rotations. "Usually at this point in the evening, after the auction, I'd be praying for a quick end to the night." He looked up and held my gaze. "Not this year." He raised his glass. "To the beautiful woman who redeemed the Fire and Ice Auction for me."

I smiled, leaning forward and really enjoying myself. "My pleasure..." I trailed off, my mouth hanging open when I spotted Scott over Sergei's shoulder. He noticed me at the same moment. Sergei twisted in his chair to see what I was gawking at. I was in shock. Scott slid a chair from under the table so the lady in red could have a seat. "What are the odds? With all the restaurants in San Francisco..."

Sergei rubbed his brow. "I'm afraid that would be my fault." I peered at him. "I heard Scott making reservations and thought it might be funny if we 'ran into' each other here and we could commiserate about our dates. That was before I knew I'd be going out with you."

I stared at him. Is that what we were doing? Going out?

"Is this a problem? Because we could maybe go somewhere else. It's still early."

I glanced behind him again. Scott seemed royally pissed. *I'm not letting him ruin my night.* "No. No problem. So, what were you saying regarding me being beautiful?"

He laughed. "Well...you were easily the most stunning woman in the room today, and all of the other Flame players probably hate my guts right now for being the one who had the privilege of taking you to dinner."

"That's very kind of you," I said quickly, the heat rushing to my cheeks. "But if you keep saying things like that, I'll think you're just trying to get me into bed."

His face drained. "That's absolutely not what I'm trying to do."

Well, you don't need to protest that much. I sighed. *Can I get any more awkward? Accusing the guy of seducing me when he was only thanking me for doing him a favor.*

"I'm sorry. That was supposed to be a joke. Sometimes my sense of humor is...a little off."

"Well...I want you to know that's not what I'm doing."

Okay. You've made that clear.

"Please forget I said anything." I needed to change the subject. "Tell me another funny story."

"Involving Scott?"

"Or you. Or any of the players."

He thought. I brought my glass to my lips but stole a look at Scott's table. The pair seemed to be having an animated discussion, but catching my eye again he stopped talking, his lips parted. She rotated in her chair and saw me. I raised my glass in a smart-assed salute to her. She had none to lift in return, so gave me a sharp nod, then she reached over and rubbed Scott's back. The hackles rose on my neck. *What I wouldn't do for a hockey stick right now.* I refocused my attention on Sergei.

"Okay. This one is about Scott too. His rookie year he was in a huge collision with—"

"Tony Whiteside," I supplied. "I remember that. It was awful."

"It was. Terrifying at first because they were both out cold. When they brought Scott to in the dressing room, he didn't even realize he was in the NHL, let alone San Francisco. When coach asked if he'd be able to play in the next period, the trainer said, 'He doesn't even know who he is.' To which Coach said, 'Tell him he's freaking Wayne Gretsky and get his ass in here.'"

I laughed. "You're kidding."

"I kid you not." He tipped his head to the side. "Funny thing was, even though he didn't know he was an NHL hockey player, once he knew there was a game, he wanted to get on the ice."

I rolled my eyes but smiled.

That's my Scottie.

The waiter reappeared, but we hadn't even opened our menus, so we sent him away again. A pop made me glance over. A waiter was pouring bubbly for Scott and his date. Like the champagne we'd had the evening before. It hurt.

What do I care? It's not like I didn't know Scott was out with different women every night of the week.

I blinked and tried to hone in on the menu, putting all thoughts of him aside. I got ricotta and wild mushroom stuffed ravioli, and Sergei ordered lobster tail. My phone buzzed on the table and I picked it up. It was a text from Scott.

WHAT THE HELL ARE YOU DOING HERE WITH HIM?

What the hell am I doing here? I stared at his table. He was focused on her. I responded to the text.

WHY DO YOU CARE?

Sure, it was a bit snippy. But I was thrown. I centered myself by concentrating on Sergei. We got involved in conversation, so I didn't see her coming until a shadow crossed our table. I thought the waiter had returned with a question and was surprised to find the infamous lady in red standing next to us. She cast a look at Sergei then faced me with a brow raised.

"Enjoying your second choice?"

I was so stunned, I had no comeback. She sauntered off with her nose in the air. Sergei took a drink of his wine, studying the window with the skyline beyond it.

"I—" My gaze ping-ponged around the tablecloth, cold shock being replaced with a red-hot rage. "I'm so sorry, Sergei. That was a horrible thing for her to say. I—" I didn't know what to say. I could tell he was hurt and trying to hide it. "I'll be right back." I slammed my napkin on the table and began to rise, intending to find that woman and scratch her eyes out, but Sergei covered my hand.

"Forget it, Elise." He stared at me with his head tilted, jaw tense.

I slowly sat down, glowering at Scott. He was peering at us. I glared at him, and he turned away. Before I could come up with anything to say to Sergei, the waiter arrived with my salad and Sergei's soup. He stirred his clam chowder and cleared his throat. "This smells wonderful." He was forcing his words to fill the silence, not looking at me directly anymore.

Not able to find the right thing to say, I reached over the table and gave his arm a squeeze. He lifted his gaze and the tension seemed to leave him.

"Uhh...how's your salad?"

I glanced at it. "Haven't tried it yet."

We started our conversation again, not as lively as before, but still interesting. I enjoyed listening to him and studied his features in the candlelight. His hair was baby fine, a dark blond that swept over his forehead. He had these incredible ice-blue eyes and an amazing smile that lit his whole face, amping his boyish charm.

When we'd arrived at the restaurant, the sun had been setting beyond the windows to my left. The sky was on fire, with molten shades of yellow and orange. The silhouette of the Golden Gate Bridge stood out in stark contrast, its edges so defined it resembled a die cut paper image of the real thing. Now the view was equally breathtaking, with the lights of Marin County across the bay twinkling like the stars at night. "Can I ask you a serious question?"

His brows shot up.

A busboy appeared at our table. "Are you finished, sir?"

"I think I am," he said with dread. He laced his fingers together and placed them on the table. "It depends."

"On what?" I glanced at the busboy. "I'm finished too. Thank you." He cleared my spot.

Sergei leaned forward. "On whether you expect a serious answer."

"Come on. I think five hundred dollars deserves an honest answer."

"It was my five hundred dollars." He laughed. "Go on." He lifted his wine glass.

I licked my lips. "Why were you and Scott not getting along the other day?"

"Mmm." He took a drink, staring off blankly. "Well, to understand that, I think you need to go into the mind of an athlete." He spun his glass on the table again. "I don't want to sound braggy...but for years and years and years...since I was four, in fact, I've been told I had a 'rare talent.'" He made air quotation marks. "I can see the ice and know where my boys are much of the time and predict what part of the ice they're headed for. Hockey is very important where I'm from. And when you're told you're special, and treated like you're special from an early age, you start to think you are special."

I began to say something, but he was gazing at his wine glass and didn't realize it and continued.

"Now Scott, from miles and miles away, was probably told he had a wicked slap shot. He was told he could skate so smoothly and so naturally he looked like he was floating above the ice. He was told he was tough, didn't take shit from anybody. That he had leadership skills and unrivaled loyalty." He held his arms out, palms up. "He was cool under pressure. Fast...I mean, there are any number of things he could have been praised for. He's even-keeled... So," he said as he picked up the salt and pepper, "Mr. Special meets Mr. Special." He brought them together. "Things don't always go smoothly." He tipped one onto its side and pepper came out. He righted it, brushed the grains into his palm, then dumped them on a bread plate which had been left behind. "So that's my long-winded way of saying, our egos clashed."

It made sense. Scott could be fairly full of himself at times.

"Is that a huge turn-off?"

I tilted my head, staring into the flame of the candle. "Well, it's a weakness to be sure." I lifted my gaze to his. "But I'd be a hypocrite to judge you for it. I have all sorts of shortcomings, Sergei. I won't hold it against you."

He exhaled, smiling. "I'm glad." He took my hand in both of his. "You are an incredible woman, Elise. It's no wonder Scott talks about you all the time." He brought my hand to his mouth and kissed it.

He talks about me all the time?

Before I could say anything, the waiter approached. "Can I interest you in some dessert this evening?"

Sergei looked at me.

"Oh, no. I couldn't eat another bite."

"If you could just bring me the check then." When he left, Sergei turned his gaze on me. "Any chance I could convince you to hang around with me for a little while? An ice cream sundae may be in it for you if you get your appetite back."

My lips eased into a smile. "I think I'd like that."

The plaintive wail of a saxophone floated to me as we exited the building. Curious, I crossed to a railing overlooking the courtyard below. Near a huge fountain a guy was playing his horn. Dressed in black pants and a matching vest, a white button-down and solid black tie, worn loose, and sporting a snappy fedora, tilted forward, he fit the part of the musician. I quickly recognized the melody—"Let Her Go" by Passenger. I'd never heard it on the sax before and was surprised by how well it lent itself to that. "I love this song."

"Do you want to go and listen?"

"Sure, that would be great."

We found a staircase to the courtyard and made our way to the fountain area. As we listened to the music, Sergei took my hand. When I glanced at him, he beamed at me. My heart lightened and warmed. I tempered the zing of excitement I felt, remembering Scott's advice to go slow. I rocked along with the melody. I don't know why my body was so connected with the sound of music, but it was something I did unconsciously. My mom said I did it even when I was too young to understand the idea of dancing. Sergei lifted our arms and considered me with raised brows. My lips twitched.

He wants me to dance.

I had an urge to scan the people surrounding the musician to see if anyone else was dancing, but the way he held my gaze was almost a challenge, and I could never turn down a challenge. I twirled under his arm and laughed, thinking maybe we were through, but he pulled me into his embrace and swayed with me held tightly against him. It should have felt uncomfortable—we really hardly knew each other—but it didn't. Damn it all if my smile didn't widen.

"Thank you for coming with me, Elise," he said, his voice pitched a bit lower than usual.

We continued to stare into each other's faces. "It's been absolutely wonderful." I released his hand and brought both of mine to loop around his neck. Motion to my right drew my attention. Another guy was holding his arm up for his date to spin beneath, and they moved deeper into the opening created by those gathered listening to the music.

I tilted my head. "Look what you started." To our left, two couples found a space of their own on our "dance floor." He didn't comment, still focusing on me, his features tight with an intensity I hadn't seen before.

My lips parted and I played with his hair at the nape of his neck, shifting my focus from one of his eyes to the other, studying all the nuances of his expression. He leaned in and I thought he would kiss me, which was weird. What was weirder still was the fact I wasn't sure if I'd stop him.

A sudden movement broke the spell. The saxist had hopped up onto the edge of the fountain and was really getting into his music. A half-dozen couples were dancing now, and others were staying to listen, growing the crowd. I glanced back at Sergei. The moment had passed.

He grinned. "You're a violinist. I should have thought of music before. Of course you like it."

"Oh, you have to love music to be in my family."

"I want to hear your family stories," he said abruptly. "I want to learn more about you. Do you want to take a walk with me?"

"Sure."

He released me, but when I looked he wasn't following me. He was drawing a hundred dollar bill from his wallet and dropping it in a funky black hat I hadn't noticed lying beside the sax's case. He hurried over and took my hand, and we split the crowd and disappeared beyond them.

This night was definitely not turning out like I'd expected it to.

Scott

This night was definitely not turning out the way I'd expected it to.

I almost choked when we walked into the restaurant and I saw them together.

Seriously? THIS restaurant?

My evening, which had been going steadily downhill, plunged even farther.

How the hell did he worm his way into getting her to spend $500 of her hard-earned cash to go to dinner with HIM? He really is a douche. And he WILL be paying her back.

"Something wrong?" My date, Stephanie, followed my line of sight. "Well, would you look at that?" Twisting to face me, she narrowed her gaze. "Is this a problem? Because, if it is, we're leaving."

Yes, ma'am.

She was every bit the spoiled little princess I had taken her to be, and an heiress to the estate of the guy who invented the "Chip Corker," apparently some sort of revolutionary way to seal snack bags. She was attractive in that 'I've-got-an-endless-supply-of-money-to-make-me-attractive' way, but it paled in comparison to Elise. I don't know why it was Elise I chose to compare her with, other than the fact that she was especially tempting this evening.

Tempting?

I tried to give Stephanie my most charming smile and helped her to be seated before sitting myself. "Not a problem at all."

She immediately ordered the most expensive champagne on the menu, possibly on the planet, downed her flute, then excused herself. I watched her leave and was surprised when she stopped by Elise's table, yet not all that surprised. Whatever she said, Elise first seemed shocked, then totally outraged. Like toe-curlingly infuriated. She jumped to her feet like she intended to beat the living daylights out of my little heiress, which I would have actually paid to see, but Sergei put a hand on hers and she lowered herself into her chair, shooting me a withering glance. I focused elsewhere.

What did I do?

When Stephanie returned to the table, I rose to again get her seat for her. I felt the weight of Elise's stare but ignored it. But it was difficult to ignore her laughter, or how much fun they seemed to be having, or the way her face looked in the candlelight.

What the hell is wrong with me? Why do I even care what Elise's face looks like in the candlelight, or anywhere else for that matter? I'm having dinner with a beautiful woman and thinking about my friend at the next table?

I gave my head a shake and vowed not to think of Elise again. Which worked until she passed us on her way to the door. Stephanie was running her hand along my thigh. "What do you say we leave and find someplace more...intimate?"

I followed Elise with my gaze. "Great idea."

I hurriedly paid the bill and rushed Stephanie through the door. I'm not sure why, because I was sure Elise and Sergei would be gone by the time we got there. Then I spotted them. Sergei was holding his arm up for her to spin under, even though no one else was dancing.

What a dork.

Then I watched the two of them together. She seemed to be having a good time. I zeroed in on his hand on the bare skin of her back and my gut tightened.

"Who is she?"

"Huh?" I glanced at Stephanie, whom I'd forgotten for a second. "Oh, just a family friend."

"Huh," she said, cocking a hip. "You seem to be very focused on your 'family friend.'"

"That's because she recently got out of a relationship, and I know—" I almost told her about the bet but luckily remembered I couldn't release any information that might get a teammate in trouble. Even a douche of a teammate. "I know she falls for guys easily, and I don't want to see her get hurt."

I was staring at Elise again. Stephanie stuck one painted nail on the side of my face and turned me toward her. "She's a big girl, McCord. She'll be all right."

"Yeah..." I said thoughtfully. Then I cleared my throat and gave her my full attention. "You're right. She's fine." I inhaled through my nose. "Now where to?"

"Let's go to my place."

Why not?

Once we'd climbed into the back of the car I'd sent for, she quickly became aggressive. She stuck her tongue down my throat and chewed on my lip so hard I was sure she'd drawn blood. She grabbed me between the legs and dug her claws in.

"Ooh. I love an athlete. So big...and strong." She yanked on my belt buckle fiercely and before I could even protest she had my pants unzipped. My gaze connected with Ben's in the mirror. He was frowning. Apparently he thought she was a bit much too.

"Uhh...let's take things a little slower." I nodded toward the front. "We're not alone."

She climbed on top of me. "Oh, he won't mind." Her frantic movements ended, and she twisted to peer at him in the mirror. "Or he can just pull over and join us. That might be fun."

Ben rolled his eyes and shook his head, laughing.

Unfazed, she slipped her hand into my pants.

"Hey, hey! Hold it a minute," I slouched in my seat more to get some room and managed to get her hand out. Once that was done, I zipped my pants, exhaled, and raked my hair back as it had gotten messed up with all the action.

She pouted and crossed her arms.

"I generally like to be the one in control," I told her.

She brightened. "Oh, I like that too." She climbed on top of me again, and I heard her dress rip a little. "Stephanie's been a bad girl and needs her daddy to spank her." She took my hands and put them on her ass, which, admittedly, was a fantastic ass, probably bolstered with silicone.

I took both of her arms and pushed her into her corner of the car. "Stop."

She bit her bottom lip. "Ooh. I'm in trouble, aren't I?" She looked around at the nearby buildings. "Let's not go all the way to the house. I've got a place that's much closer. Take a right at the next corner."

Within a few blocks, we arrived at a high-rise with luxury condos. She grabbed my elbow. "This way." She turned to Ben. "You sure you don't wanna...?"

He tipped his cap. "Not while I'm on duty, ma'am."

Behind her back I mouthed, "Help!"

"Hmm...that's a shame." She stood frozen for a second. "Oh, well. Come on, lover boy. I can't wait to get you to myself."

The next thing I knew I was sitting in the middle of a huge living room. Two sets of windows ran all the way along adjacent walls, meeting in a seam at the corner. I was on a white couch set adrift in a sea of white fur carpeting. She had removed my jacket with those dragon nails she had and draped it over the couch then disappeared somewhere and I was catching my breath. I spotted a drink cart and made myself a bourbon neat, downing one and adding some ice to the tumbler.

"Ohh, Scottie. Could you come here?"

"Uhh..." I clinked another piece of ice in and grabbed the decanter. "Be right there." I poured a half-glass, then rethought things and filled it all the way. "Coming." I searched for a plausible excuse to leave. The short hall she'd gone through only had one door, and it was slightly ajar.

"This way," she called.

I grabbed the doorknob and swung the door open, releasing it about halfway, and it continued its journey, banging against the wall. So much was going on in there I could hardly take it in. Dominating the room was a big, heart-shaped bed covered with red fur. Manacles were attached to two posts that stood at the head of the bed, and two at the foot. It was set up against a short wall and two sheets of windows angled out from the edges of that wall, the far side of the room faceted like a hexagon. Straps, harnesses, and things I didn't even recognize hung from the ceiling. I turned to the right. Some kind of chair with spikes stood in the middle of the floor with handcuffs attached to its back and legs, a big spotlight suspended above it. I whirled to assess the situation in the opposite direction. She was bent over this kneeler looking thing, her wrists bound with a red scarf. She had a choker chain circling her neck and was wearing some sort of black studded leather jumpsuit with openings for her butt cheeks. A whip lay nearby on the bed.

"I need you to tie these tighter."

"Whoa," was all I could manage. From the corner of my eye, I could see a high dresser. With shaky hands I went to put my tumbler on it and knocked it against some weird, wolf-like tribal mask. Next to it was an assortment of dildos, vibrators, and tools I didn't want to know the use for, spread on a silver tray like a doctor's instruments. I jumped and moved away.

Unbeknownst to me, she had stepped up behind me. "You like?"

I spun and she ran her tongue around her lips. Now I could see the front of her getup and it also had holes, which her other surgical assets were shoved through. Her nipples were pierced with hoops hanging from them like door knockers.

I shuffled toward the hall. "Th-that's some...some ensemble you've got there. But I have...I have practice. Yep. Gotta practice."

"What? On a Friday night?"

"Yeah. Coach is real strict..."

"Well, surely you have time for a short beating, and maybe a blowjob?" She snatched the whip off the bed and held it out to me.

"W-wish I could, but, you know...gotta go."

She followed me into the hall. "Maybe tomorrow night?"

"Uhh..." I forced a chuckle. "Got plans. Big plans." I reached the door finally and grabbed the knob, twisted, and rushed along the hall, jabbing at the elevator button again and again. I heard the door open behind me and whirled.

She was walking toward me, and I noted for the first time her thigh-high, suede boots. I actually liked those. "You can beat me in the elevator then." She wore brass knuckles with LOVE spelled on them.

Holy shit. She won't quit.

Searching frantically, I spotted a stairwell and sprinted for it. I tore down the stairs, skidding around the landing and attacking the next set of steps. I chanced a quick look up when her chains clanged against the railing. She was bent over it, watching me race, then swing across the landings, and continue to descend as quickly as possible. "Maybe after practice?"

Not even for the Stanley Cup.

An upper door creaked. "Oh, hi, Joey."

"Hey."

Oh, Joey. My savior! I love you!

I continued swirling like water in the drain, fifteen floors.

She giggled. "Hold on a minute. I have someone who will join us. You'll love him."

Shit.

Heels clicked rapidly on the steps above me. Rounding the curve on a landing, my dress shoes slid, and I rammed my hip against the cinderblock exterior wall. But I kept going.

The last five floors the walls became windows, and I took a moment to bang on the glass. Ben was leaning against the car, but he straightened, saw me, and threw his paper in the open window of the car, hustling to the driver's side.

Once at the bottom, I scrambled outside, booked it across the pavement, and jumped in the car. "Go! Go! Go!" I shouted as I grappled to get the door shut.

He squealed away from the curb as I lay panting in the back. He looked at me in the mirror. "You didn't kill anyone, did you?"

My laughter was broken up by heaving breaths. I wiped the sweat from my brow. "No." Then I flashbacked to Elise and Sergei dancing. "Not yet, anyway," I muttered.

CHAPTER EIGHT

Elise

We left the bricked area of the square, crossing Beach Street to sit on a park bench facing the ocean and talked for close to forty-five minutes. I told him some childhood stories with Scott in them, being careful to leave out any parts that might embarrass Scott or me, like the time we kissed. The breeze off the water made it chilly, so he'd insisted I wear his jacket over my sleeveless dress.

"What about you? What do you miss most from your childhood?"

"Oh, that would have to be my babushka's *zefir*," he said immediately.

"*Zefir*?"

"You don't know what *zefir* is?"

I chuckled. "No. Should I?"

His brow furrowed. "Oh, no. I guess not." Then his expression brightened. "It's kind of like fruity marshmallows. Only it's not really like marshmallows at all. It's...well, it's light and airy, mostly egg whites and— Hey! Why don't I make it for you tomorrow?"

I winced. "I can't. I kind of promised Scott I'd spend the evening with him."

"Oh, well..." He sounded disappointed. "Sunday, then. I could make it for you Sunday. We have a matinee game. You could come over after, and we could make it together."

"Okay. That sounds great." I stood, stretching. "But we should probably get going. It's late, and I have practice tomorrow morning."

"Practice?" He frowned momentarily, then his face cleared. "Oh, for your violin. I was thinking hockey practice. Duh."

I was surprised by his use of slang as a Russian. I was on the verge of asking him about it when my phone vibrated loudly in my handbag. I was half expecting it to be a text from Scott, but it was a call. My heart pounded. A call in the middle of the night couldn't be good. "Do you mind if I take this? It's my brother."

"No not at all." He looked concerned too.

I clicked the button. "Hey."

"Happy birthday!"

Jake sounded a little sloshed. "Uhh...thanks, but...isn't it two o'clock in the morning where you are?"

"Yes. Yes, it is. But I waited up so I could be the first to wish you a happy birthday."

I had to grin. "You know a text would have done fine, you moron."

"Oh, I didn't think of that..."

"Maybe because you're knee-deep in suds?"

"Yes." I could visualize his head bouncing animatedly. "It could definitely have something to do with that."

"Is everything all right?" Sergei murmured.

I smiled at him and nodded.

"Good. I'll call the car." He slid his cell from his pocket and stepped away to place his call.

"Was that Scott? Put him on for a second."

"No, that wasn't Scott." I hurriedly changed the subject. "Are you out somewhere? You're not driving, are you?"

"No, I'm waiting for an Uber. Hey, wait..." I heard him say to someone else, "Is it an Escalade? ...yeah, that's it." He returned to me. "My Uber's here. I'll call you in the morning. Or maybe afternoon. I may sleep in."

I'd put money on it. "Okay. See ya."

"Love you, sis."

"Thanks, dude. I'll talk to you tomorrow." I sighed happily, plunking my phone into my purse. He hadn't forgotten me, even though I'd moved halfway across the country. "Sorry about that," I said to Sergei.

He put his hand on the small of my back and led me forward. "Does he often call you in the middle of the night?"

"Oh, no." The sound of our shoes tapping over the brick ricocheted to us off the closed shops' windows. "We do have a habit of texting each other when we've been drinking, though. He and I have always been tight as it was just the two of us after my brother Ryan went to school." I wrinkled my nose, amused. "We usually stick to texts, though, not phone calls."

"Oh?" He looked at me with raised brows.

"Yeah, he...uh...he said he wanted to be the first to wish me a happy birthday, the dork."

His brows shot even higher. "It's your birthday?"

"Well, technically, yes."

"Well, happy birthday."

"Thanks. But it's been my birthday for a whole...five minutes, you know. You'll need to do better than that if you hope to beat Jake next year."

He chuckled. "I'll keep that in mind." I was saved from further embarrassment by the car pulling up to the curb. Sergei opened the rear door, sweeping his arm out with a flourish. "Birthday Girl first," he said loud enough to alert the driver, the Charles kid from earlier.

"It was your birthday?" he said enthusiastically, the prospect stirring him from of his previously sleepy state.

"Uhh...yeah."

"Well, happy belated birthday."

Sergei had slid into the back on the opposite side. "Not belated. It's today."

"Oh." The driver peeked at the dash. "Oh, it's after midnight. Let me be the first to wish you a happy birthday then."

Sergei and I glanced at each other. "Too late," we said at the same time, chuckling.

Charles looked confused.

"My brother just called me," I explained, realizing I had entered yet another awkward conversation.

"Oh, I see."

My purse bounced between Sergei and me. I rolled my eyes with a grin and drew my phone out, reading the display. "My other brother. Sorry about this."

"No. It's your birthday," he said as if that offered a blanketed pardon for any wrongdoing.

I may not have liked the fuss on my birthday, but I did like those little privileges. I clicked the receive button and held the phone up to my ear, smiling in anticipation of hearing his voice.

"Hello?"

"Are you seeing someone already?"

My face fell. "What?"

He sighed. I could picture him rubbing the bridge of his nose. "It's two o'clock in the morning. Let's not play games. Who's the guy with you, Elise? You said it wasn't Scott, so who is it?"

I tightened my grip on the phone. "Jake called you."

"Yes, he did. And I'm glad he did. Answer my question."

My temperature rose. Ever since my dad cheated on my mom and walked away from us, Ryan seemed to consider himself "the man of the family," much to Jake's and my aggravation. I sat forward, fighting to keep my voice calm and low so everyone in the car wasn't privy to my browbeating. "You know, I thought when I put fifteen hundred miles between us some of this brotherly bullshit would end."

"Who is he, Elise?"

"Oh my God," I huffed, glancing at Sergei. "You're not going to let up until I tell you are you?" I didn't wait for him to respond. "His name's Sergei, and—" Sergei eyes widened, making him look like a trapped dog. His gaze darted to Charles' in the rearview, and the driver winced sympathetically.

"I thought we talked over this before you left. You—"

The condescension in his voice was infuriating. I blocked out everything but my conversation. "You know, this is none of your business. I'm an intelligent adult, Ryan. I can make my own choices."

He raised his voice. "You're intelligent about some things, Elise, but when it comes to relationships—" He stopped himself.

"When it comes to relationships, what? I'm dumb?"

"I would choose to say inexperienced."

"But you would actually mean dumb, huh?"

His voice was tight. "Don't put words in my mouth." It was like suddenly we had reverted to kids and every argument we'd ever had was on the table in front of us. Every time he had stolen my radio. Made fun of my friends. Made fun of me...

I exhaled and closed my eyes, sinking into the seat and reminding myself he was being an asshole because of his love for me. "He's Scott's roommate, all right? We're out as friends. The team had this auction thing and..." I didn't want to go into the whole explanation.

Ryan was silent for a moment. He released a long breath. "I'm sorry, Elise. I should have never listened to Jake's drunk ass."

I wasn't ready to let him off the hook. "At least Jake wished me a happy birthday."

"You're right. I'm sorry. I'm a crappy brother." He sounded tired.

I softened. "Just occasionally."

He laughed at that. "Well, good. I'd hate to think I was that way all the time."

"Ry...I'm not sixteen anymore. I can take care of myself."

"I know. But you've only dated Hunter—" He seemed to recognize his mistake and held up.

His name still stung. I fought back the tears that mounted behind my lashes. "I know, all right? I'm *well* aware of that." *And I don't know why everyone has to keep reminding me of it.* "But I'm old enough to make decisions on my own. Even if that means getting my heart trampled on again."

"You're right. You're right. It's just...it's hard having you on the West Coast."

I hadn't thought about it being hard on them. "I know. But Ry, we hardly saw each other as it was. You're busy with your job..."

"I should have made more time for you."

How could the guy I'd wanted to strangle seconds ago now make me love him so much? "No, Ry. You have a life. It happens. We're all adults and that means not spending as much time together. You're a good brother."

He sighed. "I guess."

"This will take a little adjusting for all of us. But I'll come home. And you have that trip planned to come see me..."

"You're right. But I don't like to think of you being alone there. Unprotected in a big city..."

I fought not to roll my eyes. Why did he perpetually think of me as being four years old? "I'm not unprotected. Scott's here."

"Yeah, but he's always wrapped up with his hockey..."

Or women. "Ryan..." I said in a gently scolding tone. "I can take care of myself. I have that mace you gave me. I'm doing all of those safety tips in that article you sent me..."

"All right. You've convinced me. But watch your heart, little one. I'm going back to sleep."

"Goodnight, big brother."

I was about to disconnect but heard him shout. "Wait. Elise!"

I hurriedly returned my phone to my ear. "What? I'm still here."

"Happy birthday."

The corners of my lips tugged upward. "Thanks. Now go to sleep."

"You don't have to tell me twice. Bye."

"Bye." I disconnected and released a big breath. It was nice to know I mattered to my brothers, even if they were a pain in the butt.

"Everything okay?" Sergei asked.

"Oh, yeah. Sorry. I'm the only girl. Overprotective brothers."

"Well, if you were my sister, I'd look out for you too."

I patted his leg. "Thanks, Sergei." Suddenly realizing he was in the seat with me instead of driving I asked, "Why did you sit back here? How's Charles getting home?"

"My brother's following us," Charles offered.

"And I sat here so I could spend some more time talking to you."

Charles pulled in front of my place. "Oh. And I wasted it all talking to my brothers."

He patted my leg. "Don't worry about it. We'll have plenty of time to talk Sunday when we make my babushka's *zefir* and celebrate your birthday."

I batted my eyes. "Ooh. We'll be celebrating my birthday?"

He tapped my nose. "Damned right we will be."

"That'll be great." I collected my purse. "Will Scott help with the cooking?"

When I glanced over, he was staring at me with his head tilted. "No. I thought it would just be the two of us."

I didn't know how to respond.

"That's okay, isn't it?"

"Of course." I swatted his arm. "Scott would only get in the way."

"Most definitely." His voice held an odd tenor I couldn't decipher. He got out and came around to open my door, but I was already standing beside the car. Looking up the long walkway, I spotted a figure sitting on top of the metal picnic table on the lawn.

"I'll walk you to the door. Keep you safe. Like your brothers wanted," he joked.

"Umm..." The figure had slowly gotten off the table and now stood in the middle of the sidewalk, appearing somewhat intimidating. "I think I'll be okay."

He followed my gaze and must have recognized Scott too. His face clouded for a minute, then he turned to me. "Okay. But I want to do something first."

Before I could even blink, he stepped forward and covered my lips with his. A soft, quick kiss, but enough of one to make my heart skip a beat.

"Goodnight."

I slipped his jacket from my shoulders without saying anything, because, quite frankly, I couldn't, and held it out to him.

"Keep it. I'll get it Sunday."

Charles had bailed, leaving the driver's door open, so Sergei got in and drove away.

I walked sluggishly toward Scott. Because I knew him so well, I could tell he was steamed simply by the way he was holding himself. I could always tell when it was him on the ice, even if I couldn't see his number. They all looked similar with their helmets on, but I could always recognize him by the way he skated, the way he passed, even the way he checked. As I neared him, there could be no mistaking his foul mood. The light was coming from behind him, so he was mostly in shadow, but I could make out enough to know he wore the same expression he had every time he got called on a ticky-tack foul. When I got within a couple of feet, I saw his pupils had flames jumping within them.

What does he have to be angry over?

My insides tightened in response to him, and I could feel the level of sarcasm rising like bubbles in boiling water.

"What the hell were you doing at that restaurant with him?" The words jetted from his mouth like he'd been holding them in the entire time he watched me saunter along the sidewalk.

I kept my voice steady. "Eating dinner. I would have thought that was obvious."

He tilted his head back, crossing his arms and staring down his nose at me. Seconds passed as he worked his jaw, a vein pulsing below his cheekbone serving as a warning that he was close to snapping. I mimicked his posture but added a cocked hip and a raised brow. Our standoff was short-lived. He clicked his tongue and looked to the side. "I thought you'd be eating dinner with me." He returned his gaze to me and the hurt that briefly floated through them did more damage than the anger had done. "That's what we agreed on. Right? You'd bid and help me to avoid the hell of having to take someone else to dinner."

"But..." I huffed. "You saw what happened. She outbid me. My bank account isn't stuffed full like yours is, Scott. I need to eat next week."

"What are you talking about?"

"I haven't got a lot saved up yet..."

"But you bid like two thousand dollars."

"Two thousand and fifty."

"You were planning on paying for that with your own money?"

"Yes." *How else did he think I'd pay for it?* "Along with the five hundred you gave me. I didn't have any more than that to spare."

"But...I would have paid you back for whatever you bid."

My heart sank. I hadn't even thought of that. "Oh," I said flatly, then I dug deep into my well of indignation. "Well, we never discussed what would happen if someone bid over the five hundred you gave me. How was I to know that?" When he was silent I continued, looking down as I swept the toes of one shoe through the loose dirt at my feet. "Besides, you seemed pretty happy with Mama Long Legs." I lifted my face at the end to see his reaction.

Maddeningly, he didn't say anything, and I couldn't read his expression.

"You freaking kissed her." I hadn't meant to say it, but it came out anyway. And shakily, at that.

He held up a finger. "Correction. *She* kissed *me*."

The way he said it, like he was proud of that fact, ticked me off even more. "Well, good for you, Scottie. I'm so happy for you. Now, if you'll excuse me, I want to go to bed." I tried to shoulder past him.

"Sergei kissed you."

I whirled around. "That was different. That was a birthday kiss."

"It didn't look like any birthday kiss."

I will not blush. But the heat was already rushing to my cheeks. "You don't know what you're talking about." I spun on my heels and prepared to stomp away, but he rushed to get in my way.

"Elise, wait."

I clenched my teeth and glared at him. "What? What is it that you want?" I was on the edge of losing it, with a stiff wind behind me.

"I'm...sorry. Okay?"

This is new. Scott McCord apologizing? I took a step back. Literally and figuratively.

He exhaled, the tension leaving his shoulders. "I guess I got a little caught up in everything." I didn't speak, blinking and looking to the side. "I've never had two beautiful women bidding over me, okay? It went to my head." He bent his knees to catch my gaze, giving me a disarming smile.

Did he just call me beautiful?

He clasped my hands. "You're the woman I wanted to have dinner with."

Oh, God, no. Don't do this to me, Scott. Don't be charming.

He glanced down. "Are we still on for dinner tomorrow night? Or, I guess I should say, later today?"

I shrugged. "Yeah, sure."

He pinched my chin and raised it, slipping an arm around me, and drawing me in. "Maybe *I* should give you a birthday kiss..." He brought his lips so close I could feel the heat of his breath on mine. "Huh, Elise?"

Everything inside me rose up, wanting to meet his lips so badly I could hardly take it. My traitorous heels actually lifted from the ground as I stretched, yearned toward him. I broke free from his grip and stumbled backward. "Don't do that to me." My voice was gravelly.

"Do what?" he said, indignant. "You gave him a kiss."

I was shaking with emotion. *How can he not understand this?* "He and I do not have a past."

"What difference does that make?"

I wanted to scream. I wanted to slap him. I wanted to cry. "Are you really that clueless?" I left before he could say another word.

CHAPTER NINE

Scott

I stared at her door for a long time, trying to make sense of her words. A couple returned and shook me from my stupor, giving me the evil eye until I walked away. Words and images floated around in my head like pieces of a jigsaw puzzle. Except it was like I was forcing pieces together that didn't belong together and mashing the edges.

Once home, I found the place dark, barring the light under Sergei's door. I toed my shoes off, folded my jacket over a chair, and stood for a moment grasping the top of it. Slowly, I turned and moved to my wet bar with only the light from outside guiding me. I poured myself a rusty nail and took it across to an armchair. Savoring the flavor of good scotch and Drambuie on my tongue, I flopped down, setting my drink on a table, the whole while thinking of Elise. The lights remained extinguished while I yanked my shirt from my pants, unbuttoned and rolled my sleeves, and opened my shirt halfway, as the combination of alcohol and my thoughts was making me hot.

When Sergei kissed her—man. I was filled with an urge so strong it scared me. An urge to seek and destroy. Obliterate. Annihilate. End him. On the walk home, I contemplated doing just that, in numerous creatively violent ways, but my anger had dissipated by the time I got to my place. Still, I didn't tempt fate by talking to him, and I hoped he'd be smart enough to stay in his room for the rest of the night. I decided I needed to tell Elise about Sergei's bet, even if I had to pay off every single guy who'd taken him up on it. I couldn't risk her getting further involved with him and getting hurt.

For some reason, I remembered a time in school I was also worried she'd get hurt. I overheard a guy making fun of her. Elise was on a rampage to get the city of Lincoln to be more conscientious with battery disposal, attending town meetings and somehow getting interviewed by the newspaper. She was almost single-handedly responsible for ordinances that saved our landfills from batteries that could have leaked hazardous chemicals into our environment. I was proud of her, but not everyone looked at it that way.

"Elise Scofield," the guy said, watching her ass as she walked in front of him on the way to class. "Shit, with a body like that, she should be a Playboy bunny, not some freaking Energizer Bunny saver. What a waste of flesh."

The hairs on the back of my neck rose. I waited until Elise turned the corner then tapped the kid on the shoulder. When he faced me, I said, "You need to stop talking Elise down."

"Oh, yeah? Why's that?" I recognized him as a linebacker from the football team who was rumored to have gang connections. His three buds hung back but looked interested in what was going on. The bell rang, but the five of us didn't react. Since people were supposed to be in class by this time, the hallway was fairly deserted. Plus, it was a short hallway that connected two of the buildings and had a courtyard on one side and the library on the other. I was outnumbered. He had his friends and I had nobody. But I was pissed. "You just need to." I ground my teeth.

He got in my grill. "And who's going to make me?" He shoved me and advanced a foot. "You think I'm worried about your dad suing me, little rich boy?"

Because my dad was a lawyer, everyone assumed that we were rich. They didn't understand the amount of debt he had from law school, or how much raising a family of five could cost. Up until that point, I'd never been in a fight. Sure, I'd finally gained some muscle mass after junior high, but it took more than that to win with a guy like this. Inside I was slightly shaky, but there were some things I couldn't let slide.

He dropped his backpack, and it was the same as dropping the gloves at a rink. It signaled that it was game on. Another backpack hit the ground with a *thud*, and I looked over to see that Elise's boyfriend at the time, Hunter, had just come out of the library and was ready to join my side. That brief distraction cost me the initial advantage. The altercation didn't last long, though, as two of the football coaches had entered the hallway at the far end and they rushed to break it up. Worried they might lose some of their athletes they needed for Friday's game to a suspension, they agreed not to turn us in and made us go our separate ways.

The memory came and went, as memories do, and I refocused on my present problem. Namely, Sergei and her. I slouched in my chair for a bit, then rose and took my drink onto the balcony, staring out over the views I'd paid thousands to have without even seeing them and finally coming to the conclusion that none of it mattered. The things I'd filled my life with, the distractions—expensive baubles, easy women, and hockey. Always hockey. Hours of time on the ice. And at the moment, it left me empty, and I'd never felt so alone.

Leaning on the railing, I kept thinking of the ways she'd reacted to things—my usual even-keeled, at times almost flat, Elise—emotional with hardly any provocation at all. I wanted to blame it all on Hunter, but I could see now I'd played my part in it too. I realized, in retrospect, she had feelings for me, and how much I'd hurt her, and that killed me. And my own emotions when it came to her...what the hell was going on there?

I began a text to her a half dozen times, edited it, deleted it, and started again, never sending it. I revisited moments since she'd come to San Fran. Her face, glowing when she'd first arrived and rushed down the stairs at the arena. Smiling at me from inside a hockey helmet when we'd played together. Etched with pain at the restaurant. Relaxed and content in the limo as she rested her head against the seat. Studious and tense at her orchestra practice. And less than an hour ago, *wearing Sergei's jacket*, the incredible blue of her eyes made liquid by her tears as she turned to leave.

Then my mind drifted farther. To any number of scenes from our childhood. And times later, when seeing her with Hunter had driven such intense pain into me I had to leave. But it always came to that fateful day I'd kissed her. First, under a tree in her backyard. Later, as I pressed her against the garage and we could be hidden while we tested, tasted, and touched. I remembered the silk of her hair. The way her skin felt under my fingertips when I explored her. The way I responded internally to her lips, her stroke, her body under mine... We were kids, but I felt the first stirrings of manhood that day.

We broke apart finally when Jake returned. I stared into her face as he called our names, then stepped from our cover and acted like nothing had happened. Throughout the rest of the day, I couldn't stop thinking of her. It would never work. She lived in Bloomington; I was in Lincoln. And even if we were together, how could we possibly have a relationship with my family and hers constantly around us?

So, I'd ended it before it began. Or so I thought.

As the night progressed, I realized with crystal clarity it had never ended. All those times when others saw it, and I'd vehemently denied it, came back to mock me. I'd tried to convince myself I was over her. What a joke. I'd never be over her. I couldn't will away these feelings I had for her. Time and distance hadn't changed them.

Holy shit. I'm in love with my best friend.

It was like this incredible epiphany, and yet, in some ways, I'd known it all along.

But her words when we'd parted still rang in my ears. When she'd said why it was she could kiss Sergei and not me. We *had* a past. The real question was, could we have a future?

Elise

I groaned and slapped at my alarm clock to silence its unrelenting noise. My sleep had been filled with a jumble of Sergei and Scott. The way Sergei'd kissed me, and the way Scott threatened to. And threatened was the right word because his kiss was dangerous to me. And the way he approached it so casually...like I needed another reminder it meant nothing to him. And...a "birthday kiss?" Was that a thing in Russia? And he wanted me to come over and bake...whatever it was? What was that all about?

Beyond my open window, someone was whistling incessantly, being far too chipper for the hour, in my opinion. Then I recognized the tune. If Scott and I had a song, "Broken" by Seether and Amy Lee was it. I gasped and scrambled to get to the window. And there he was, sitting on top of the picnic bench like he had been when we came home last night.

Shit. I so do not need this.

I sighed and convinced myself he'd be gone by the time I'd showered and got dressed, but he wasn't. I waited as long as I could before I needed to get to practice on time, but he still didn't leave.

When I walked through the door, he waved as if it was the most normal thing for him to be sitting outside my building at eight o'clock in the morning, but he was surprised I was there. "Oh, hey."

"Hey...?"

He picked up a white paper bag at his feet and unrolled the top, peering inside. "Nice day, isn't it?"

I glanced around. Birds were singing. The sun was shining. "It appears to be."

He nodded, making a humming noise and drawing out a donut which he proceeded to eat.

My stomach growled. I'd forgotten breakfast. But I wouldn't be drawn in to a conversation with him just because he had fried dough of the sweetened variety. "Well, I've got to get to practice." I took two steps then backtracked, giving the bag another look. "Is that the donut shop you're always going on about?"

"What? This?" He checked the bag. "Why, yes it is." His shit-eating grin was both annoying and, damn it, heartwarming.

"Hmm. Well enjoy it." I cursed under my breath and had crossed two squares of sidewalk when he spoke loudly.

"And I've got a powdered sugar cream-filled one. You used to like those, didn't you?"

I stopped but didn't turn. He knew darn well they were my favorites. "You don't fight fair."

"Oh, come on," he cajoled. "Surely you can spare me a minute or two."

I twisted my head. He dangled the donut in front of me like a puck in front of an opponent he intended to deke.

Son. Of. A. Bitch.

I growled and came back to snatch it from him. Stuffing it into my mouth, I glared at him, then my eyes widened. "Oh. My. God." I looked at the powdered sugar confectionary like I held the Holy Grail. "This is incredible."

"I told you." He patted the table next to him. "Sit down."

I gave him a small smile. "I really only have a minute."

"That's fine." He held out his hand to help me up.

"Why didn't you ever ship these to me?"

"I would have if I'd thought about that as an option. But I think it's something you have to experience in the San Fran air to appreciate fully."

"Is that so?" I said with my mouth full.

He chuckled. "That's my answer and I'm sticking to it."

"I see," I said with a faux frown. Sitting as near to him as I was, I could recognize the scent of the cologne he once told me cost him a hundred dollars a bottle. That was way more than I would have spent on myself, but I guess it wasn't too over the top, if one took into account the fact that he had once invested in a five-hundred-dollar bottle. A fragrance they offered payment plans for was so not my thing considering my pear-scented one cost less than $20. And I couldn't see it beating his current combination of essential oils—sage, bergamot, and patchouli. Whenever I caught a whiff of any one of those, it made me think of him...in a very non-brotherly way. I chewed more slowly before asking my next question. I stared at the crack in the concrete slab in front of me. "Why are you here?"

He had wolfed down his donut and had his fingers interlaced, his forearms on his knees. "You mean, like, in the cosmos? Or here at your doorstep?"

I tilted my head. "The latter."

"Oh." He sighed and gazed across the lawn. "I couldn't sleep last night because the way I had acted was weighing on me."

"You've been out here all night?" I joked.

He winced. "No, but I might as well have been." He took my hand. "Listen...I'm sorry for being kind of a jerk. I have to admit, seeing you and Sergei together bothered me."

I blinked. "It did?"

"Yeah. I mean, he's not my favorite person in the first place..."

I could feel another big brother lecture coming on how I shouldn't be involved with someone on the rebound, and I'd had my fill of it the previous night. I hopped off the table. "I know you told me to steer clear of him, but he felt like he owed me for bidding on him, and—"

"He *will* reimburse you by the way," he said adamantly.

I wrinkled my brow. Did he really think I'd pay $500 for a date with a guy I hardly knew? "There's no need for him to reimburse me. I was bidding with his money. Like I intended to do for you. Anyway...I had a nice dinner with him, and I'd rather not go into it because I haven't got time. And as much as I love to hear you grovel, I haven't got the time for that either, darn it," I teased. I bent in and kissed his cheek lightly. "Thanks for the donut." I walked backwards down my front walkway. "We can discuss it tonight."

"So we're still on?"

"Of course." I stopped. "Maturity looks good on you, McCord, by the way."

He laughed and got to his feet. "Is that what this is?"

"God, I hope so."

"Get out of here," he growled, but his grin widened. I turned to go, but he called to me. "Hey, Elise..." He tossed the bag to me. "Another one's in there."

I opened it up and peeked, lifting my gaze to his. "I could kiss you for this."

"I thought that was what got me into trouble last night."

"It was." I hurried away to the sound of his low laughter.

At the end of practice, I was surprised to see him leaning against a tree with his hands in the pockets of his khakis. He straightened as I approached, and I was able to fully appreciate the way the lightweight blue sweater he wore emphasized the icy blueness of his eyes and accentuated his muscular frame.

"What are you doing here?"

Sergei gestured to the stage with his chin. "I wanted to see you in action."

I exhaled, looking back. "It's not quite like a hockey game."

"No." He took a step closer. "But it probably would be counterproductive to check your seatmate."

He's got a good sense of humor. "Yeah, they frown on that."

"Besides..." He shifted near enough to grasp my upper arms gently. "I wanted another chance to give you a birthday kiss."

Remembering my conversation with Scott, I pulled away, shaking my finger at him. "No, no, no. I have a strict one birthday kiss a year policy."

"I must not have done it right then." His eyes became smoky, and his voice was low and sexy. I stopped moving, enjoying the way his words slid along my skin and entered my core, igniting small shivers of arousal.

"Oh, no," I said, my voice equally low. "You did it right."

His cocky grin made him almost edible. "Good. I'd hoped I did." We stood for a moment without speaking. At least not with our mouths. We were having a whole delicious conversation without using words. "We're still on for tomorrow night, right?"

I was tempted to cross the sidewalk and show him how on we were by indulging him with that kiss he wanted, and then some. I imagined it, but I stayed put. "Oh, yeah," I said slowly, smiling at him. "We're on."

His face glowed and he bit his lower lip, giving his head a little shake. "Mmm...I can't wait." He lifted his gaze, taking in something over my shoulder. "Hi." He looked at me again. "See you." He spun and walked, no, strutted away, his hockey player's ass ratcheting up my hormones even more.

"Who was *that*?" Carrie asked.

I twisted partially in her direction but kept watching him as he slid into his Porsche. "A friend."

"You have the yummiest friends." She giggled and I turned. She was flushed and her eyes bright.

I laughed and put my arm across her shoulder as we moved toward our cars.

She fanned herself. "Whooo!"

Whooo is right.

Scott texted at one to tell me—even though he was cooking me dinner at his place—it was a "dress up affair." I inquired further and learned this meant "nothing too crazy, but maybe something like that black dress of yours." After much debate, I finally chose a black cropped knit sweater that left my midriff bare and a long cheetah-print skirt with slits on both sides, pairing it with strappy black heels with a little bling. I spent most of the afternoon preparing for my dinner with Scott. I gave myself a mini-pedicure and had enough time to crash for a bit before getting dressed.

At seven o'clock I set out on the short walk to his place. He hadn't been happy about my coming by myself, but I insisted, knowing he would need the time to get dinner ready. He relented when I agreed to let him walk me home when it would be dark.

When I got there, Sergei was in the hall locking the door to the condo. "Hi."

"Oh, hey." He ran his gaze along me. "You look fantastic, as usual."

"Oh..." I tucked a piece of hair behind my ear. "Thank you. Do you...have a date, this evening?"

"Nah. Just meeting up with the guys."

"Really?" I returned the gesture, sliding my gaze over him. "This doesn't seem like a hanging-with-the-guys kind of clothing choice." He had on jeans with a button-down white shirt and brown suit vest. It looked great on him.

"Oh. Perhaps you are right. Maybe I should change." He swung around to open the door.

"Oh, no. Don't do that. You look very nice. I'm guessing professional athletes in a big city like San Francisco, might dress a little differently than your standard Lincoln, Nebraska, guy." I wrinkled my brow. "Are you locking Scott in?"

"Oh, yeah, umm..." He scratched the back of his head. "He's...He's not here right now."

"Oh. Did he forget something and have to run to the grocery store? Sounds like him."

"Uhh...so..." He was acting very strangely. "He...went somewhere...but not to the store."

"Where then?"

"Uhh...well, to be honest, Elise...he left with that lady from the other night about a half hour ago, and he told me not...to...wait up for him." He kind of trailed off.

I stood with my mouth hanging open.

He...forgot my birthday dinner? He never forgot my birthday.

He glanced at me and shifted his weight. "I'm...so sorry."

I found my voice. "It's all right. I just...he said he was making dinner."

"I know." He scratched his arm. "Tell you what...why don't I take you for that sundae you didn't have?"

"No," I mumbled. "It's nice of you to offer, but you had plans."

I turned away from him and pushed the elevator button feeling like shit. My mom and Kyle wouldn't be here until next month, so I would be alone on my birthday. Alone without food.

"Plans can be canceled."

The elevator dinged far too cheerily, and the doors opened. I shuffled inside, still a little in shock. Sergei followed me.

"I'm texting them and canceling right now. That is...if you want to go with me...?"

"Go?" I said in a daze.

Go. Go to Ghirardelli's. Ice cream is exactly what I need at the moment.

"Are you sure? You don't have to..."

"Are you kidding? After all the fun we had last night?" He elbowed me gently. "Besides, I promised you a sundae." He squeezed my arm and gave me a smile. "And maybe we'll get another chance to dance. You never know." He let my hand go and texted whoever he was supposed to meet.

I stared at him. Scott—the asshole—may have stood me up, but Sergei was being a standup guy. I slipped my arm through his and hugged myself to his side. "Thanks."

"I should be thanking you." He looked over from his texting. "You're probably saving me from a major headache tomorrow morning. And we have that game too. Probably shouldn't have agreed to go out anyway," he said as if to himself.

CHAPTER TEN

Scott

After I left Elise's, I purchased a cake at a little place across the bridge in Oakland. It was a bit of a drive, but it was the best place I knew, and I wanted everything to be perfect. Tonight would change our lives. I had decided, on top of letting Elise in on Sergei's little dirty secret, I would tell her I loved her. Part of me just wanted to propose to her right away. Now that I'd finally realized I loved her, I knew what I wanted was a life together. But, at the same time, I knew I had to take my time. Not rush her. I would need to prove myself to her after all the damage I'd done, but that was okay. I was up for the challenge. I was very goal driven. It was what had gotten me to the bigs. Grit, determination and some good old-fashioned stubbornness.

Cake in tow, I went to the mall, one of my least favorite places. But for Elise, I'd do it. As a bachelor, I only had the basics, as far as setting a table goes, so I needed to get some things. The china was a struggle, as all the patterns seemed too girly. After wandering in a department store for over an hour, I finally found one with a gray, scrolled rim with gold accents I thought was nice. Then on the way to the checkout, I spotted some solid black plates with grooves in them that appeared rugged and decided to also purchase a set of those to use every day. By the time I got around to drinkware, I was so tired I asked a saleslady to choose something "manly" for me. She came back with these cool squared off wine glasses I liked so much, I got the same style for water glasses, tumblers for the wet bar, and several other kinds of drinkware as well.

After she rang me up, she asked if I had flatware and linens, and I didn't even know what she meant until she showed me. Luckily, by that time she knew what I liked and went right to a set of silverware I thought looked good, grabbed an "onyx"-colored glass vase she said went well with the china, and these funky silver candlesticks made with smooth, twisted metal that kind of cinched in the middle like a bowtie. She added a pair of candles to go in them and a set of cloth napkins, and I was on my way. I was so grateful to her for all the time she'd spent with me, I told her she could text me a date, and I'd leave tickets to a game at Will Call for her, which she seemed thrilled about.

I made a quick stop at a florist—worried I'd be short on time—took everything home, washed the dishes, and recycled all of the boxes and packaging materials. Halfway through, I had a moment of sheer panic where I thought—shit, maybe I should have waited and let Elise pick out some of this stuff with me. Then I figured, I needed something tonight anyway, and we could always get more at a later date. It wasn't like I was hurting for money. And after my shopping trip, I could finally fill most of the kitchen cabinets I had.

Sergei had come in while I was unpacking things.

I glared at him. "Well, look who's up? Tired from your evening of giving unsuspecting girls 'birthday kisses?' That was so weak, you know."

He stretched. "Yeah, I'm beat. All the erotic dreams I was having starring Elise kept me awake, if you know what I mean?"

He was trying to get under my skin. No way would I let him know he had. I frowned. "Dreaming is as far as you'll get with her."

"Oh, I wouldn't be too sure of that. She was pretty turned on when I left her. How was she when you left her?" He was baiting me. I ignored him and kept removing glasses from boxes and putting them on the counter. "What's all this?"

"I'm making dinner for Elise, so I need you to make yourself scarce."

He worked his jaw, studying me, his eyes shooting sparks. "I will if you clear out on Sunday after the game. Elise and I are planning to make my babushka's *zefir*."

I shook my head. He probably got the recipe from a Betty Crocker cookbook. "No way are you using my kitchen to seduce the woman I—"

He arched his brows, staring at me.

"—grew up with."

He meandered around the island, taking a plate and examining it, then appraising a wine glass. "Well, if you want me to tell her you refused to let us use your kitchen..."

The man was evil. It didn't really matter, though, because after tonight Elise would know exactly what kind of snake he was. "Fine. If you and Elise want to use the kitchen on Sunday, I'll stay clear."

"Great." He came to the box with the cake in it. "Ooh."

"Get your hands off it!" I warned. "That's Elise's birthday cake. Chocolate cake is her favorite dessert." I smiled smugly. "Not your granny's zephyrt, or whatever you called it."

"That's because she hasn't tried *zefir* yet." He opened the refrigerator and snagged an apple. "See, you knew her a long time ago. You didn't realize she's into new things now. And new people." He polished his apple on his chest. "She and I will be cooking here tomorrow on more than one level." He gave me a shit-eating grin and took a bite from his apple. "See ya." He left the kitchen, and I took a moment to fume then got back to my unpacking.

Having completed that, I set the table, first Googling how everything was supposed to be arranged. I only had a small, dark wood table, but it was nice. When I moved in, I knew I didn't exactly have the skills it took to host a dinner party, and therefore I didn't need anything bigger. What I had was perfect for a romantic meal, which is what I hoped to have with her.

I took a shower while the steaks marinated and put them and the little aluminum foil potato packets on the grill afterward. I finished getting dressed, opened the wine so it could breathe and put the fresh green beans I'd snapped earlier in a pot on the stove.

I wonder if I could add some almonds to them. But would I have to sauté them? Better stick with what I know.

I'd already called Dani, my stepmom, three times with questions. She seemed to enjoy helping me though. I checked the table one more time, dimmed the lights, and lit the candles. I had to admit, it looked pretty good. But we still needed a little ambiance.

"Alexa play...dinner music?"

"Playing solo classical piano."

I listened. *Too sleepy.* "Alexa, stop. Alexa, play soft jazz music."

"The station, Vocal Jazz, free on Amazon music."

Louis Armstrong belted out "What A Wonderful World."

I said soft. This isn't soft.

I sighed. "Alexa stop."

What would Elise like? Oh. I know.

"Alexa, play violin music."

"The station, Classical Violin, free on Amazon music."

She played some song they always had at weddings. "No, no, no, no, no." I didn't want the girl to freak. "Alexa, stop." Maybe we don't need music. I turned to go, then spun back. "Alexa, play romantic music."

"The station, Love Songs, free on Amazon music." A soft, slow, soothing female vocalist accompanied by piano filled the air. *Perfect.*

All I need is my woman.

I smiled. Now that everything was in place, I was dying for her to arrive. I glanced at the clock. There were still five minutes before I told her to arrive, but I'd added in fifteen minutes for Elise to be late, which she almost always was. I went ahead and poured myself a glass of wine to calm my nerves a little, glad Sergei had agreed to vacate without a fuss. I opened the box with the cake and put it on the counter. It looked incredible. White frosting with chocolate dripping across the top and down the sides, chocolate-covered strawberries and bonbons sat on top, and chocolate spiraled cookies were stuck at angles in the middle. Elise would love it.

I flipped the steaks, hoping the smoke's odor wouldn't overpower my special cologne, although the meat was smelling pretty darn good too. Coming inside, I took a seat in the chair I had occupied the night before, setting my glass of wine on the coaster my rusty nail had sat on, and checked my watch. Any minute. I popped to my feet and moved her presents—which I'd luckily gotten a few weeks ago—from the wet bar to the hearth then changed them back again. They were better on the wet bar. That's when I remembered I hadn't put water in the vase with the flowers. I jumped and rushed into the kitchen, encouraging the water to come out of the faucet faster.

"Come on. Come on." I was aggravated when my hurrying caused me to spill some water on the table. I mopped it up with a kitchen towel and threw it under the sink to temporarily hide it. I took a breath. I'd told her 7:30, planning on her arriving at 7:45. It was 8:00. She was half-an-hour late. I made some adjustments, shifting the steaks and potatoes farther from the flames, lowering the heat on the green beans.

Maybe I should have waited to start things until she got here.

But I'd wanted to be able to concentrate on her. It was okay. I'd know better next time. Everything was still looking good.

At 8:15, I began to get worried.

I hope she didn't run into any trouble on the way here.

I debated texting her. I didn't want to rush her if she was having some sort of wardrobe emergency, which she was known to have. But she'd usually text when she was running late. I decided to check on her.

JUST SEEING WHAT YOUR E.T.A. IS. WANT TO MAKE SURE I TIME THE FOOD RIGHT.

At 8:30 I was really getting worried. It wasn't the best neighborhood. Maybe I should turn the grill and stove off and walk her way. I texted again.

ME AGAIN. DON'T WANT TO RUSH YOU IF YOU'RE HAVING ISSUES, BUT I WANT TO MAKE SURE YOU'RE OKAY. IT'S DARK. DO YOU WANT ME TO COME WALK YOU OVER?

I was pretty sure the steaks were dry now, and the foil on the potatoes was flaking, the green beans, mushy. I switched everything off.

As I waited for the elevator, I wondered if I could maybe order something from Jilani's if I had to, the restaurant in the lobby of our building. The elevator dinged, and my phone vibrated in my hand simultaneously. I read the text as I got on board.

SORRY. I ENDED UP HAVING A DATE TONIGHT. MAYBE WE CAN GET TOGETHER LATER THIS WEEK.

Later this week?
I reread the message, slumping against the rail at the back of the elevator.
Who the hell could she have a date with? Someone from her building? The symphony? She made it sound like they hated her there. Why didn't she let me know earlier? That's not like her.
I was totally deflated. The elevator came to a stop and the doors opened. A family of four was waiting with groceries, backpacks, and gym bags. I slipped past them to let them have it, then decided to step outside and get some fresh air, because I was beginning to feel a little hot under the collar. I'd put a lot of work into everything, and she couldn't at least call and let me know she wasn't coming?

Jimmy was closing a car door for someone but looked over. "Evenin', Mr. McCord."

"Hey, Jimmy," I said flatly.

"You not feeling good tonight?"

Not so much.

"That why you're not with your friends?"

What was he talking about? "Huh?"

"Mr. Duskin and Ms. Scofield?"

I frowned. "What do you mean?"

"I just...I saw them leave together earlier. Oh...maybe you're meeting them somewhere?"

"No. I'm definitely not meeting them anywhere," I said with disgust. "See ya, Jimmy." I whirled and went inside. I was glad when the elevator was empty. "Son of a bitch!" I screamed, glaring at my reflection in the gold doors. I'd chosen my clothes so carefully, worked on my hair, for *nothing*. "What a chump." They were having a good time, and I was down...I don't know how much money. I had two dried up steaks, two charred potatoes, and a pot full of green bean soup. I entered my apartment and leaned against the door, scrubbing my face. "Shit." I twisted my head. I'd forgotten the candles and they were melted all over the table. I exhaled, plodded to the table, and blew them out. I snatched the water glasses, took them into the kitchen and dumped them in the sink.

I wouldn't let them come back and see what an idiot I had been, preparing everything for someone who didn't even care enough to be honest with me and give me a call. I would get rid of all evidence of this evening and go to bed. With a sigh, I bent over the counter, my arms spread wide. Elise's birthday cake sat in front of me. I lifted it, stepped on the pedal for the trashcan, and dropped it in there.

Elise

I stared at the mound of melting ice cream and hot fudge in front of me, my spoon poised on the rim of the bowl.

"You don't like it?"

I glanced up at Sergei. "Oh, no. It's great." But a few seconds later, I pushed it away. "I'm sorry, Sergei. I'm just not very good company tonight."

"Do you want me to take you home?"

Did I want to be home, by myself, on my birthday?

"Not really. But you've been so nice, and I've already ruined your plans for tonight."

"No, you didn't." He took my hand and brought it to his lips, kissing my knuckles. "Come on. Let's take a walk. Maybe a little fresh air will make you feel better."

I doubt it.

But, strangely enough, it did. We crossed Beach Street and took off our shoes to walk along the beach. It was a bit chilly, but that seemed right somehow. Like the weather was sympathizing with my mood. He held my hand as we strolled and left me alone with my thoughts.

I was an idiot for thinking maybe Scott had changed. He was still as full of himself as he'd always been. Still as thoughtless and inconsiderate. Still thinking solely of himself and thinking of me as a side note. But I wasn't so much mad at him as I was mad at myself. Why had I fallen for his charm again? If anyone should have known better, it was me. But how could a guy who made me feel so good at times, so valued and taken care of, make me feel the exact opposite at other times. I mean...he frigging stood me up on my birthday. He made me feel like crap on a day that should have been special.

Sergei left me to my thoughts. I liked that about him. Communicating with people wasn't my strong point and continual conversation required a lot of effort and drained me. I bent to pick up one of those plastic ring things that held six-packs of beer or soda cans together. I stretched it with all my might.

"Umm...what are you doing?"

I glanced at him. "Trying to break this so some seagull doesn't get it tangled around its neck."

"That's really a thing? I thought that was something that only happened to penguins in animated movies."

"No. As many as one million seabirds and 100,000 marine mammals are killed every year by six-pack rings," I blurted out without thinking.

Oh my gosh. I sound like a complete nerd.

I had worked on curbing my tendency to spout environmental statistics. But apparently not hard enough.

"Really? I had no idea."

I checked to see if he was teasing me, but he seemed genuinely interested. I shrugged. "Well, that might not be true anymore. It was a study from the late eighties."

He held out his hand and I passed him the can holder. He stretched it until one circle snapped open, then continued until they were all taken care of and ran up the beach a bit to throw the remains in a trashcan. When he returned, he simply smiled and took my hand.

As we walked, the comforting sound of the waves, the cold saltwater surging between my toes, together they somehow soothed me. I twisted to gaze at my companion. Guy could have been having a good time with his friends, but he was here with a moping girl on her birthday. He looked over. "Thanks for hanging with me."

He grinned. "My pleasure."

"Liar."

"No, really. Who wouldn't want to be out with a gorgeous woman like yourself, strolling along a moonlit beach?"

Something sharp touched me and I squealed. I glanced down to find a small bird bopping near my feet, chirping and peering at me like he was trying to tell me something.

"Did he peck you?" Sergei asked in surprise.

"I think he did." I squatted, and he flew off but curved back to land about fifteen feet in front of us, continuing to hop around like a Mexican jumping bean.

"Whoa. I can't tell if he's upset or if he has a thing for you."

"Maybe there's a nest in the area he's protecting." We searched but kept walking, and the bird continued with us.

"Did he hurt you?"

I checked my feet. "No. It only hurt for a second. Like dropping something light on your foot."

Sergei looked down the beach. "Maybe he wants to thank you for saving his other marine friends. Is that what you want? Are you trying to tell us something, little fellow?"

The bird bounced erratically and tweeted up a storm.

"Oh." Sergei turned to me. "He wanted to wish you a happy birthday," he said as if he should have understood that before.

I had to smile. "Oh, he did, did he?" The bird came closer again. It wasn't one of those sandpipers, just a tiny bird with brown wings and back, and a white underbelly.

Cheep, cheep, cheep, cheep, cheep-cheep.

"What did he say that time?" I asked with a smirk.

"Oh. He suggested you go have a beer to celebrate your special day."

I raised a brow. "A beer is it? He mentioned a beer specifically?"

"Yes." His eyes twinkled. He addressed the bird. "That's what you said, right? A beer?" He twisted his head and held a hand to his ear. His feathered friend continued his tirade. "Okay, okay. I've got it. Yes, definitely a beer."

The little guy took flight as if he'd finally gotten his point across and could go.

"Well, then," I said, feeling a lot better. "If the cosmos is sending us instruction via animals, I think we should go."

"Good. Me too." He leaned inland, taking my hand and pulling me. "Come on."

We made our way to San Francisco Brewing Company and took a seat at the bar. The kitchen was closing shortly, so we ordered some burgers to-go and had a drink while we waited for them. Shortly after we ordered, Sergei excused himself. Curious, I observed him. He first talked to the hostess, who left him and came back with a gentleman who he then chatted with briefly and shook hands with before returning to me. Catching me watching him, he smiled brightly.

"What was that all about?" I asked when he got close.

He lifted his shoulders and took his seat. "Well, they're closing up soon, so I just asked if we could stay in the beer garden for a while, and they were fine with that."

"Oh. Cool."

When our food arrived, Sergei paid for our pint glasses and had them refilled. We took our dinner onto the patio/beer garden. A fire pit was going. He gestured to a picnic table.

"Do you want to sit at a table while we eat?"

"Sounds good."

Only one other party was out there, four people at the other end of the garden. The burgers and fries were excellent. Or maybe it was because I hadn't eaten in hours. When we were finished, we discarded our containers and shifted over to chairs by the fire. Sergei moved them next to each other before we sat and we talked and talked. He held my hand from time to time, and it felt surprisingly natural.

"So, what's Moscow like?" He'd spoken very little of his homeland.

"Well…" He leaned forward, staring into the fire. "Have you ever been to Vegas?"

"No. But you're not telling me Moscow is like Vegas, are you? Because that is *so* not the mental image I have."

He chuckled. "No, no, no. I was using it as a comparison point." He sat back in his seat again. "Moscow is a lot like any other big city, actually. Like San Francisco, or Chicago, or New York. If you took a picture of the skyline, it would be similar to those cities. Of course, there are a lot of cathedrals with older architecture. Those are the ones you probably picture, with colorful, Hershey Kiss-shaped towers. But you'd also find some incredible skyscrapers, including this really funky one that twists. Hold on, let me show you a picture." He pulled something up on his phone and offered it to me.

"Whoa! That can't be safe."

He glanced at it again. "Yeah, I wouldn't think so either, but I'm sure they had loads of architects checking the plans and people who inspected it."

"Is that why you were comparing it to Vegas?"

"Not exactly. So…the buildings may appear similar, but the people don't look American. They look European. Less makeup. Less dentistry. Less plastic surgery…less money. I think something like 40% of the wages there go to housing, where the U.S. has so much more…what's the word? Expandable income?"

"I think it's expendable income." It was the first time I'd heard him stumble when using a word. I guess he'd been living in the U.S. long enough to pick up on a lot of the language.

"Yes. Ex-pen-da-ble," he said carefully. "So…I was going to say that the way Vegas is outrageous and extravagant, that's what the U.S. seems like when compared to Russia. Most Russians live in apartments. Your average three-bedroom home in the United States would be a mansion in Russia." He played with our fingers between us. Lacing and unlacing them. The other table had long ago left, and we were alone.

"Your family lives in an apartment?"

He nodded. "And a small one at that. Lots of people under one small roof. Now...I have a question for you."

I smiled tentatively. "Okay..."

"Why are you way over there?"

I laughed. "I'm practically on top of you."

He wiggled his brows. "And yet, you are not on top of me."

He wants me on top. Oh my God. I can't believe I thought that.

I hesitated. "I feel like I don't know you that well."

He sighed exasperatedly. "You're right. I'm rushing things. It's only..." He looked at me and stopped.

"What?"

"I'm going to come right out and say it. Elise...I'm insanely attracted to you, which is no surprise."

My cheeks flushed.

"But what is a surprise is...how much I like you. You're so...genuine. I mean so many of the women I meet are either out to bag a professional athlete, or out to bag a professional athlete's salary, which, to be fair, is usually not a problem for me. But you...you're different. You talk to me...like you would anyone else."

I giggled. "Yes. How else would you want me to talk to you?"

"No other way. That's the thing. I like spending time with you. In fact, I love spending time with you."

I leaned in. "And I like spending time with you too. But I'm not a big city girl. I'm from the middle of the cornfields of Nebraska. I'm—"

"Living in Lincoln is not like living in a cornfield."

"How do you know that? How long have you been in the United States?"

"Long enough to know Lincoln is a big city."

I tucked a piece of hair behind my ear. "Maybe. But...let's just say we Midwest ladies take it a bit slower than West Coast females." Before he could say anything, I amended my statement. "I'm using a huge generalization. I'm sure some West Coast women take things slow, and I know for a fact some Midwest girls are hussies." I said it to make him laugh. And it worked. I spoke carefully now. "I'm...slower than most. Think turtle. Or sloth. I want to get to know a guy a little before I jump right into things."

"I understand. I shouldn't rush things. But I feel like you know every-thing about me. What else can I tell you?"

"It's not so much telling me things. I don't need a rundown of your med-ical history, your grades from senior year, or your waist size."

"What then?"

I need to know I can trust you. I went for humor again, rubbing my palms together. "I need to know your deepest, darkest, slimiest secret."

"I was afraid you'd say that."

"What? Does Sergei Duskin have something to hide?"

He hesitated a smidge too long for my liking, then narrowed his eyes on me. "Does this have to do with Scott?"

Can he tell I have a thing for Scott? I felt exposed.

"Listen," he said, "I know Scott doesn't like me, and, to be honest, I can't blame him. I kind of act like a jerk sometimes. But that's how you have to act where I'm from. You have to act tough, and crude, and kind of heartless to survive. It's all an act. And I've been doing it so long, I'm afraid that's who I've become."

I took his hand. "Well, I don't see you that way."

He gave me a crooked smile. "Well, that's because I'm on my best behav-ior with you." He gave my hand a squeeze and released it, lifting a poker laid nearby and stabbing at the fire. I was sorry he'd lost his playful mood. "Okay," he said. He cleared his throat. "You want to know my dark secret?"

I'm not so sure I do.

"There was this girl...Arina. A Russian from where I'm from. We were young. I thought we were in love, but I was really too inexperienced to know any better. But...I did love her. Anyway...one night, I'd been drinking. I wasn't even close to the legal drinking age. We'd gone to this party together. She drove home because she didn't want me behind the wheel. We hit a patch of ice..."

My stomach dropped.

"We spun and crashed into the side of a bridge...that's how I got this." He pulled his hair back to reveal a scar an inch from his hairline. And these." He twisted his arm to reveal several long, jagged lines, from biceps to elbow. "But...Arina...she died." He got choked up. "And to make matters worse," he swiped at a tear, "the autopsy showed she was pregnant. I killed my child and my girlfriend."

I immediately rose and went to sit on his lap, brushing his hair then hugging him to my chest. "Oh, no, you didn't do that. It was an accident. That's not your fault."

"But if I hadn't been drinking, and I had driven…"

"The same thing could have happened."

"Yeah." He exhaled. "Maybe."

"Does…Scott know that?"

"No, I don't think so." It was quiet. "I think I told a couple of the other guys, though, one night when we'd been drinking. I'm pretty sure Scott wasn't there." He lifted his head, staring into the flames. "It's not exactly something you talk about with the guys, for the most part."

I turned his face toward me and stroked it gently. "Sergei…I'm sorry that happened to you."

"Thanks." He studied me. "I don't even know why I told you that."

"I'm glad you did. That you felt comfortable enough to share yourself in that way."

"Yeah. But it's your birthday. It's supposed to be fun. Wait…hop down for a second."

I scurried off his lap. "I thought you wanted me on top of you."

He covered his heart and took on a comic expression. "Oh, God. Please don't say that. The images it conjures up…"

I swatted him, but he spun and dug into the bag which had held our food, drawing out a small box. "Close your eyes."

"Close my eyes?"

"Yes. Close your eyes." He fiddled around with something. "Keep them closed." I waited. "Come on, come on," he said quietly.

I peeked. He was trying to light a long skinny candle from the flames and having to change hands and shake them because the heat was getting to them.

"Hey! No peeking."

I squeezed my eyes shut again.

"There. Finally." A few seconds later, he said, "You can open them."

He had the candle stuck in a single piece of chocolate cake that looked wonderfully decadent within an open Styrofoam to-go box. "Happy birthday to you, happy birthday to you…" Balancing the box, he carefully brought it to me, finishing the rest of the song in Russian, which was stirringly sexy. He had a good voice. The candlelight and firelight made his face glow, but I was mostly focused on his lips.

When he reached the end, I clapped. "Hey, you're not half bad."

"Yes," he said, his accent thick again, "that is because I am all the way bad. Now…" He gestured to it with his head. "Blow it out."

I puckered my lips.

"No, wait."

I glanced up.

"Make a wish first."

What do I wish for? Peace. Not like world peace, but peace within me. I wanted to heal my broken heart and be whole again, and to try to regain the confidence I'd fought so hard to build.

"You have it?"

"Yes." I blew on the candle.

"Do you want to eat it over there?"

"No. I'll come to the table."

He straddled the bench on the near side and set the box on the table, digging a fork from the bag and passing it to me. I couldn't straddle the seat like he did because my skirt was too tight, so I sat backward, resting against the table and holding the box with one hand, fork with the other.

I took a taste. "Oh my gosh."

"Is it good?"

"It's heavenly. Have some. Didn't they give us another fork?"

"No. One's in there, but that's for you."

"No. Have a bite." I speared a piece on my fork. "Here." I held it out to him, and he angled forward to eat it, cleaning the fork as he pulled away. "It is good."

I wasn't entirely listening, because, for some reason, all I could focus on was his freaking lips. "I think you earned another birthday kiss."

"I did?" he said excitedly.

I set the box aside and crooked my finger at him. He leaned in and I brushed my lips over his experimentally, then took them. We both opened wider on the second kiss and his tongue danced with mine. I touched his leg and he moaned into my mouth, the vibrations filling me, and arousing me all the more. He spread his legs wider and drew me closer, his palm sliding across the bare skin at the small of my back, and I flopped my legs on top his. I skimmed my hand along his jeans, almost moaning myself as I sensed the muscles beneath them. My fingers roamed farther but I was frustrated to find his shirt securely tucked in, denying me access to his skin.

I put space between us and ripped through the buttons of his vest. "Mind if I undress you a little?"

He laughed. "Are you kidding?"

I undid the rest of the vest buttons, yanked the sides apart and undid a few shirt buttons so I could feel his abs while he continued to destroy me with his kisses. "Holy crap, you're built," I said against his lips.

He chuckled again. Then he quickly covered my exploring hands with his and held them. I peered at him, and he was gazing beyond my shoulder.

"I'm locking up now."

My eyes widened, but I didn't turn.

Sergei cleared his throat. "Okay, Josh. Thanks for everything."

"My pleasure, Sergei. And thanks for the tickets."

Sergei grinned. "No problem."

"Do you want me to take some of your trash?"

"No," Sergei said quickly. "We'll make sure not to leave a mess."

"Okay. Have a nice evening." A door closed and deadbolt clicked.

Sergei remained tense for a couple of seconds, still staring in the direction of the restaurant, then relaxed his grip and looked at me. His lips curled up. "Sloth-like?"

I grimaced. "Too slutty?"

He growled, sliding his hands to my wrists and holding me against his chest. "Not in my book." He released me. "Uhh...you have something at the corner..."

I licked my lips. "Did I get it?"

He tilted his head. "Not quite." I moved my tongue to the side he was focused on. "No... I'll get it." He snagged a napkin and leaned in to wipe it off but at the last second, he flicked his tongue over my lips instead, and when I laughed he took the opportunity to urge my mouth open wider with his. I laced my fingers behind his neck. He was a wicked good kisser. My phone vibrated in the pocket of my skirt, but I ignored it. When it repeated its buzzing, I slipped it out and put it on the picnic table, but I caught a glimpse of the caller ID. Scott. Sergei's lips had traveled down to my neck, and he hit the sweet spot, forcing a moan from me. I stretched to read the message.

ARE YOU WITH HER?

"What the hell?"

Sergei pulled back. "Who is it?"

"Scott."

His shoulder muscles tensed. "What does it say?"

"Are you with her?" I looked at him, wrinkling my nose. "With who?"

He returned his attention to my neck. "Who knows? Ignore him."

"You're right." I slid it to the middle of the table and concentrated on him. He was the one who had made my birthday special, not Scott.

The *thud-tap* of steel-toed boots over the brick courtyard alerted us to the fact we were again not alone. We stopped kissing but remained within each other's arms.

A figure swinging a flashlight approached. "You kids finishing up there?" When he got nearer, he amended his statement. "I'm sorry, folks. I thought you were a couple of teenagers making out."

"No. We're a couple of adults making out," Sergei responded with a smirk.

"Oh," he said surprised. "So I wasn't that far off. Just keep it clean, folks, and we'd like to see you making your way to your car soon. All the businesses are closed."

"You've got it."

As he continued walking, I snaked my hands under Sergei's shirt again. He twisted, watching the retreating form of the guard. I alternately nibbled on his earlobe and kissed his neck. He released a soft groan. "You're going to get me in trouble." He lifted my hair from underneath and tilted my head so he could attack my mouth. "I like that."

Our tongues tempted and teased furiously. He might have women chasing after him every night, but it had been a bit since I'd had a man touch me, and he was driving me insane. "Elise," he managed between kisses. "I have to tell you something."

"No." I attacked from a different angle. "No more talking."

He seemed about to press it, but he mumbled, "Fuck it." Then he dove in again. Things increased in speed and intensity to the spot where Hunter would have normally cooled it down, but Sergei turned it up. We both withdrew at the same time, an arm's length from each other, panting and staring at each other. It was back off or have sex-on-the-table time. We laughed.

"I think we'd better stop."

He nodded as he gulped in air. "I should probably take you home."

"Yeah," I got out between gasps.

We ate a few more bites of cake and cleared our trash as promised.

"Do you want to keep these glasses?"

I huffed. "Yes, rich boy, I do." I held one to the light. The logo—The Golden Gate Bridge, a couple of pieces of wheat, and some hops—was etched on the glass, along with San Francisco Brewing Co. "These are nice."

He took my hand and kissed it. "Then they are yours, m'lady. Come on." He helped me over the rope barrier separating the beer garden from the rest of the courtyard. When we'd gotten halfway across the courtyard, the security guard rounded the corner again, approaching us.

"Have a nice night, folks."

"You too," we called back.

But within thirty seconds, Sergei slowed and twisted to look behind us.

Wondering what he was doing, I asked, "Is he watching us?"

"Not yet." He stopped and set the bag with the glasses on the ground. Before I could even think, he had me pressed against the side of a building and was kissing me dizzy. He laced his fingers through mine, pinning them against the wall.

"You know," he gestured beyond my right shoulder with his chin. "That's a hotel right there. And there's one down the street if you don't want that one."

My heart was crashing against my ribs. I'm sure he thought he was talking to someone who'd done it before. Who'd ever heard of twenty-four-year-old virgin? And I was not exactly repulsed by the idea. He, no doubt, didn't usually have to suggest it to women. They were probably dragging him to the nearest bed. But that wasn't who I was. Part of me was sorely tempted, if only to get it over with. Rid myself of the whole v-tag thing. Satisfy my curiosity. But my hesitation spoke for me.

"Never mind. Forget I said that. I don't want to rush things with you. We have all the time in the world if it's something we both want. I'm just...uhh..." He licked his lips. "You are insanely sexy, you know?"

I almost laughed. "Sexy? Me? The drinks must have gone to your head." I looked away from his penetrating gaze. "We should probably go."

He released one hand and rotated my chin so I was facing him. "No way, Elise. You are...so beautiful. Inside and out." He lowered his lips slowly to mine and slipped his arms around my waist. Even minus the heat and fury of the previous few moments, these kisses were making my body pulse against his, to a different beat, but equally strong.

"Hey."

We both jumped. The security officer was coming toward us.

"Shit. Come on," Sergei said, yanking my arm, and we ran off laughing.

On the way back to my place, we held hands whenever he wasn't changing gears. My phone was on the console between us. It glowed and vibrated loudly against the hard surface. Scott had texted. Before we left Ghirardelli Square, I'd replied to his earlier message of *are you with her?* My question to him was, *with who?* Now I read the short response in the glow of the dashboard.

ELISE. DON'T PLAY GAMES WITH ME.

"Play games with you? You're the one playing games!"

"What?" Sergei said, sounding alarmed.

"I'm sorry. It's...Scott again. He's accusing me of playing games after he—" I got choked up and turned to stare at the window so Sergei wouldn't see.

"Hey, Elise," he said softly.

I pulled it together and looked at him.

"Just ignore him. He's acting like a jerk."

"Yeah," I forced out, trying to give him a smile. For the rest of the ride, I watched the scenery slip by and he was quiet too.

His car glided to the curb in front of my place, and he switched off the engine. He exhaled. "I had a really great time with you."

This time the smile was genuine. "Me too. Thanks for making my birthday special."

He laughed. "Well, I didn't do much, but I'm glad I could spend it with you." He glanced at the dash. It was a few minutes before midnight. "I was able to give you your first birthday kiss today. Any way I could be honored again with the last birthday kiss?"

Instead of answering verbally, I gave him a long, sensual kiss, my gaze roaming over his face as I drew back. He brushed his fingertips along my arm. "I..." His voice was rough. "I should walk you in." He was cheerful, but I could tell he was disappointed. I observed him as he moved around to my door. Wouldn't I love to wake up next to him...

He put his arm across my shoulders, and we ambled down the sidewalk without speaking at first. "So...I'm making you my babushka's *zefir* tomorrow, right? After the game?"

"Yes. Should I bring anything?"

We'd stopped at the door. "Just your cute little self."

"Are you sure? I could get the ingredients...?"

"Nope. It's my treat. I'll take care of it."

I frowned, tilting my head. "But you treated tonight."

"This is like...a birthday extension. Totally falls under the birthday umbrella."

"All right. But if you change your mind...I could give you my number and you could text me?" I indicated my phone.

"I can get it from Scott if I need it. Now," he glanced at the windows above. "You should get some sleep. You have practice tomorrow, right?"

I sighed. "Always."

"Okay." He gave me the bag with the glasses in it.

"Thanks," I said, lifting it. "Thanks for everything."

"Totally my pleasure." He brushed a knuckle along my jawline and my senses awakened. He looked like he was going to say something else, but he closed his mouth and stared at our feet for a second. "Goodnight." He spun on his heel and walked quickly away, but when I was closing the door behind me, he had halted a few yards off and was facing the building with his hands in his pockets.

Alone for the first time all evening, I took the opportunity to think over everything. And sure, I thought of Sergei. How nice he had been. How easily he ignited passion in me. But, like a beat dog who returns to his master, I kept coming back to Scott.

I was angry at myself for letting Scott hurt me again.

How many times does a guy have to dump on you before you get it, Elise? You're not a priority to him. He doesn't care about you the same way you care for him. Stop letting yourself fall for his charm. You, of all people, should know better.

But even as I thought it, I recognized it was useless to scold myself. Something inside of me just couldn't let go of Scott. No matter how many times he did things to hurt me.

CHAPTER ELEVEN

Scott

I was beginning to wonder if, after all these years of teasing Uncle Kyle for being prone to violence, I was actually the one who was the savage. I came to this conclusion as I sat in my dark living room, for the second night in a row, talking myself out of doing physical harm to my roommate. My thinking went somewhat like this...

I cannot beat my teammate because we have an important game tomorrow. I cannot tear him limb from limb. That would upset Coach. I cannot, in fact, dismember him in any way. I cannot castrate my teammate because that would make it hard for him to skate. I cannot burn any of his digits...

While I cleaned the kitchen and ordered a pizza—because my dinner was destroyed—the anger stewed, festered, and threatened to explode in every direction. Then, for the next hour, while I sat in the dark waiting for Sergei to return, it cooled, but remained equally as deadly. I texted him and asked him if he was with her, and he had the gall to act like he didn't know what I was referring to.

I was thinking these murderous thoughts about Sergei, as it hurt more to think of Elise. I'd texted her a simple,

JIMMY TOLD ME YOU LEFT WITH SERGEI????

It took her an hour to reply to that with,

YEAH.

Yeah. No explanation. No excuse. No apologies. Just four letters, Y-E-A-H.

I drafted a smartass response to that, deleted it, started a new one, more toned down, and then deleted that too. As I continued to struggle, I could hear my dad saying, "If you have something important to say, don't text. Call." So I called. Six times, in fact. She didn't pick up. I texted her, asking her to answer, if she could, as I wanted to talk to her. Crickets.

I couldn't believe she had spent her birthday, her special day, with *him*. It had always been kind of our thing to spend our birthdays together if we could. I was an idiot for going to all the effort I did when it obviously didn't mean that much to her.

Then, once it hit eleven, all I could think of was *what the hell are they doing?* If they went to dinner, that should be done by now. Were they at her place? I kept seeing him kissing her...and imagining her liking it. I saw him doing things to her that I wanted to do to her, and my hormones took command for a while. I saw her rolling around on her bed with me when we were kids, and then it morphed into Sergei and her. It was so wrong. And I was at least partly to blame for it. I'd let it go on too long. I'd underestimated how vulnerable Elise would be after her breakup. I debated trying to find them and tell her what Sergei was doing. Would he have taken her to Ghirardelli's for that sundae she wanted? No. I would have done that, not him. Would he have taken her to one of his favorite places? Maybe I should just go to Elise's to prevent them from doing it, if they weren't doing it already. But...was that stalkerish? My brain hurt from thinking.

As I sat brooding over it all, I heard the sharp sound of the key in the lock. My anger rocketed back to its original high. He opened the door and, not seeing me, spun to shut it quietly. I flipped the lamp on, and he whirled, taking in a sharp breath.

"What the hell are you doing lurking in the dark like that?"

"Did you sleep with her?" I said evenly. My voice sounded strange.

"What? I'm not talking to you." He made an attempt to storm down the hall, but I moved quickly and got in his way.

"Did you sleep with her?" I shouted.

"What the fuck is wrong with you?" he tried to push past me, and I threw him against the wall then stepped up and grabbed fistfuls of his vest.

"The only thing that's saving your ass right now is the fact we have a game with the Sharks tomorrow and they're ahead of us in the standings."

"Whatever, man."

"You're messing with my family here. Someone I care for. Do you think I'm sitting around and letting that happen?" I shoved him again. I wasn't really doing anything to hurt him, but it felt good to do something physical with the rage inside me.

He pushed me in turn. "Get off me."

I wasn't giving ground. "I asked you a question. Did. You. Sleep with her?"

"No. Okay? I like her."

That shocked me. "What?"

He caught me unprepared and pushed me back enough to squirm away. "I don't have to answer any of your fucking questions!" He snuck into his room and slammed the door.

I stood frozen for a second. *He likes her?* I glanced down the hall. *If he thinks he's safe in his room, he's got another think coming.* I covered the area in two big strides and threw his door open. He was standing near his bed, running a hand over his face. "That's bullshit. You don't care about anybody but yourself."

"Have you lost your mind? Get out of my room. I don't care if you're a teammate. I'll beat your fucking ass!"

His appearance surprised me. He wasn't wearing his usual smug expression. What was going on?

"I'm telling her tomorrow, Sergei."

"What? You can't do that."

"Watch me. I don't care if I have to pay off every single one of those bets. I'm gonna—"

"You can't do that, man. It'll hurt her. You can't do that."

Who is this?

It was throwing me, and I didn't like it. I could handle the asshole Sergei. This guy I didn't know.

"Either you tell her, or I'm telling her," I said distinctly. I stuck a finger in his chest. "This is where it ends. It's over."

I turned around and walked out, but I was shaken. Could there actually be something real between the two? Was I too late?

I actually considered going to her place right then and pounding on the door until she let me in and I could tell her what Sergei was doing and profess my love. Then I remembered a keycard was required to enter her building. I contemplated the whole throwing the rock at the window thing, but I wasn't sure which window was hers. I finally talked myself off the ledge. I'd tell her right after the game.

Even though I had a plan of action, I slept fitfully. I was a tad nervous that my lack of sleep might affect my game. But, the truth was, I often performed my best when I felt my worst. I didn't understand it, but that's usually how it worked. As the team captain, I had to attend the Fire and Ice Brunch, where we gave the children's hospital the giant check and they took a whole lot of pictures. I could hardly keep still during Coach's speech. I was filled with this anxiety or maybe even dread. I only knew I had to talk to her, and then I'd feel better. It was difficult to deal with all the small talk and pleasantries, especially after my huge role of presenting the fake check was finished. By the end, I may have been a bit rude even, as some little old woman told me about her niece's wedding, for some reason. I just wanted to get home.

By the time things wrapped up, I had to go straight to the stadium. Luckily, I'd packed what I needed for a contingency such as this. Sergei and I did not interact. Unbelievably, he looked like he felt even worse than I did somehow. It would be a long game for both of us. I caught him scanning the stands as I had been, searching for Elise, but not finding her. Maybe she was running late.

We were playing San Jose, whom we didn't like. Well, we weren't fond of any of our opponents, naturally, but, if it weren't for the Knights, the Sharks would probably be our most hated team. And the animosity didn't even stem from the players or coaches; it was because of two radio personalities. These two jokers had a local morning talk show and loved to play practical jokes on visiting teams. Particularly us, for some reason. Moreover, these guys were as obnoxious as they could be, corny and unduly impressed with themselves. They thought they were hysterical, and apparently had a fan base who concurred, but they were a pain in the ass. In addition to this rivalry, it was an important game because if we could come out with a W, we'd take first place in the division from them. We relished the idea.

I loved those first moments when I hit the ice, before I was required to put a lid on top of my flow. I'm not exactly sure why I liked it so much, but there was this addicting sense of freedom and excitement at pre-skate. When I hummed across the ice at top speed, the rush of air blowing my hair back, the cold bracing on my cheeks, the sound of my blades alternately gliding or biting into the ice with twists and turns...it all made me feel alive. I fed off the energy of the crowd, the anticipation of a good hockey game almost as desirable as the hockey game itself.

As would be expected, chirps were filling the air. A shark player, Ted MacNamara, skated up to one of our rookies, Troy Grinder—with a name like that the kid was born to be a hockey player. I observed the exchange because—even though this was only my third year in the bigs—I hated it when veterans took advantage of rookies, and I wanted to know if any retaliation would be necessary.

"Hey, I used to have a stick like that," he commented, running his gaze lovingly over Grinder's Alpha Flex Stick.

Kid fell for it, seeming pleased a player of MacNamara's caliber had noticed his twig. "You did?"

"Yeah," MacNamara shifted his focus to the rookie's face, "then my dad got a job."

Troy deflated, probably as much from the fact that he had fallen for the comment as much as the comment itself. I skated across, taking aim at Mac. "Nice helmet, there, Teddy boy. Does it come in men's sizes too?"

He just grinned and skated off.

"You were looking good in warmup, Grinder." I gave him a friendly elbow. "But remember, keep your stick on the ice and your head on a swivel, and let's get us a little shark for dinner."

He bobbed his chin, brightening some.

We got a feel pretty quickly for how the game would go when we got called for two lame penalties in the first five minutes.

Frustrated, Sergei yelled, "Hey, ref. Your old lady is gonna be pissed when she hears how much you've been screwing us."

"Careful, man," I said under my breath. It was important to know which refs could be joked with and which took it personally, and with Terry Hollister, it was a crap shoot.

Sure enough, before the end of the first, Sergei was hooked but the call went the other way and he ended up in the box for embellishment. It wasn't a penalty handed out very often, but I'm pretty sure the refs hated players taking a dive as much as we did. Problem was, Sergei really was hooked, and it was pretty obvious to everyone other than Hollister. His supposed "dive" had nearly crammed his chin into the back of his skull.

Sergei growled at the ref on his way to the sin bin. "Yeah, you haven't called a game this bad since last night."

"Watch it," he returned, "or you'll get another two." I could tell by the expression on his face he had already chalked up another penalty for later in the game.

As Sergei passed me, I caught his eye. "Hey, bad call, but keep your head in the game. We need you."

He nodded but didn't say anything. We considered ourselves lucky to walk away from the first with only a one-point deficit. Coach must not have been real happy about The Douche's mouthing off either because he moved him down to the second line in the third and switched the rookie to the top line. Kid had two assists in the second period and two amazing shots met by two even more amazing saves, so he was being rewarded for his hard work. I knew Coach was hoping he'd score his first NHL goal.

The opportunity came three minutes into the third. We were on a power play after Liam Bouchard had been boarded and had to leave the game. We were working the puck around, looking for an open lane, when an errant pass sent the puck behind the net. I was able to retrieve it and tap it to Mansford in the slot and, with hardly any movement—tic, tac, toe—he dished it immediately to Grinder on the other side of the net for a redirection, leaving Alex Munyard, their goalie, out of position. The rookie one-timed it and scored his first goal, tying the game. He was so excited, as was the rest of the team. We all remembered that rush of getting our first. I joined in the celebration, then got the puck and took it to the trainer so he could put tape on it and mark it as Grinder's first. I had a feeling a lot more were in his future.

The rookie's goal must have set MacNamara off, because on the kid's next shift the veteran was gunning for him. But aware his opponent was coming in for a check, Troy put on the brakes at the last second making Mac miss and sending him crashing into the boards.

"Hey, Abe Lincoln," Grinder sniped as he skated into the o-zone. "You ever finish a play?"

I grinned. Kid had some gumption. He drove hard to the net, and I increased my speed to get into position for a pass if he was jammed up. Grinder waited a beat too long before taking a slap shot and hit the goalie right in the breadbasket. Seeing we were both there for a rebound, the tender held it.

As we were getting into position for the resulting faceoff, Big Mac issued his own verbal attack, saying derisively, "Nice shot. I've seen better hands on a digital clock."

Grinder's jaw tightened, but he didn't respond, focused on the puck, but before it could be dropped, Mansford got himself kicked out of the circle, so I got my chance to square off against their centerman, Rusty Simms. As I went to take my place, I murmured under my breath to Grinder, "Be ready."

I was decent in the circle, but Rusty was one of the best. If I went for a straight win, he'd probably beat me. That being the case, I wasn't going for the puck, I was going for his stick, while at the same time intending to lean in and push him backward, giving Grinder free rein to get the puck and, hopefully, shoot. I got into my crouch, legs wide, choked up on my stick, and watched the ref's hands. When he dropped that little vulcanized rubber beauty, I took Rusty and his stick out of the play. Grinder must have read my mind, because he glided closer and toward the boards so he would be in position to shoot, angled his blade to go top shelf, and buried it.

It gave us the lead with ten left, which was too much time when one was playing the Sharks. We needed an insurance goal or two. If they tied it and it went to four-on-four, they'd have the advantage as they were faster on the whole. I made several attempts to get it past Munyard, but he was on fire, stopping everything we threw at him. But there was one thing we hadn't tried yet, and I wasn't the guy to do it. At 6'6, 228 pounds, Grinder had a hell of a reach, and he was amazingly fast for a big man. I let the other players know what my thoughts were. We all wanted to coordinate it so the rookie got the hattie.

The plan was for our defensemen to bring it up the ice and feed me at the point. Grinder would charge the net on the opposite side, and I would try to feed him near the corner of the net. Mansford's job was to park in front of the net and lift any sticks threatening to block my pass. The goaltender would have to focus on me but would be aware of Grinder coming in and ready to shift to that side with the pass. What we hoped he wouldn't suspect was Grinder using that quickness and long reach to loop behind the net to the opposite end and tuck it in. Wraparounds weren't high percentage shots, but we were hoping the combination of it being late in the game and Moony probably being tired, plus Grinder having the physical attributes he had, he could sneak it in on the goalie. The timing had to be precise. I needed to hit him at roughly two feet from the crease, going at full speed.

The play didn't go exactly as planned. Blane was in a shoving match with MacNamara, so I didn't have him elevating any sticks. But the skirmish screened the goalie some, which helped throw his timing off more as he was ducking between bodies to see me. I laid it right on the tape, and Grinder added a dirty deke after he got the puck, shifting his shoulders to make it look like he was going for the shot and Munyard bit. Then Troy pulled the puck back in, turning his stick over to protect it, swung around the net and dived at the last minute to give himself that extra half-second on Moony, which he probably needed as the goalie pushed off then dove to try to block it. But the puck found daylight and he lit the lamp for his hat trick. Hats rained down on us as we celebrated, and it took several minutes to clear the ice. We finished the game with no further scoring by either team.

My earlier dread was replaced with the high of a victory, until I got my phone out and had a message from Coach asking me to stop by his office. No one wanted to get called to the coach's office. It might be a player being informed of a trade. I doubted it was that. I would have heard rumors. Still, my heartrate was accelerated when I knocked on the door's muted glass window. When he hollered to come in, I took a deep breath and slowly twisted the knob.

"You wanted to see me?"

"Yes." He didn't say anything further, just stared at the giant desk calendar in front of him. I stretched to get a look at it myself, but it didn't give me any clue as to why he sent for me. "I don't know how to say this..."

I swallowed, a wave of cold hitting me that had nothing to do with the ice not far away.

"I know I told you I'd take care of the Fire and Ice closing..." he waved his hand about, searching for a word, "...thing, but Dottie called. She was pretty upset..." he said hesitantly, as if not wanting to reveal too much.

Instead of alleviating my fear to hear him say his wife called, it doubled it. Dottie was going through cancer treatments for a very aggressive form of uterine cancer. "Is she okay? Did something happen?"

"Uhh...no. Not really. But...this whole thing has her pretty worked up, as you can imagine..."

I couldn't, but I understood.

"She asked me to come home. You probably have plans."

"You want me to do the check thingie at the fire station? Not a problem. I've got this. You get home to your wife."

The tension oozed out of his body briefly. "Are you sure? I don't want to—"

"I'm sure. Go." Telling Elise could wait a couple of hours, in this circumstance.

"I owe you," he said sincerely.

"Don't worry about it." I took a look at my phone. Twenty minutes. I'd need to hustle.

"Do you want me to tell Sergei you're not coming home?"

"No. He wasn't expecting me anyway."

He got to his feet. "So you did have plans."

"No. He wasn't expecting me, but I was going home anyway." I knew I had promised him free rein of the kitchen; however, I figured his hijacking my date with Elise made the deal null and void.

As I turned to leave he shouted, "Wait. Damn."

Whatever it was couldn't be good. Vincent LePaige was one of the cleanest mouthed hockey players I had ever met. *Ever.*

"You can't do it for me. I have to make a speech too. Damn," he repeated.

"No problem, Coach. I'll just give them the one you gave this morning."

"You...you remember it? All of it?"

Yeah. In the same way I remember most of the team's stats, people's phone numbers, and all sorts of other trivial trash, but I can't remember to pick up the dry-cleaning half the time.

"Uhh...yeah. I sort of have a photographic memory. At times."

He clutched the top of his chair. "Well, I'll be... That must come in handy."

I grinned. "Sometimes. But listen, don't worry about anything. I'll take care of the Fire and Ice thing, and you get home to Mrs. LePaige."

He thanked me again and I headed out, grateful I still had my suit and had actually put it on a hanger instead of crumpling it at the bottom of my locker as my first instinct had told me to do. The dinner was due to start at seven.

What's the longest it could last? A couple hours?

That meant I'd be home before ten. What could happen in that short amount of time?

CHAPTER TWELVE

Elise

When he opened the door wearing nice fitting jeans and a Fire T-shirt he was almost bursting out of, a thrill ran through me.

"Hi."

"Hey. Come in." He stood aside and I sauntered in. "You look great."

I wore an ivory "bodysuit" which was simply a blouse which snapped between my legs. It had an elasticized sweetheart neckline which tied in the middle, and it was tight across my stomach, with ruching. I'd chosen tan, strappy shoes and faded, rolled jeans with several "ripped" patches.

I threw my purse and small bag on a chair and turned to take him in again. "So do you."

He was trailing on my heels and his hands came to my hips as he leaned in to kiss me. When he separated from me, he tugged lightly on the ends of my bow without undoing it. He raised his brows and sucked in a breath between his teeth. "I like this."

"Mmm." I played with the hair along his nape and smiled up at him.

He gestured. "What's in the bag?"

"Oh, whipped cream. I wasn't sure if you guys would have any, and I want to share some of my heritage with you and make you a wicked Irish coffee."

He wriggled his brows. "You brought whipped cream."

"Is that all you heard?" I shot him a faux frown. "We are making some sort of yummy dessert, aren't we? Or was that merely a story to lure me into your place?"

He brushed his lips over mine. "What answer do you want to hear?"

I laughed and pushed him playfully. He took the hint and backed away. "You didn't start making it yet, did you? I want to follow it step by step."

"I got the ingredients together to make sure I had it all, but I haven't combined anything yet."

He had the recipe visible on his laptop screen. It sounded more like a meringue than a marshmallow, in my book. Before we'd gotten too far, it became obvious he was pretty clueless. "Are you sure you've made this before?"

"Yes, it's just been a while."

I narrowed my eyes at him, although my lips tugged up at the corners. "Oookay." We'd first made the raspberry Jell-O we would be flavoring them with, then we whipped egg whites until they were stiff. Next we had to make some agar gelatin, which he said he purchased at an Asian store, which made no sense to me. We were making Russian merengue-mallows with Asian gelatin? We cooked that until it thickened and then added everything together, with a little lemon juice, and put it in this ginormous pastry bag. I had almost finished spooning the goop into the sleeve to pipe it when Sergei took the bowl to put it into the sink. I rotated to take in his backside and he caught me at it. I whirled, acting like I was concentrating on getting the pastry bag closed.

"Umm..." He stepped behind me, placing his hands on the counter on either side of me, pressing that marvel of a body against me and speaking into my ear. "What are you doing?"

I cleared my throat. "Making *zefir*. What did you think I was doing?"

"I think," he brushed my hair over my shoulder, nuzzling my neck and sending sexy shockwaves through my core, "you were ogling my ass."

I couldn't quit smiling. "I have no idea what you're talking about. You must be full of yourself."

He chuckled. "Oh, I am, am I?" His lips grazed my skin.

It took everything inside of me not to spin and attack him. I was well aware one-night stands happened all the time. I was also aware this was the proverbial third date...but I wasn't sure if I was ready yet. Although I sure felt ready at the moment. He was turning my willpower to overcooked noodles and my desire to lava. I twisted the pastry bag a trifle too strongly and some leaked onto the counter. "What do you think *you're* doing?"

"Well...it seems ...you got a spot of *zefir* here." He licked and sucked and teased between words. Sliding his finger across the counter he found the place I'd accidentally squirted out, scooped it up, and dragged it along my neck. "I'll clean you."

I rolled my head back, on the edge of coming unglued. "Mmm...what you're doing doesn't seem to be cleaning to me. In fact, it seems..." I sighed. "Downright dirty."

"Mmm...I must be doing it right then."

"Oh, God, yes," I breathed. He reached around to grab my chin and move my mouth into range so he could absolutely devastate it. I was going down. I had morals, but I was only human...and my brain had totally checked out.

I'm supposed to be doing something...something important...

"Stop!" I shouted.

He jumped away. "What? What did I do?"

I tried to recover. "Nothing. I...uh..." I looked at the pastry bag in my hand. "It said we have to do this fast before it hardens." I escaped from him, crossing to the section of the island he'd draped plastic wrap on, since he didn't have parchment paper, and "dusted" it with powdered sugar, as much as an NHL player could dust something. It was pretty much carpeted with the stuff. I piped miniature piles onto the area.

He was quiet. "Did I do something wrong?"

"No," I replied without making eye contact, but my voice even sounded weird to me.

He dropped his head. "I'm sorry, Elise." He lifted his chin and peered at me with a pained expression. "When I'm with you, I...kind of...get a little crazy."

My face flushed, and blood rushed elsewhere too. "Well," I glanced at him with a smile then continued my work. "It's just that a guy usually at least buys me dinner before he starts mauling me."

"Is that what I was doing?" He winced. "I'm sorry."

I stopped, straightening. "Sergei, I'm kidding."

"Oh." He absorbed this. "Sooo what you're saying is, after dinner I can maul you."

I rolled a shoulder. "Well, dinner and *zefir*."

He gave me a crooked grin. "It's *zefir*." He pronounced it with a long E sound where I had been saying it like zepher.

I scrunched my nose. "I've been pronouncing it wrong this whole time."

He shrugged. "It's cute." He gripped the top of one of the chairs. "So, let's review. After dinner and *zefir*, I am free to maul you as I see fit."

I flashed him a big smile, lengthening my words. "Ohh, yeahh."

He clapped once, loudly. "Let's go, then."

I laughed. "Let me clean things a tiny bit."

"Clean?" he whined. "Come on. You're killing me. Just throw that shit away."

"I'm only putting it in some hot water and leaving it, okay?"

He rolled his eyes. "Fine."

When we got into the elevator to dine at the Italian restaurant on the first floor, he put his arm around me, but kept his distance all the same. At dinner, he held my hand some, but to my frustration, played the gentleman during the entire meal.

What do you want, Elise? You're the one who freaked out on him, and now you're upset he's standoffish? Make up your mind.

By the time we got in the elevator to go back to the condo, I'd worked myself into a giant ball of insecurity. We were alone. He was watching the numbers in one corner, with his legs wide, arms in front of him, fingers circling the opposite wrist, reminding me of the stance soccer players take so as not to be racked. I was across from him, biting my lip and searching for a way to undo what I had done. About five floors into our journey, I couldn't hold it in any longer.

"Are you mad at me?"

He twisted his head to stare at me, blinking, but not answering for a moment. "No, of course not. Why would you ask that?"

"Because...you aren't touching me anymore." I hate that I sounded like a child.

He turned to me and ran his hand along my arm, then brought it to lightly clasp my fingers, looking down. "I...I'm trying to do what you asked. Give you space."

I stepped into his embrace and placed my palms on his chest, gradually moving them up until they met behind his neck. Naturally, he grasped my hips and a slow smile spread over his face. "I don't need that much space." Gazing at him, I stretched onto my toes, intending to give him a quick kiss at first, but knowing milliseconds before our lips made contact it would go deeper than that. I closed my eyes and sunk into that kiss. He received it and returned a little heat of his own. I slanted away, a bit dazed by what he did to me.

"Mmm." He gave me two more quick kisses then peered at me with such longing, it caught me off-guard. "Elise...do you believe people can change?"

I was confused by his question. "What?"

"I mean, in your experience, have you ever known someone to fundamentally change and become a better version of themselves?"

"Why do you ask that?"

He shrugged. "I don't know. Just curious, I guess."

"Well..." I thought about it. "I would have said no except for what's happened with my dad."

"Oh?"

"He cheated on my mom and was a terrible father until...I don't know...something happened and he...well, he's not perfect. I still see the old dad sometimes...but he's way better, and so is our relationship."

"Your mom's still married to him?"

"Oh no. She's remarried now to a great guy. Kyle. He's the best."

"Hmm..."

The odd conversation came to an end as the elevator *dinged* and stopped. I walked backward, tugging him along. "Are you ready to get your Irish on?"

"As long as you're ready to do it Russian."

"Ooh," I said coyly. "Is it different with a Russian?"

"You bet it is." Everything sounded sexy coming from his lips with that Russian accent. He opened the door and let me in without taking his gaze off me.

I led the way to the kitchen to see if the *zefir* had hardened properly. He snatched one up and popped it in his mouth. "Oh my God! These are fantastic. I made this?"

"*We* did." I slapped his hand as he reached for another one. "We're supposed to sift powdered sugar over them."

"They don't need it." He snagged another one and brought it to his lips. "Trust me."

It seemed like he was referring to something other than the dessert. "I do." He stepped closer and I narrowed my eyes. "I think."

Instead of eating his purloined sweet, he held it out for me, looking at me with an intensity that made the whole thing a little erotic. I opened my mouth and let him feed me. I ate it, licking my lips a smidge more than was necessary. "You're right," I purred. "It is fantastic."

He tilted his head toward me.

"It really is," I added hurriedly. "But I bet it would be even better with Irish coffee. I'll get the coffee brewing if you could just grab the Jameson's from the wet bar?"

He stood for a moment, leaning on the counter, then spun on his heel and left without a word.

I exhaled. "Holy shit, he's hot!"

"What?"

He heard me?

"Uhh...I said, could you grab my bag for me?" I grimaced, waiting for his response.

"The one with whipped cream?"

I relaxed. He hadn't heard me. "Yeah. Thanks."

Am I ready for this? I don't really know him that well...but it would be such a relief to...get that monkey off my back. Satisfy my curiosity, as well as my desire. And...I knew enough to know he wasn't using me and wouldn't hurt me, didn't I?

Bottles knocked together in the wet bar, reminding me I was supposed to be doing something. I rushed about, getting the coffee brewing, pleased to find glass Irish coffee mugs in the cabinet that looked brand new.

He returned. "Here you go." He set the bottle of whiskey down and took out the can of whipped cream and the little bottle of maple syrup I'd brought.

"Syrup?"

"Yeah. I use it instead of sugar. The flavor works well with the whiskey and coffee." I stopped. "You do drink coffee, don't you? I guess I should have asked that before."

"Oh, hell, yeah. Lived off the stuff in college." He casually picked up another piece of *zefir*. "Uhh..." he moved nearer, "...you ready for another one?"

I set the mugs on the island. "Bring it."

Focusing on me, his face tense, he fed me the treat. As he was pulling away, I grabbed his hand.

"You must be sticky." I closed my mouth over a finger and sucked on it, twirling my tongue around it with no subtlety whatsoever.

"Holy *fuck*! You're making me crazy. Is it mauling time yet?"

I flipped my wrist, pretending to check a watch. "Yes."

I knew we would make love now. The way the electricity was firing between us, there could be no other conclusion. We crashed together like two tidal waves surging against one another. He lifted my hair at the nape of my neck, cupping my head to tilt it and take command of my lips. Each kiss set a new shimmer of pleasure through me until it was absolutely imperative I have more of him. I yanked his shirt out of his pants, and he whipped it off, chucking it into the corner and bringing his rock-hard body back to me. My fingers started above his waist, gliding upwards to scale the mountain of his chest to the summit of his shoulders. I climbed farther, exploring the indentions of muscles, telling me the story of his strength and fitness.

"I love hockey."

We both laughed for a millisecond, then got serious again about ravaging each other's mouths. He tried to untuck my shirt, mumbling against my lips, "What the hell is with this shirt?"

"It's a bodysuit."

He stopped, parting from me briefly. "Meaning?"

"It snaps between my legs."

"You're fucking kidding me?"

I couldn't read his expression. "Uhh...no..."

He grinned. "I like that." He dragged a stool over from under the island with his foot. "Come here."

I wasn't quite sure what he doing, but I was game. I came to him, and he kissed me again, slower, but equally as effective, if not more so. He slid his hands around to my backside, following the curve down, then up again several times. Dropping his lips to my jaw, then my neck, he rumbled, "You feel so good."

I love the way you touch me.

I thought it, but there seemed to be some sort of disconnect between my brain and my voice. He hoisted me and I circled him with my legs as our mouths fused again. He lowered onto the saddle-shaped stool, bringing me onto his lap. He had to adjust and move deeper onto the seat so I could rest comfortably, freeing his hands. Pulling the elasticized top off my shoulder he kissed the skin he revealed. Then he suddenly dropped his forehead onto my upper chest. I thought he would go lower, and I ached for him to, but he stilled, then rolled his head from side to side before lifting it to peer into my eyes. He brushed the hair back from my face, then left his palms on my cheeks, his fingers laced in my hair.

"Elise, I want you so badly. I want all of you."

That's evident.

I wrinkled my brow. "Why are you stopping then?"

His gaze raked over me. "I really care for you, and I don't want to hurt you. I should tell you something..."

My heart sped up. Was he poised to make some sort of declaration of his feelings? I didn't need that. Didn't want that, for some reason. I wanted to give myself to him mindlessly.

I brushed my thumbs across his lips, searching his face. "Let's not complicate things..." I parted from him and tugged on the ends of the bow on my shirt. "...with words right now."

"But—"

I covered his mouth with mine, writhing against him. He hesitated, then I felt him give in. Taking his hands, I led them to my blouse. Putting space between us, he studied me for a moment, then dropped his gaze. All at once he jerked my top below my breasts. Bracketing my ribs with his fingers, he moved his thumbs over my bra, making my nipples come to life. He looked at me again. "Are you sure?" he said distinctly.

I don't think I can be sure of anything when you're doing that to me.

"I want to..." I hunted for the words, make love to you sounded old fashioned and stupid, have sex with you cheapened what we were doing, have intercourse was too clinical. "I want to be with you." It was the only way I knew how to say it, at the moment.

He nodded and lowered his lips to my collar bone, bringing the tempo down again. I moaned and arched my back, offering him more of me, but he continued his torture for a bit, approaching the edges of my bra, then veering away until I thought I would lose my mind. I clutched at his head, holding him near, praying he would make the feverish ache dissipate and satisfy me. Finally, his lips skimmed over the satin, the warmth and moisture of his breath a further tease before he abruptly closed on my nipple, sucking on it through the fabric of the bra. I exhaled, my heart rate relaxing a little, enjoying the sensations branching from my core outward. He shifted to the other breast, clawed the cloth aside and alternately lapped long and slow, then short and fast, pulling whimpering noises from me. I watched him as he circled with the tip of his tongue, then drew me into his mouth, his movements strong and sure, even a touch painful, but enjoyably so.

The next thing I knew, he was lifting me and setting me on my feet. My mind reeled.

Why are you stopping?

He smiled at me, and grasped the top of my jeans, jerking me in and kissing me in a more demanding way. Even as I responded, my lips turned up in pleasure. He unbuttoned and unzipped my pants, and I toed off my shoes while he did it. After a combined effort, my jeans lay on the floor. Once back in his embrace, his hands found my butt cheeks.

"Is this a thong?"

"Uhh...yes."

He caressed my skin. "I *really* like this shirt."

Before I knew what was happening, he spun me to face the counter. He tugged my shirt down again and worked at my bra clasp. "You won't be needing this." He removed and threw it in the corner with his shirt.

"Now." He moved my arms over my head, pressing my palms against the cabinet. "Close your eyes."

"What?" I asked breathlessly.

His mouth was at my ear as he gripped my waist. "*Close* your eyes," he growled, nuzzling me.

My lips quivered with nervousness, arousal, and amusement. "Okay." I shut my eyes.

Pop.

"What's that?"

"Never you mind." I reached behind for him. "Uh-uhh. Hands on the cabinets."

"Ooh. Bossy."

Sht, sht, sht. There was a noise like someone shaking a spray paint can. Followed by what sounded like the release of air. *Pssst.* Something soft was molded to my breasts, spreading wetness across my skin. "Oh my God. This is like one of my wildest fantasies come true."

"Can I open my eyes?"

"Yes." The can of whipped cream sat on the counter, foaming over at the top. It looked a little erotic itself. He removed one hand from my breasts and licked whip cream from it, the wet sound in my ear sending shivers through me. "You taste good." His other palm slipped down to my stomach, dragging sweet white foam there too. He snagged a towel from the countertop. "I better clean you up. Spin around." He shifted, giving me room to rotate and face him. He wiped away a small strip.

"Really?" I said, incredulous. "You're not licking it off?"

"Nah."

I leaned on the countertop, with a disgruntled exhale.

He smirked, crouched, grasping my hips, and began to trace sensual patterns on my stomach with the tip of his tongue. I threw my head back with a moan.

"You like that, do you?"

"Oh, hell yeah."

He chuckled, then made his way higher, taking one of my nipples between his teeth. My eyes flew open, and my knees started to buckle. He tightened one arm to support me while turning on the water for some reason and continued his quest to eliminate all signs of whipped cream from my body. When he was finished, he stretched to hold the towel under the stream in the sink. "You probably don't want to be all sticky." The towel he cleaned me with was soothing, as he had let the water get warm before wetting it. When he was finished, he set the towel on the counter.

"Now, there's something else I want to do to you."

"Well, shit," I joked. "I hope it doesn't involve the coffee."

He laughed low. "No." He looked at the pot. "On second thought..."

My heart raced as he took the pot from the maker. He poured a glass half-full, and to my relief, brought it up to take a drink. He moved over to set it on the island then returned to me, lacing his fingers with mine and pulling me as he took a few steps backward. "Only one thing is standing in the way of what I want to do." He lifted me onto the counter and ran his hand between my legs. "These snaps."

All I could do was follow him, speaking out of the question at this point, and it was clear he enjoyed being watched. He put his hands behind my tush and slid me to the edge then gently pushed my legs wider. "Lay on your elbows," he said, his voice husky. I did what he asked, pretty sure my mouth was hanging open, and there was a definite possibility I was drooling. He held my gaze then lowered between my legs and unsnapped the flap with his teeth. Then his tongue was stroking, flicking, fingers were inserted... I collapsed onto the table and stared at the lights hanging from the ceiling, the air caught in my throat. My eyes rolled back into my head with the first mini-wave of bliss. I struggled to let any thought into my bombarded brain other than *yes, this feels so good*, but I fought through it. I pushed onto my elbows.

"Wait." I panted.

What was I going to do?

"We should go to your bedroom."

CHAPTER THIRTEEN

Scott

By the time I dragged my ass home, I was exhausted. It was only shortly after ten, so I was surprised to find the place quiet.

Did Elise and Sergei go out together? Hopefully, she saw the light and told him to take a flying leap.

Then I entered the kitchen.

I first thought, illogically, that Sergei had finished his little cooking session with Elise, drove her home, picked up some girl and brought her home and it made me mad. It seemed like an insult to Elise. I sighed and gathered a pair of heels and some jeans and...some other contraption...a shirt with a snap crotch? What the hell? I dropped them in the corner with a bra, and what I presumed was Sergei's shirt, so I wouldn't have to keep stepping over them.

I am wiping down EVERY surface in here.

The coffee machine was on, with a full pot ready, which seemed strange, until I saw the Jameson's and the mugs. Irish coffees, then. That makes more sense. But just one of the mugs was used... I brought that to the sink and for some reason smelled it. No one had put any Jameson's in there. The whipped cream was foaming onto the counter, which looked a bit obscene, to be honest.

Clearly this woman was still in the condo. Could they have fallen asleep? If so, should I clean with the possibility of that waking them?

What the heck. All the stuff for Irish coffee is available, might as well have some. It's my place, after all.

I took my drink to the living room and that's when I saw Elise's purse and my mind exploded. I knew she was a grown woman and capable of making her own decisions, but I wanted to pulverize Sergei. She was vulnerable after her breakup and had no idea what his motive was, the sleaze bag. To outright use someone to...what? Win some bet? It infuriated me.

But I didn't have enough energy to stay furious for long. I lowered myself into a chair and stared at the one across from me where Elise's purse sat. I dropped my head into my hands.

I can't believe…if only I had gotten home in time to warn her. She…she slept with him?

I was reeling. My mind's eye returned to the kitchen, formulating a scenario of what had happened.

Oh my God. This is sick. I pulled at my hair in frustration. Then the thought came that would be my undoing.

How could she do this to me?

And I did something I hadn't done since I was a little boy. Cried.

She didn't do anything to you, you idiot. You took freaking—I don't know how many, but far too many—years to realize you loved the girl. How could I have been so stupid? How could I not see I had the most wonderful, perfect woman in front of me and I ignored her?

But that wasn't the truth. The truth was I had been scared of my feelings for her from day one, and I took the coward's way out, ignoring what I was feeling, and oblivious to what she was feeling.

I've fucked everything up.

I drank my Irish coffee and then made another one. I would be wired, but I didn't care. No way would I be able to sleep with Sergei and Elise…she had to be naked. All of her clothes were in the kitchen.

Right now, Elise…

Merely thinking her name made my heart ache.

…is in bed, naked, with that son of a bitch…! When I get hold of him, I'll crush him.

But instead of Sergei making an entrance, at about two o'clock in the morning I woke, realizing there was a presence in the room. Elise was tiptoeing along the hall in one of Sergei's shirts, the moonlight painting her bare legs in white. I switched on the light and she screamed.

"Scott! Holy crap! You scared the shit out of me." She had covered her heart.

I sat up. "Searching for your clothes?"

She didn't say anything, but her chin trembled. And damn it all if she didn't look so beautiful I wanted to just take her into my arms and kiss her myself. But some other man had already done that.

"Elise…" My voice sopped with disappointment. "How could you have—?"

"Don't!" she screamed, throwing a hand out like a traffic cop. "Don't you say anything." Her eyes shone with tears, but I pushed down the part of me that felt bad for her.

"You slept with him. In my house. Under my roof. In my freaking kitchen, for God's sake! What kind of animal—"

She rushed at me, getting so near I could freaking smell that florally, citrusy scent of hers that drove me crazy. "Shut up. You shut up. Don't you say another word. You have no right to judge me!"

Then my mouth took over and hurled things at her indiscriminately. "Don't you think it's a tad fast to be jumping into bed with someone? You were with Hunter a week ago."

Her jaw dropped open, she blinked, and took a step backward. She looked so vulnerable, barefoot, swimming in a man's shirt... Then she found the fire. "Don't you think that's my decision? And why would you care anyway? You didn't care enough to not stand me up on my birthday. You were too busy with that dark-haired, leggie chick from the auction."

"What are you talking about? I was here all night. You were the one who decided to go out with Sergei and not answer any of my texts."

Sergei stumbled into the room. "What the hell's going on—?"

I charged Sergei, who was wearing only sweatpants, pinning him against the wall as best I could with nothing to hold on to. "You son-of-a-bitch!"

"Scott, man, calm down."

"Don't fucking tell me to calm down."

Then she was touching me. Her little hand on my arm where the veins were bulging with anger. "Scott, don't! Leave him alone."

"You're defending him? This guy? This guy who—" My voice broke. I didn't want to hurt her, but she had to know.

Sergei must have seen it in my eyes. "Oh, God, don't, man. *Please* don't. I'm begging you. I—"

"He bet the other players he could sleep with you."

"Wh—" She stumbled backward, looking from Sergei to me, tears now escaping from behind her lashes. "What did you say?"

It felt like someone had stuck a knife in me. "I'm sorry, Elise, but—"

She peered at him, her lips trembling. "You did *that*?"

"No, Elise. It's not like that." He shoved me off and moved in her direction, but I got between them.

"Get away from her."

He stopped, staring around me at her. "I wanted to tell you..."

"Quit lying to her." I twisted a fraction to talk to Elise. "He's not even Russian."

"He's not—"

"Yes, I am."

"He's got Russian in him, sure. But he's from Brooklyn. Born and raised in the U.S. That's a fake accent."

"Is that true?"

He stood for a moment with his mouth hanging open, then dropped his head. When he spoke, it was without the fake Russian. It must have been disconcerting for Elise. "Yes, I—" He lifted his gaze to hers. "I wanted to impress you."

She didn't respond at first. "Your babushka's *zefir*?"

"She did make it...but I found the recipe online and copied and pasted it to a document."

"I can't believe I was so stupid."

"You're not the first girl who has been fooled by his *Russian schtick*," I told her, adopting my own fake accent for the last two words.

"You know what, Scott, I'm sick— You know what? Fuck you." He came at me, and we grappled. He pushed me, and with my dress shoes on I slid back, giving him enough room to throw a punch.

Elise screamed. "Oh my God!"

My shoe heels hit a chair and I got some traction and took a swing at him, hitting him squarely in the chin. Then I pushed him against the wall again.

"Stop!" Elise shrieked. "Stop this!" She was tugging on my arm, nearly hysterical. I couldn't make a move without risking hitting her.

I stared daggers into Sergei. "I can't believe you slept—"

"Oh, don't get self-righteous with me. I wasn't the only one making a bet. Are you going to tell her that you did too?" He glanced at Elise and seemed to realize his mistake. "Oh, fuck. I'm sorry, Eli—"

"Scott?" Her voice wavered. "Is that true?"

"No. Well, yes, but I bet you wouldn't sleep with him. I thought—" Her face, the look of betrayal on it...

"Oh my God." She turned, squeezing her temples between her palms.

"Elise?" I was so distracted by her, I wasn't paying attention and he broke away from me, crossing to her and putting a hand on her shoulder.

She whirled and shoved him. Five foot nothing against an NHL forward. "Don't you touch me!" Her shouted words vibrated and hung in the air, and it was silent for a moment. She shifted her gaze from him to me and I wanted to disappear. "Is that all my life is to you? A game?" Her voice was low but steely. Sergei and I glanced at each other. "Huh?" She sobbed, and I took a step, but her head whipped up and I froze in her glare. She eyed Sergei again. "Let's see what we can get Elise to do. Is that how it works? Let's see how much of a fool we can make of her."

He moved toward her, a far braver man than I. "It did begin as a bet. But...along the way, my feelings for you grew."

She pulled at her hair and walked around in a circle. "Do you hear yourself speaking? You put money down to see if you could sleep with the virgin."

Holy shit! She and Hunter never did it?

"Oh." She seemed to realize what she'd said and seemed like she was about to lose it altogether.

"Wait...what?" Sergei was as dumbfounded as I. "You were a virgin? Why didn't you tell me?"

"Because it's not something you advertise, Sergei." She held her hands up in the air. They were shaking. "I— I have to get out of here."

Sergei and I watched her leave, stunned by her revelation. Then he started moving toward the door, and I grabbed his arm.

"Stay away from her," I growled.

"The hell I will!" he spat back. "I really care for her. I'm finding her."

He rushed after her and I hurried to follow. The elevator doors were closing, and we just got a glimpse of Elise covering her face, sobbing uncontrollably.

"Shit!" He paced in short lengths, his fingertips on his temples. He stopped, facing our apartment.

I stared at the numbers above the door lighting in descending order. I couldn't let her leave like this. I dashed for the stairs. When I got to the lobby, short of breath, a couple was getting on the elevator. I took a quick peek. No Elise. I went out on the street.

Jimmy was helping a lady with a walker maneuver it onto the curb.

"Have you seen—?"

I didn't have to finish my sentence. He nodded his head to my right. "She was real upset. Took off that way. Some sketchy looking guys were over there. She was—"

I didn't hear anything else because I was running down the street. I came to the alley on the north side of our building and took it all in within seconds. Somewhere between six and eight guys in leather jackets and hoodies surrounded her. One held Elise's forearm while she thrashed around. One had his hand up under her shirt.

"Whooee! Ain't got nothing under there either."

"Leave her the fuck alone."

They turned to peer at me, straightening. The one who had been messing with her spoke first. "Hey, boys. It's Scottie McCord."

"Who he?" a skinny one asked.

They were walking toward me. The one holding Elise shoved her away.

"He's a big-time hockey player. Ain't you, McCord?"

"Elise." I glanced at her, scared for probably the first time in my life. I'd survive getting the shit beat out of me. It wasn't like it hadn't happened before. But if they did *anything* to Elise... "Come over here and get behind me."

She scurried in my direction but stopped and grabbed her foot. "Oww."

I had to take my gaze from her because her attackers were getting closer.

"Let's just see how tough you are without your pads on, big boy."

Sergei skittered in the loose gravel at the top of the alley to my rear. "Oh, shit. Call the cops!" he shouted at Jimmy.

Then all hell broke loose. It probably took all of thirty seconds. Blows were coming from all angles. Elise vaulted onto one of the guys' backs, screaming. Sergei yanked someone off me and decked him. The guy Elise was riding had grabbed her and was trying to flip her over his shoulder, but she was clinging on. Sergei pulled someone else away and I caught his attention. "Get her before she kills herself," I told him. He nodded and went to detach her. I guess the guys had their bit of fun kicking a hockey player's ass because they hightailed it down the alley, dropping me to my knees. I pitched forward, wrapping an arm across my middle and catching myself with the other arm to lower myself to the ground. I fought my head up. Elise was all right—thank God. Sergei's lip was bleeding, but I don't know if it was from my punch or if one of the thugs had tagged him. I moaned and collapsed to the ground.

"Scott!" Elise was by my side, turning me to help me but causing me a considerable amount of pain. That's okay. I deserved it. I flopped lifelessly on my back, staring at a streetlight coming into and out of focus. All of my separate areas of pain were fighting to be heard above the others. "Oh my God, Scott," she sobbed. I must have appeared pretty bad because she was nearly hysterical. She extended a trembling hand. "Look what they did to you."

I concentrated on her. "I'm fine. It's nothing." I coughed and my ribs sent a stabbing pain through me I couldn't ignore. I closed my eyes, suddenly needing to concentrate on my breathing.

"No, it's not. It's not nothing."

Sergei was crouched over her shoulder. "You okay, buddy?"

Jimmy came tearing into the alley. "Cops are on their way. Ambulance too." He fought to catch his breath, gazing around. "Where are the punks? You mean I don't get a chance to hit nobody?" He bent, clenching his knees. "You have all the fun, Mr. McCord?"

"Yeah, sorry about that, Jimmy." I laughed, then groaned.

"Where's that ambulance?" Elise said, staring at me.

"I'll go wait for it. Flag them down." Sergei took off.

I managed to lift my arm and touch Elise's face. "Shh-shh-shh. Don't cry. Why is it I always make you cry?"

She sniffed, the question distracting her momentarily. "I don't know."

I gathered my energy. "Elise...I shouldn't have taken Sergei's bet, but he egged me on, and I thought you'd see through his bullshit and toss him out on his ass. I didn't think you'd get involved with him and get hurt."

She leaned into my palm. "I probably should've seen through it. I was just in such a bad place when I came here, and instead of clearing things up, it only got worse here with you. All we've done is fight."

"I know. And it's all my fault. I'm sorry." I took her hand. "Will you forgive me?"

"Of course I'll forgive you. You're my best bud." She struggled to keep her voice steady.

"Good. Now...can someone take me to the hospital? I think I broke something."

Sergei returned. "The ambulance is here. They're getting their gear."

"You can't tell coach. He may not play me tomorrow night."

He nodded. "Okay."

"Are you crazy? You're not playing tomorrow night."

Sergei and I laughed.

"You guys are freaking lunatics. I'm getting dressed quickly." She kissed my fingers. The medics approached behind her. "Listen to these guys."

"I will."

She struggled to get to her feet and hopped around.

"They need to examine your foot." The guys set their stuff on the ground. "She hurt her foot."

"Ma'am? Can we have a look at that?"

"Uhh..." She glanced down. "I need clothes."

"I've got a blanket in the rig. I'll be right back."

I shut my eyes. "Listen to them," I mumbled.

CHAPTER FOURTEEN

Elise

They had to remove several shards of glass from my foot. Little cuts dotted the area, and the big cut ran from the ball of my foot to the start of the heel and required 34 stitches to close it. But all I could think of was Scott being swallowed up by those guys and the stomach-rolling sound of their blows and his grunts. At this point, I think I was in shock. From all that was revealed, as well as all that happened.

Once I was stitched and bandaged, I changed into the clothes Sergei brought me, which I had taken from him without a word. The nurse had told me Scott's room number, so I was on my way there when Sergei intercepted me.

"Can we talk?"

I stared at him. "I want to check on Scott first." I didn't wait for a response, pushing the door to Scott's room open.

"Elise." They'd cleaned him, but he still looked like hell. "Are you okay?"

I inhaled shakily, trying to pull it together, and nodded.

"Come here," he lifted his arm, although it seemed like a struggle, and I ran to his side, laying my cheek on his chest.

"I was so scared."

He kissed the top of my head. "I know. But I would have never let them hurt you."

I straightened. "Not scared for me—although, I was, at first—scared by what they were doing to you."

"What? This?" he joked. "This is nothing."

I surveyed the cuts, bruises, and swelling. "It doesn't seem like nothing to me." My voice came out rough.

He bookended my face with his hands. "Elise," he shifted his gaze from one of my eyes to the other, "I'm *fine*."

I drew away from him because I had an overwhelming urge to kiss him. "Don't give me that macho shit. Your bruise hurts just as much as my bruise."

He drew his brows together and examined me. "Did they bruise you?'

"No. Hypothetically."

"What about your foot?"

"It's fine. They stitched it up." Although I was wishing like hell I had my tennis shoes instead of heels. I looked at his features and wanted to cry again. "Don't do that again. Don't rush in and save me when I've done something stupid."

"Elise, I'll always rush in and save you," he said matter-of-factly, and it tipped the scales. I covered my face and cried, my shoulders shaking.

"Hey. Come here. Come here."

I went to him, and he drew me against his battered body and let me cry, holding me and stroking my hair. "I'm so sorry, Elise. This shouldn't have happened to you. You don't deserve—"

I shook my head, raising it. "I should have listened to your warnings. I can't believe I—" I stopped, images of the things I'd done with Sergei running through my mind. They made me sick. I wiped my cheeks. "I need to talk to him. He's waiting in the hall."

"Do you want to wait until I can be with you? You don't have to talk to him, you know."

"Yeah, I do." I straightened and gave him a smile. "It won't take long. I'll be back."

"Okay," he said, sounding unsure.

I walked out of the room. Sergei was leaning against the opposite wall with his hands in his pockets but crossed to me. "Do you want to go into this waiting room? No one's in there."

I let him lead me around the corner to an empty room and stood silently before him, rubbing my arms. I felt naked and exposed and so, so foolish. I couldn't look him in the eyes. It was too painful because...I had come to care about him...

No. About someone who never existed.

"Elise. I've been going over what I want to say to you, but none of the words can express how sorry I am to have hurt you. I wanted to tell you, Elise, I swear. I tried to a couple of times, even..."

"But you didn't. You let me...give myself to you, or to some ridiculous phony version of yourself..."

"The things I made up, the stupid accent, and all that, those weren't true. But the feelings I have for you are genuine."

"You know, even now, part of me wants to believe you. That's how...warped I am."

He touched my arm. "*You* are not warped. You are a wonderful woman and I—" His voice broke. "I can't believe I threw that away."

I wrung my hands. "I don't know what you want me to say..."

"Say you'll forgive me."

"Sergei..." I turned from him and plopped into a chair. "I could maybe forgive you, but it would be pretty unwise for me to trust you again, wouldn't it?"

He sighed, then began again. "I'm not proud of the man who made that bet, who thought nothing of using someone else for his gain. But I feel like...I know this sounds stupid because we haven't known each other that long, but I feel like being with you has changed me. Has made me see I am capable of...caring for someone other than myself."

I stared at him for a long time. "If that's true, I'm happy for you. I am. But...I can't trust you anymore. And not only that, but I also can't trust me. I don't know if I'll ever be able to trust another man again."

His jaw tightened. "And then there's the fact that you're in love with Scott."

I blinked several times. It was no use denying it. "Yes, there's that." I looked at my hands in my lap. "I'm sorry."

"And if that's the case, two of us were lying in that bedroom."

To hear him mention what we did...it hurt. And to have him blame it on me. But, in a way, he was right. "Maybe you're right. I was lying to myself, and I was lying to you."

He was silent for a moment. "No." He squatted before me, holding onto the arms of my chair. "You weren't lying, Elise. There was a difference between what I was doing and what you were doing. I was trying to exploit someone. You were trying...to mend a broken heart. To start over. To make a life for yourself and let go of loving someone who—for whatever reason—doesn't understand what he could have, if he simply woke up to what's right in front of him." He hung his head. "It was wrong of me to try to blame this on you. You were the *one* person acting in good faith here."

He seemed so miserable, I couldn't help myself. I reached to stroke his hair. "I'm sorry, Sergei."

"For what?"

I shrugged. "For the way things turned out, I guess."

"Yeah, me too." He ran his hand across his face, leaving it on his chin for a long moment. He inhaled deeply. "I have one thing I need for you to believe after all this. While I'm sorry for my actions, I'm not sorry for a moment I spent with you. I'm grateful to you for...helping me to look at myself more honestly and want to change who that person is. I will forever be thankful for that." He put a palm on my cheek and peered into my eyes. Leaning forward, he gave me one last heartbreaking kiss then rose. "Goodbye. If you ever need anyone in your corner, I'll be there." He left.

I bent in two and sobbed.

When I got a hold of myself, I dragged myself down to Scott's room. "How'd it go?"

I shrugged. "He said he was sorry. I said I was too. He left."

"Mmm."

I needed to change the subject. "So, what did the doctor say?"

He clapped his hands together. "Good news. No broken bones."

"Okay, that is good, but what else did she say?"

He grinned. "That I was a fine specimen of a man."

My lips twitched. "Not looking like that, she didn't."

"They're coming back in a few minutes to take this IV out and bring in discharge papers and I'm going home," he said brightly.

"And you didn't bribe anybody?"

"In the strictest sense of the word, no. Can you pass me my shirt?" He gestured to a stack of clothes on a chair.

"Did you give anybody tickets to a Fire game?"

"Huh?" he said innocently. "What do you mean? I do that all the time."

"Uh-huh." I dropped the pile of clothes on top of him, then considered them. "Hey, how'd you get clean clothes?"

"Uhh...Sergei...brought them to me. I didn't even ask."

"Hmm."

A nurse came in and I stared through the window at the cars passing below.

He brought Scott clean clothes without asking.

"I want you to know I asked Sergei to call Coach, and I now officially have 'an upper body injury' and won't be playing in tomorrow's game."

"Good."

I kept rehashing my conversation with Sergei and coming back to his, *and there's the fact you're in love with Scott.*

Yeah, there's that. That thing with him that makes me ache and there's nothing I can do about it.

"Elise?"

"Yeah," I replied, still spacing out. Several seconds passed without a response so I turned to see what was going on.

He was standing by the bed buckling his belt, his hospital gown discarded on the bed. His perfect abdomen was a mass of black.

"Oh my God, Scott." The tears pressed again. I put a hand over my mouth, staring at what his gown had covered.

He glanced down. "It looks bad, but it's not."

I forced myself to gaze up at him. "What if no one had come, Scott? No Sergei. No Jimmy. No ambulance. No cops." They had shown up after Scott was already in the ambulance and had met us at the hospital for questioning. "What would they have done to you?" The idea made my stomach drop.

He lifted his arms and dropped them on my shoulders, unable to hide the wince, the sharp intake of breath, and the need to close his eyes to keep it together. "Fuck that hurts." He opened his eyes. "But it will heal. It's fine."

"Your definition of fine and mine are way different." I inspected the deep bruises again. "What if they had killed you, Scott?"

"But they didn't."

A rap on the door interrupted us and it cracked open. "Everyone decent in here?"

"Yeah, come in, doc."

"Ahh...Mr. McCord. You're up and going. I see those pain killers we gave you are working."

I moved to the side.

"Yeah," he said, his voice tight, "they're great."

"Well, let's go over your discharge papers, then, and you can be on your way."

I stayed by the window to give them some privacy and again immersed myself in my thoughts. How had my life become this? Hunter, gone. Living in San Francisco instead of Nebraska. Talk about culture shock.

I really wish Mom was here right now.

"Ms. Scofield?"

"Hmm? Yes."

"I understand you received quite a cut on your foot. How are you doing?"

"Oh, fine. I just...I stepped in some glass, and I didn't have shoes on. It's nothing like what happened to Scott."

"Well, thirty-some-odd stitches is no little thing. And I imagine, going through something like that was pretty scary."

"Uhh, yeah, I guess. I'm okay." *Why is she talking to me?*

"Well, if it were me, I'd be pretty shaken up. If you want someone to talk to, both of you, there are people here who can help you."

Scott looked at me. I didn't know what to say, so I said nothing.

The doctor filled the awkward silence. "I'll write the number on your discharge papers in case you decide to take advantage of that."

Scott took it from her. "Thanks."

"And no more taking on eight guys at a time."

"It was only six."

"Six is enough. Take care." She left.

"So, want to catch a taxi home?" He grabbed his T-shirt. "Or I could call a car. It might take longer, but..."

"A taxi's fine."

He sucked in his breath while struggling to work his way into his shirt.

"Let me help you." I tried to ease him into his shirt, but I could tell it was still agonizing.

"Let's get out of here."

When we finally got into the taxi, I could tell he was exhausted. He gave the cabbie my address.

"No. Could you please take us to the McDermot Building?"

Scott started to protest.

"I want to see you settled in."

He was in no shape to argue, which was good. He lay back onto the seat and shut his eyes. I thought he'd fallen asleep, but he grabbed my hand. He swiveled his head to peer at me without lifting it. "Are you all right? You're awfully quiet." His voice was pitched lower than usual.

I forced a smile. "I'm fine." I patted him. "Don't worry about me."

He closed his eyes again. "I'll always worry about you," he said sleepily. I think he was asleep in minutes. He woke when we pulled to the curb.

Jimmy opened the door. "There he is. Rocky Marciano. Welcome home, big guy."

"Yeah. Hi, Jimmy. Thanks for your help last night...or was it this morning?"

"What do you mean? You already had them taken care of when I got there." Jimmy laughed.

"Oh, yeah. I was bruising their knuckles with my face and abs. They never had a chance."

Jimmy slapped him on the shoulder, and he winced. "Oh, sorry. How are you, Ms. Scofield? How's the foot?"

"It's fine," I said hurriedly. "I just want to get this big galoot into bed."

"Oh. Need any help with that?"

"I think we've got it," Scott answered for me. "Thanks anyway. And, seriously, thanks for calling the ambulance and the cops."

Jimmy hesitated, then responded seriously, "I only wish I could have helped more."

"You did what we needed. See ya later."

Strangely enough, it didn't occur to me until we were in the elevator that I was returning to the scene of the crime, so to speak. I scratched my head. "Umm. Is...is...he—"

"Is Sergei there? No. He's staying at Blane's house. He brought my phone to the hospital with my clothes and texted me around an hour ago."

"Oh. Okay." I was quiet for the rest of the ride to the condo, but my nerves amplified when we entered it. I tried to focus on Scott.

"Let's get you to bed."

"Well, that's a tad forward, don't you think?" he said with a lopsided grin.

"What? Oh, shut up." But it did make me smile. When we passed the kitchen, my heart skipped a beat, but I had to take a look. I was surprised to find it all cleaned and straightened.

When I got him to his room, he wanted me to help him remove his shirt.

"Wouldn't it be easier to keep it on?"

"I can't sleep with my shirt on. It's a thing I have." I worked if free as carefully as possible. "Would you mind helping with the pants too?" I stared at him. "I'll put a blanket on top of me. You only have to pull from the bottom."

"Fine." He got situated. "You must be starved too. I'll make you a grilled cheese if you have the ingredients."

"Ooh! An Elise Grilled Cheese? Totally worth getting my ass kicked over."

It did warm me a little. "Sure it is." I tugged on the cuffs of his jeans, but his leg musculature made it difficult. All at once, they gave, and I stumbled backward and put too much pressure on my cut foot. I yelped then fell on my ass. For some reason, that was the last straw. "These stu-pid..." I yanked one off. "Shoes." I hurled them across the room, then drew my legs in, laid my head on my knees and cried.

"Elise?"

"I'm fine," I shouted, completely out of control. I scrambled to my feet, which made the injury hurt even more. "I'll just...get your stupid grilled cheese sandwich." I rushed from the room, leaving him dumbfounded. I stopped to gather myself and realized my hand was on Sergei's bedroom door. I withdrew it like it was burned and hurried to the kitchen. I held it together pretty well until I went to throw the cheese wrapper away and the *zefir* was in the trash. I sat in the middle of the kitchen and had myself a cry while the grilled cheese burned. It only lasted a minute or two though. I needed to quit feeling sorry for myself. I struggled to my feet, and resolutely dumped the sandwich in the trash on top of the Russian treats we'd made together without shedding another tear. I whipped up another batch, deciding I wanted one myself, and Scott would probably eat two, at least.

I knocked on his door and entered sheepishly when he said to come in. "I'm sorry it took so long. I burned the first batch. I didn't know what you wanted to drink. You want a Coke?"

"Sure, that would be great. Man, I haven't had one of your grilled cheeses in ages."

"Well, it won't taste quite the same with no mayo. Sorry."

He blinked. "Mayo? You put mayo on them?"

I nodded.

"But I don't like mayonnaise." He took a bite.

I smiled. "Neither does Kyle." My stepdad was the biggest fan of my grilled cheeses. I had to laugh, thinking about him. "You know, he said once if the house were on fire and one of my grilled cheeses was on the table, he'd run back into the burning building."

He chuckled. "Sounds like Kyle. Yeah, it's not quite the same, but still damn good. Thanks."

"It's probably because you're so hungry," I reasoned.

He grabbed my hand. "No, it's because you made it." He had a strange expression on his face and being near him, shirtless, was making me nervous.

"Let me go get you that drink. I think you can take a pain pill now," I said over my shoulder. I brought the drink to him and hunted for his meds, surprised to find he'd already finished one of his sandwiches. "Do you want a third?"

"Do you have it made?"

"No, but it wouldn't be a problem."

He carefully moved from a sitting position to lying. "No. I'm fine." But when I'd reached the door, he called to me. "Elise...I don't want you to go home by yourself. Those guys might still be hanging around. Plus, your foot."

"Oh, they're probably long gone." But the idea still worried me. "But I was planning on staying, in case you need anything. Would you have any extra blankets?"

He hesitated, then answered as he rolled over. "Top of the closet on the right."

"Thanks." I had to get a hanger to snag the blanket and pull it down. All was quiet in the bed. I gathered up his plate and glass. Once in the kitchen, I washed them and tidied the area. When I came back, the light was off and he was turned on his side, but he made some movement that indicated he wasn't quite asleep yet. "Do you need anything else?" I whispered.

"Come here," he mumbled.

"Okay." I crossed to the bed.

"No," he said petulantly. "Here." He slapped the empty side.

"In your bed?"

"Yes."

I tilted my head. Maybe the drugs had gotten to him. He didn't know what he was saying. "Uhh...why? Exactly?"

"Just come here." He sounded disgruntled. It made me chuckle a little. "I need to know you're okay. I'm worried about you."

Worried about me? "But I'm fine, Scottie," I assured him softly. "The door's locked. No one can get in."

"But I want to feel you're safe. I won't be able to sleep if I can't feel you're safe."

Is he messing with me?

"*Please*, E. I need you."

I drew in a breath and with it a cold, sharp feeling which made my heart squeeze and feel heavier. *I need you.* Words I'd kill to have him say for real. But...he sounded upset, and I wanted him to sleep. That's what his body needed to heal.

I sighed and circled the bed. "Ooo-kay." I peered into his face. His eyes were shut. Maybe he'd forget and fall asleep.

"You're not in the bed."

I chuckled. "Okay. I'm getting in already. Geesh."

I lay on my side, facing away from him, riding the edge of the bed. *This is ridiculous. Ridiculous, but amusing.*

"That's not close enough. I can't feel you," he grumped.

I twisted around. His eyes were still shut, and he looked cross. I flipped back and huffed, inching nearer. "If you are messing with me, Scott, I won't hesitate to roll your bruised ass out of this bed." I wouldn't, but he didn't know that.

"No, you won't," he said smugly.

"I wouldn't push me," I replied, but my lips turned up.

I thought I'd finally satisfied him, but thirty seconds later he mumbled. "Closer."

"Scott! I'm practically on top of you." I could feel the heat of his body. I moved infinitesimally nearer. "You'll regret this in the morning."

"No, I won't."

"Yes. You will." I pulled the covers to my shoulders, murmuring, "I should be freaking recording this. Can you imagine the hits on that?"

I settled in, and although I thought it would be impossible to sleep this close to him, I started nodding off.

Suddenly he lifted his head and his deep voice slid into my ear, sounding a little too clear for my taste. "I can't *feel* you." His arms wrapped about me, hauling me in. "Mmm."

I was going to chew him out, but his last utterance seemed to contain pain. "Did you hurt yourself?"

His sole answer was a sigh of contentment.

This is ridiculous. Every nerve was on edge. My heart was pounding against my ribcage. My eyes were wide open. No way would I sleep now.

As if reading my mind, he whispered, "Relax, Elise. I've got you. I won't let anyone hurt you. Ever."

I squeezed my eyes shut and tears tumbled over my lashes. He meant to comfort, not be cruel, but it hurt. It was like torture, and it was like heaven. I concentrated on breathing evenly.

Relax, Elise. This is the only time you'll be able to lie beside him. When he's drugged. So, you might as well enjoy it.

I consciously released the tension in one muscle at a time.

It's okay. I can pretend for one night we're together. That he cares for me in the same way I care for him. I can take this one night and hold on to it forever. I don't need to think about how much it'll hurt in the morning. Just this once.

He smelled so good, even though he'd been lying down in a filthy alley. Like a forest. Or a lumberjack...something sharp and sweet at the same time, and very masculine. Headily so. And the strength of those arms around me was reassuring. I let go and fell into him. Drowned in him.

His embrace tightened for a moment. "That's it."

That's the last thing I remember.

CHAPTER FIFTEEN

Scott

She was gone. For a second it filled me with an illogical terror. Like they'd come and got her. I flew up so quickly the pain made me sick to my stomach. After I'd breathed through that, I left the bed, pulled on some sweats, and went in search of her. Once again her purse was in the chair, but I couldn't find her. I even checked *his* room, dreading finding her there. When she wasn't, I was relieved for a half-second before again wondering where the hell she was. Leaving his room, I saw the blanket pooled at her feet. She was slumped in the chair so much only a hint of her showed over the top.

I opened the door to the balcony. She was sound asleep, still wearing the clothes she had on the day before. I crouched in front of her and touched her knee. "Elise?"

Her head wobbled on her shoulders, then she slowly opened her eyes, and jumped when she saw me. "Oh."

"Hey. What are you doing out here?"

"Uhh..." She looked around as if trying to determine where *here* was. "I think I came here to watch the sun rise."

I touched her hand. "You're freezing." The balcony was usually fairly protected close to the condo, but the wind must have been blowing in precisely the right direction to catch it. Her blanket, which I originally thought had slipped, was probably blown off. "Let's go inside." I grabbed the blanket and put it over her shoulders when she stood. Once in the living room, she lowered herself onto the couch, and I sat next to her, rubbing her arms to warm her.

"Do you want me to make you some French toast?"

"That sounds great..."

She started to rise.

"...but can we talk first?"

"Sh-sure," she said uneasily.

"I've been going through everything in my mind..." I studied her. "Something's bothering me. You said something about me not being here Saturday, but I *was* here. The whole time. Did you ring the bell? Knock on the door?"

"No." She scooted forward and straightened some already straight magazines on the coffee table. "Sergei told me you'd already left with...What's-Her-Name...and..." She stood. "That you told him not to wait up. So, do you have any jelly for the French toast?"

I grabbed her leg as she turned to the kitchen. "Why would I have gone out when I was making your birthday dinner?"

She shrugged. "Don't ask me. Well, I know you have syrup, because I brought some with me." She tried to squirm free from my grip. She'd changed so much. She used to come at me, not walk away. I missed that girl. But I loved this one just as much. I wouldn't release her.

"Would you forget the damned French toast?"

She glared at me. So, the fire was still there. Folding her arms, she threw herself into a chair. "If you didn't want French toast, why didn't you say so?"

Oh my God. This is so not about French toast. I inhaled evenly and asked her quietly. "Is that why you didn't return my texts? Because you were mad at me because you thought I'd...forgotten your birthday or something?"

"What texts?"

"What texts? Come on. I had to send you a half dozen."

"The only text I got from you was that weird one saying something like...are you with her? What did you even mean by that? Was it autocorrect or something?"

"I sent that to Sergei. I was asking him if you were with him because Jimmy said he saw you together. But you got it... Did you respond?"

She unfolded her arms slowly. "No...but you replied with..." She scrunched her forehead. "Wait. Where's my phone? It's in my purse." She jumped to her feet to get it.

"Mine's on the kitchen counter. Can you get it for me?"

"Sure." She was looking at her phone as she crossed to the kitchen and grabbed mine. She tossed it to me as she spoke. "You texted 'Elise. Don't play games with me.' Wait... It's Elise, period, don't play games with me."

I unlocked my phone and pulled up my texts. "I texted that to Sergei too. I texted you..." I scrolled. And scrolled. "They're not here... None of my texts to you are on here. Or the texts I sent to Sergei." I gaped at her. "He erased them. No one else has had my phone."

She paled. "You really were here? You did...make me dinner?"

"Yes. That's what I've been telling you." I struggled to my feet, grimacing but realizing the pain wasn't as severe as earlier. I came and clumsily kneeled in front of her, holding on to her knees. "How could you think I would ever invite you for a birthday dinner and then go out with another woman?"

She stared at me, her mouth moving, but no noise passing her lips at first. "Oh, God, Scottie. I'm so sorry. He told me...and I simply believed him." She slapped her palm on her forehead. "You made me dinner?"

"Dinner. And I had a cake. My presents are right there." I gestured to the bar where they still sat.

"I'm *so* sorry. What's wrong with me? He lied. He lied about everything, and I gobbled it up like a fool. I took the word of a guy I'd known for a day over...my best friend." Tears rolled past her lashes.

"Don't do that. Don't blame yourself. He fooled me too. I should have known you would never blow me off like that." I put my hands on each cheek and wiped away tears with my thumbs, looking from them to her eyes. "Oh, Elise. Here you are crying again. You'll get dehydrated." She laughed, which was what I'd hoped she'd do. "Could we maybe sit together on the couch?" My knees hurt from when those guys dropped me, dead-weight, before they bolted. She nodded and we crossed to the couch. I spread the blanket across us and cautiously lifted my arm to put it around her, happy I could do that with less pain now. "This has been one hell of a week."

"I know. I've kind of made your life a living hell moving here."

I stared at her. "No. Don't you get it?" I licked my lips, searching for the words. I had to show her I loved her, that she meant everything in the world to me. I brushed the hair from her face. "I want you here. With me." My throat ached with emotion. I wanted to explain how I felt, but I was no good with words. I was a man of action. I brushed my lips over hers, her nearness stealing my mind from me. "I want you." I kissed her tenderly and pulled back, waiting for some sort of reaction. She didn't cry; she didn't scream; she didn't throw her arms about me; she just sat there. "Don't you know how much you mean to me?" I kissed her again, and she responded this time.

Her hand came up slowly to my cheek, and she stroked it. "Scott," she breathed, one syllable full of so much emotion.

It was pure gasoline. I reached behind her head and shifted to bring her closer.

Oh my God. I love this girl so much.

Suddenly, I couldn't have enough of her. All the emotion of the last several days, the anger, the frustration, the longing, the worry when she was hurt, the guilt...it all poured out and everything inside was screaming for her. My kisses became faster, harder. My fingers trailed down her neck, along her skin and then under her shirt a little and she came unglued, pushing me away and jumping to her feet.

"No. I can't do this."

"Can't do what?"

"Can't be your freaking plaything."

"What?"

She crossed to the chair with her purse in it and grabbed it.

"Who said you were my plaything?"

"I can't let you do this to me again."

Do what? Love you?

"Elise, wait. Stop." Her purse got caught on the chair arm which gave me the chance to catch her, but she abandoned it, running for the door and fumbling with the lock. "Elise. Elise!" She got the door open a fraction, but I slammed it shut, one hand on it, one on the wall, caging her in my arms. I caught my breath, closing my eyes. And in an instant, I understood. She didn't need Scott, the guy she thought was a playmaker. She'd certainly had enough of that with Sergei. She needed me to lay it bare, which filled me with anxiety. I laid my forehead on her back.

"Elise..." I inhaled deeply and straightened. "Why do you think I moved to the West Coast?"

She turned slowly and leaned against the door, studying me. "Beeecause you got an offer from the Fire?" she said it like it was the stupidest question in the world.

"Well, yes. But why do you think they extended that offer?"

"Because you're a damned good hockey player?"

I hung my head, shaking it. How did I make her understand? "They gave me a contract because I courted them. I made it clear San Francisco was where I wanted to be. That I'd give them one hundred percent here. Make my home here. Stay as long as they'd have me."

She furrowed her brow. "Why are you telling me this?"

"Because..." I pushed off the wall but forced my feet to stay planted. I ran my tongue over my lips again and glanced to the side. "I— I tried to be happy for you and Hunter. In fact, at times I could almost convince myself I was okay with it." I peered at her. "You were happy, so I should be happy for you. What kind of prick wouldn't be happy for their best friend finding someone? But..." I dropped my gaze to the delicate necklace she always wore, a teardrop-shaped S for Scofield that rode along her collarbone gracefully. So tantalizing. "Sometimes," I said carefully, "when I would see him...kiss you...or touch you...I would run cold. It literally made me sick to my stomach." I continued to stare at the necklace like it was some sort of talisman that would help me speak and express the things I felt in my heart. "And there were times—I hate to admit this—but times I wanted to plant my fist in Hunter's smug-looking face." I chuckled humorlessly. "And then the asshole would do something cool to ruin even my fantasies of destroying him." It was like saying all of it sapped me of my energy. I turned and trudged to the couch, plopping down and exhaling, putting my head in my hands.

She stood still for a moment, then came to sit next to me. "Why didn't you say something?"

"Why would I? I'd already blown it with you." *Be honest with her.* "To tell you the truth, the feelings you stirred up in me scared the shit out of me." I folded my fingers together but stayed hunched over my knees. I exhaled through my nose. "I could square off with a guy three times bigger than I was at the rink and not blink an eye. But seeing you in the stands at one of my games..." I said slowly. "Every once in a while, it rocked me to the core. Not all of the time. Sometimes I was able to think of you in more of a sisterly manner. Like, for some reason, it didn't bother me as much when you came with Hunter. As long as you guys weren't being all cozy. But when you came by yourself..." I finally gazed at her. "Didn't you notice I always played really well when you were around, because I was trying to impress you, or really shitty, because I was so distracted by you?"

"How could I have known that? You never said anything."

I stood, suddenly agitated. I moved to the window, crossing my arms and staring out at nothing. "It wasn't easy for me. *Isn't* easy for me. Do you know what it's like to practically live with a girl your whole life and not be able to kiss her even though that's what you want to do more than life itself?"

She stood and followed me. "Yeah, I kinda do, Scott. Been there. Done that."

This has been my fault. My fault from the start. All this time wasted. And, at this point, maybe it's too late.

"Why didn't you say anything?"

Now that's the question, isn't it?

"If you felt that way, why didn't you just...kiss me?"

Because I'm a freaking idiot, Elise. Anger bubbled to the surface for some reason, and I had to put space between us again. I strode halfway across the room and stood there. "It's not easy for me, okay? It's not easy for me to open up. My own mother didn't give a damn about me. I meant so little to her she walked away and left me and never looked back." I turned on her for some reason. "So you'll forgive me if it's a bit difficult for me to be vulnerable with women."

She wrung her hands and took a step forward. "Oh, Scottie..." She came over and pushed the hair out of my eyes, which felt good at first. "I'm so sorry."

I grabbed her wrist and shoved her arm aside. "No, stop that." I fought to keep distance between us. "I don't want to be one of your stupid save-the-world projects."

Her expression changed from soft and tearful to hurt, to cold and pissed as hell.

"Okay. You won't have to worry then. You won't." She grabbed her purse cleanly this time and marched toward the door.

At first, I was going to just let her go. "No. Elise. Wait. I didn't mean it."

She spun on her heel and shouted at me, tears flying everywhere. "No. I'm done with this crap, Scott. I've let you break my heart for years. I love you," her voice broke, "but I need to take it back now and fix it." She glanced down, drawing a deep breath. "I don't want to see you. I don't want to see Sergei." She looked at me and the pain etched on her face was like a dagger. "I think it's time for me to stand on my own two feet for a while. I need to think and clear my head and get my damned feet under me."

I stood—frozen, emptied—and watched her leave, hating myself for what I'd done.

Elise

He texted before I even hit the lobby.

YOU NEED SPACE. I GET THAT. I'LL BACK OFF, FOR THE MOMENT. BUT I WILL PURSUE YOU, ELISE SCOFIELD. YOU ARE DULY WARNED.

Before I had time to wrap my mind around that, he shot me another one.

OH, AND SORRY FOR BEING SUCH A JERK. MAYBE I AM PRONE TO VIOLENCE. ;)

SERIOUSLY, THOUGH, I'M SORRY I HURT YOU. IF I WEREN'T GIVING YOU SPACE I'D TELL YOU I LOVE YOU. BUT I CAN'T. BECAUSE I'M GIVING YOU SPACE.

I was in trouble. The boy knew me. He knew my sense of humor. But could he honestly be in a committed relationship with me?

By the time I'd walked home, my foot was killing me, plus I had a raging headache. All I had to wear was a pair of guy's socks Scott had given me, but, seeing as I'd been seen in only Sergei's dress shirt the night before, it was kind of a "step" up. I wasn't supposed to be walking on the damned thing at all, but guess what, doc? I couldn't pay the rent by playing "My Immortal" for the landlord, so I'd actually need to go into work. God, how I wanted to sleep, but I couldn't. I had practice in an hour. I pushed all of my thoughts aside so I could focus on performing, which seemed to go pretty smoothly despite my lack of sleep.

As I was walking out to the rental I was still hanging on to, my attention was drawn to the window on my left. The choir director's office was in the long, tunnel-like hall leading to the lot where we were required to park. As I approached, I could see Ms. Van Hoof and Isabelle, who seemed to be double-teaming Carrie. They stood in front of her with their arms crossed, their bodies leaning away from her. Carrie was teary-eyed and wringing her hands. What could have possibly made them this upset with Carrie? She was a sweetheart and a damned good violinist. As I was approaching the door, I caught Carrie's gaze and she stopped in the middle of what she was saying.

Isabelle noticed and took a look back. I hurried past, but still caught the furious statement she seemed to hurl at Carrie. "This is exactly what we're talking about. We warned you."

Warned her of what?

I continued down the hall, but held up in the parking lot, pacing, until she exited, trying to keep it together, but tears visible on her face.

"Oh, Elise." She swiped at her cheeks. "What are you doing here?"

"Waiting for you. What's wrong, Carrie?"

She peeked over her shoulder. "Oh. Nothing. Just...uhh...stressed, I suppose."

I held her upper arms. "Come on, Carrie. What's going on? What were those two harpies saying to you?"

Her features crumpled. "Oh, Elise. I don't know what to do. They fired me."

"Fired you?" I cried in shock. "Whatever for?"

She fluttered a hand. "It doesn't matter."

I didn't know what to say. "I'm so sorry, Carrie." I patted her arm in an awkward attempt to console her.

She glanced off to the side. "I've got three kids to support, and my husband ran out on me last fall. I haven't heard a word from him since. How will I take care of my girls? I can't go back to my parents.' That's not a good environment for them..." She was rambling on to herself.

"Why would they do that to you?"

She shrugged, not looking me in the eye. "Not happy with my performance, I guess."

"I heard them say my name."

Her gaze snapped up. "It doesn't matter. Everything will be all right. I need to go."

She tried to get past me, but I shifted in front of her. "Carrie, I don't know exactly what's going on here, but I don't want you to worry over this. I'll handle it." I pulled out my phone. "What's your phone number?"

She stared at me, blinking. "What?"

"Your phone number." I opened my contacts. "I want to call you later and make sure you got home all right."

"Oh." She rattled off a number, and I entered it.

"Got it. Good. Now, you drive safe, and I'll call you later. Take a nice hot bath and try to relax." I opened the door to return and face them.

"But Elise...you shouldn't—"

"I'll be fine, Carrie. I've got to get to the bottom of this."

Whatever their reason was for firing her, it had something to do with me.

When I got close, I could hear those witches cackling. I threw the door open. Ms. Van Hoof sat behind the desk, leaning back in her chair, and Isabelle sat in one of the two chairs on the opposite side of it. They gawked at me, annoyed by my abrupt entrance. They were about to be annoyed even more.

"Why did you fire Carrie?"

The director slowly sat forward, lacing her fingers and placing her folded hands on the desk. "I think you know I can't tell you that."

"You need to unfire her."

"Excuse me?"

"Unfire her. In exchange..." I took a deep breath, "I'll leave."

The two women stared at me, then at each other, their eyes dancing. "You'll leave?" Ms. Van Hoof's brows joined her hairline.

"Yes. That's what you want, isn't it? You want me to leave. In fact, you've never wanted me here."

Again, they stole a look. "I wouldn't say that, Elise," Van Hoof said, drawing out her words.

"No," Isabelle seconded, insincerely.

"Look. I'm giving up my job here. The least you can do is be honest with me and tell me why you've been trying to sabotage me this entire time. What did I do to you?"

Now the director seemed truly taken aback. "You've done nothing. And we definitely haven't sabotaged you."

I put a hand on my hip. "So you didn't switch my music the other day?"

"Why would we do that?" Isabelle huffed.

"Because you don't want me here. You never have. You—" And suddenly it came together. "It wasn't you who wanted me here, it was Mrs. Prentiss. You were never hot on the idea, were you?" She didn't answer. "So why did you agree?"

I saw a crack in the façade. "It's not like I had a choice," she huffed.

I waited.

"The woman contributes a half-million dollars every year. She thinks she knows about music, but she wouldn't know a baton from a...a boa constrictor."

"And I was totally unqualified for the position." I could tell by her expression I'd hit the nail on the head. Or in this case, the baton on the music stand.

"Well...yes. You've never played in an orchestra before... I mean, you undoubtedly have talent...but it takes more than that. It takes talent, and experience, and know-how..."

I mulled it over. "So, you couldn't risk pissing her off, so you went along with it, then set out to show her how wrong she was by making sure I failed."

"Well, we hadn't originally planned on having to create problems for you, but you were just decent enough we couldn't risk you succeeding."

"You know what, I get that. I'm sure it's difficult having patrons constantly tell you what to do. To think their donation entitled them to...choose the music, dictate the schedule, hire the people they want..."

"Exactly," she said.

"And it's not easy for the rest of us either," Isabella piped up. "Having to work with incompetent people—no offense—"

Offense taken.

"It slows us down, makes us look bad..."

I could tell that was the clincher.

"I mean, I worked hard to get where I am. Don't I deserve to get my orders from a director, not some frumpy, over-the-hill woman who thinks she's still all-that? Writing a check and playing recorder in fourth grade doesn't make you some musical expert." They nodded to each other and smiled at me, thinking I was in their court.

"So, instead of having an uncomfortable conversation with a benefactor, you chose to play with people's lives. To uproot a girl—" I splayed my hand on my chest "—me— from my home and have me move halfway across the country even though you knew I would eventually lose my job and be put in a desperate situation."

"Well, I-I—"

"And you fired a woman who is the sole support of three small children merely because she was helping me to figure things out."

"I didn't know she was taking care of children on her own, did you?" Ms. Van Hoof asked her violinist.

"Well, I...might have..."

"Listen." I put my palms flat on the end of the desk, peering from one of them to the other. "I will keep my part of the deal and walk away from here. *You* will hire Carrie back, *a-pol-o-gize,* and if any kind of retaliation takes place toward her, I will go straight to Mrs. Prentiss and let her know what the two of you have been up to. Capisce?"

They looked at each other openmouthed, then their faces brightened. Ms. Van Hoof offered her hand. "It's a deal."

If I'm leaving, I'm having one last hurrah.

"Now," I inhaled slowly, "I forgot something in the auditorium. I'll get that and be on my way."

I traversed the hallway and crept onto the stage. The lights were still on, but the place was empty.

One last time on stage.

I set my case on a chair and drew my violin out. It wasn't my preferred electric violin, but it would do. I put my instrument to my chin and sighed. I would miss this. We had a show coming up—scratch that—*they* had a show coming up, featuring Disney music. I had been insanely excited about that because Disney did hire some of the greatest composers, in my book. Pulling the bow across the strings, I made my violin sing to "A Whole New World" from *Aladdin*, and I, in turn, danced. I used my entire body to create the music, as I so loved to. Just me, alone, in the spotlight—sort of. It was more a whole bank of lights, but I could pretend. Playing like that, I swear it was the most freeing, most soul-soothing, life-giving action a soul could perform. I let the music totally take me away. Away from thoughts of Hunter, of Sergei, of Scott. Of joblessness, Carrie, my rent. Away from missing my mom and Kyle, away from feeling anxious and awkward, away from everything but beauty and harmony. I got too immersed, though, and came down hard on my injured foot.

"Shit! Ow! Ow! Oww!" I hopped around, trying to shake off the pain. "Elise!"

I gasped. "Who is that? Who's there?" I shaded my eyes and came forward, thinking I recognized the voice, but unable to tell for certain in the blackness beyond the stage lights.

Scott ran out of the darkness. "Did you break it open again?"

"I don't know." I sat on the stage. My black pants were getting dirty, but at this point, that was the least of my worries. I was wearing black slip-on tennies, the closest I could get to appropriate foot attire and still be reasonably comfortable with the bandage on. "I think I need to define this giving me space thing. I actually was meaning more than two hours."

He stuck his hands in his pockets and rocked from heel to toe. "I know. But I...had a question."

"One you couldn't text?" I asked wryly. Having worked the shoe loose, I removed it to check the bandage. "No blood's showing, so I guess it's okay. Although it stings like hell."

"Should you even be walking on it?"

I frowned. "Is that your question? The answer is no. You can leave now."

"Wow. Somebody's grumpy."

"I've gotten like zero sleep and—" I almost told him I was no longer with the symphony. I couldn't do that. He'd want to help me, and we definitely didn't need that added to the mix. "Let's just say things haven't improved since we parted."

"All the more reason for us to be together," he said hopefully.

"Sco-ott," I said, a warning in my tone.

"Okay, okay. Space. I get it. But I needed to ask you...are your mom and Kyle still planning on coming in for the game Saturday?"

"As far as I know. Why? Do you want the tickets back?"

"No. No. Of course not. I...uhh...wasn't sure how you'd feel about the possibility of... Well, I was looking forward to hanging out with Kyle when you and your mom went for those manicures—which, can you still do that with the stitches?"

"Yes. Seeing as they'll be working on our hands, not our feet."

"Oh, yeah." He grinned. "Anyway...is it still okay with you if Kyle and I meet up?"

"Yes. He'd be disappointed if you didn't. And we were supposed to have dinner together too..."

"I'm guessing that's not allowed," he said, discouraged.

"We'll see."

I loved the glimmer of hope in his eyes. "Cool. Are you finished? Do you want me to carry you to your car?"

Do I ever.

But I promised myself I would stay away from him until I got my shit together, which didn't appear like it was happening any time soon. "I'm pretty sure that would be outside of the whole 'give me space' guidelines."

"Oh." He shifted his weight, glancing down for a moment before returning his gaze to mine. "And I guess a kiss..."

You're freaking killing me here.

"Scott. You're making this hard."

"All right. All right. I'll be good. You won't see me again until you tell me it's okay. Or until I can't stand it anymore," he added hurriedly.

I rolled my eyes. "You didn't see me for months at a time when I was in Nebraska, and you did perfectly fine."

"Yeah, but that's before I realized I'm in love with you."

It shocked me to hear him simply come out and say it like that. "Scott. You know you should probably sit with this whole thing, too. Make sure it's really something you want to pursue and not..." I swallowed, staring at my lap. It hurt to think about it. "A passing fancy."

I was surprised again when he gently lifted my chin so I would look at him. "You are not a passing fancy, Elise Scofield. In fact, this isn't actually anything new at all. I've always loved you. I just didn't know it."

I slowly withdrew from him, blinking to clear my vision from tears. "Uhh...this...see, this isn't space. What you're doing right now isn't space."

He took a step away from me. "I'm sorry." We studied each other for a long moment. He tilted his head. "You've changed, you know."

I was taken aback again. "What?"

He started to move toward me, then shifted his weight, putting his arms behind his back. "You've changed. You're not the girl I knew as a kid. You...I don't mean this in a bad way. It's only an observation, but you seem more fragile."

I knew he was right, but I didn't like hearing it. "I— Well, I guess that's the toll love takes on you."

His eyes widened, then he stared at the floor and nodded. "Especially my love, right?"

"I-I didn't say that."

He peered at me. "You didn't have to." He exhaled. "I messed this up from the beginning. I took advantage of you, of our friendship...and then later, in high school...I was such an ass. So cocky...or maybe that was a way of fooling myself, too. Convincing myself I could live without you. But I can't, Elise. I can't anymore." He released his hands from behind his back and waved them about. "The last few hours have been hell with you not around."

"Scott..."

"No. Don't worry. I'll give you your space. I deserve a little hell for the ton of hell I put you through."

"You've changed, too."

"I hope for the better..."

"I think— Could you maybe help me down from here? It's hurting my neck to look at you."

He immediately moved forward and scooped me off the stage and gently put me on the ground, letting me use his body to ease my weight onto my feet. After an instant of indecision, he retreated a foot or two. He cleared his throat. "You were saying I'd changed..."

"Yes. You're...very forthright these days."

"That's the new Scott. I'm not hiding from my feelings anymore or leaving questions unasked. I'm putting it out there."

His grin infected me and mine grew as a mirror image. "I guess I'll have to get used to that."

"I guess you will."

"You know..." I took a step toward him and touched his hand. One touch couldn't hurt. "If we try this, and that's a big if, but if we do...I'll need you to prove yourself to me." On one level I was teasing, but I kind of meant it, too. I shifted even closer. Dangerously close. I was an idiot. "You know," I ran a finger down his other arm. "It's like in a game when you get called for hooping..."

I knew it was called hooking. And he knew I knew. "You mean hooking."

"Oh, yeah," I said, still playing dumb. "Hooking." I smiled at him. Our bodies were almost touching now. "Well, when you get called for hooking and you have to show the ref you're truly remorseful before he'll let you out of that box thing..."

He leaned in. "You know that's not how it works, right?" he growled.

I ran my nails along the nape of his neck. He tentatively gripped my hips. "You need to prove yourself to me, Scott." I let some of my seriousness sink into my words.

"You don't think I can do that?" he said softly, swaying his hips with mine. "I'll win you over. I'll be so romantic it'll make your head spin."

A low laugh rumbled from my throat. "You forget. I grew up with you. I've known you since before you knew what romantic meant. You don't have a romantic bone in your body."

"How do you know? Maybe I haven't had anyone I really wanted to be romantic with."

My heart leaped, but even as it did, I called it back. I looked from one of his eyes to the other filled with such an intense longing I ached. "Do you really think we can make this work?"

"Oh, it'll work."

Warmth trickled across my skin. God, how I'd needed this. But was it too good to be true? "I've always admired that part of you. You've always been so sure of yourself. I'm always so...flighty. And insecure."

He grazed his fingertips along my face. "That's not how I see it. You knew the whole time you loved me. I was the jackass who took...what? Over ten years to realize it. You don't give yourself enough credit."

I laid my cheek on his chest. "Maybe." I sighed. "I should probably get going."

"Okay." He gave me a long squeeze and released me. "I was serious about carrying you out to the car if you need me to."

"No. It's really not that bad. Luckily, it's on the instep, not the ball or the heel, so it's not too bad to walk on." It wasn't the entire truth. "How are you feeling?"

"Better."

I gasped with a sudden realization. "I asked you to help me down from the stage. That had to have hurt."

He shrugged. "Not too bad."

"You should have said something."

"It's fine." He exhaled. "I guess a kiss goodbye is out of the question?"

I bit my bottom lip and let my gaze drop to his mouth, leaning in. He came within inches, and I poked him lightly in the chest. "Don't. Push. It."

He laughed then stood quietly. "It will make it all that much better when I do get to have you."

Have me. It sent a tingle through me. I wanted him to have me. I wanted him to have me in front of row A, seats 1, 2, and 3. But he was right. It would be better if we waited.

"Can I walk with you to your car?" When I hesitated, he added, "To keep you safe. I heard the streets of San Francisco can be pretty rough." His eyes twinkled.

"Fine." I tugged on his arm. "This way to the stairs." I led him to the stage entrance and picked up my violin and bow and secured them in the case. At the door I turned back and gave the room one more look.

"Did you forget something?"

"No. No. I'm good."

He held my hand. "I'm sorry I interrupted you playing earlier."

"Oh, it was no big deal. I was only doing it for myself."

"I got that sense. What I meant, though, is I'm sorry because I was enjoying it so much. You have a real talent, you know."

My face flushed. "Thank you for saying so." Ironically, we were passing Ms. Van Hoof's office. She and Isabella waved to us.

Scott glared at them. "That's not too suspicious." I didn't comment. "You mentioned not having a good day earlier." He tipped his head toward his shoulder. "Did it have anything to do with them?"

"No. Just tired and cranky."

"Okay." I could tell he didn't believe me. We came to the car.

"Well, thanks for walking with me. Where did you park? Do you want a ride to your car?"

"I'm in the front." He checked around. "It would be a bit of a walk. Are you sure it's okay? I don't want to invade your space or anything."

I unlocked his door, my mouth quirking. "I think that ship has sailed."

After he got in, he surveyed the interior. "Is this still your rental?"

"Yeah." I started the ignition. "I need to turn it in, though." *I can't afford to keep it anymore.*

"I can help you find a car."

I gave him a sidelong look.

"I'll behave myself. I promise."

"Thanks for the offer. I might take you up on it." He directed me to his car, and I pulled behind the sporty, blue BMW. He had told me when we drove from the amphitheater to the arena a few days ago that most of the guys had big honking SUVs, but he hated parking those, so he had chosen something smaller. It mostly occupied a spot in the parking garage anyway, which was a shame as it was a beautiful car.

"Well, since you already shot me down on the goodbye kiss, I guess I'll just get out. Thanks for the ride." He went to open his door.

"Scott?"

When he faced me, I grabbed his shirt, hauled him in, and kissed him like crazy. I loosened my grip on his shirt, happy to see him appearing a little blown away. "I like things on my terms."

He cleared his throat. "I am like, so okay with that. Please be careful with that foot."

"I will. You take care of yourself, and I'll see you Saturday. I'll text you the deets when I know them."

"Yeah. I'm not sure I'd remember them after that kiss anyway."

Yeah, living without you this week may be the hardest thing I've ever had to do.

CHAPTER SIXTEEN

Scott

When I walked into that concert hall and she was on the stage alone, I was captivated all over again. The way she played...it was like she put her everything into the music, like she was pouring out her soul through her bow and strings. And it was beautiful. She was beautiful.

And something was so right in my finally allowing myself to love her. Even if she ended up rejecting me like my mom did, at least I would have been honest with myself and her and given the two of us a chance. Better to have loved and lost and all that shit.

But after she left I began to think of the challenge she had thrown down—how I needed to prove myself to her—and that confidence she said she admired wavered. What did I know about winning women's hearts? Other than the physical kind of seduction, which wouldn't work here. The more I thought on it, the more panicky I became. Until lightning struck. Kyle. Kyle was the most romantic son-of-a-bitch I'd ever known, and I would be seeing him on Saturday. This would be a cake walk.

The week was harder than I thought it would be. I kept thinking of things I wanted to share with her, then realizing I couldn't because of the whole giving her space thing. But...if it was patience she needed, then patience I would give her. I'd be the most patient fucking guy on the planet if it meant she would give me a chance.

When Saturday rolled around, I was on edge more than ever as I headed to the hotel where her mom and Kyle were staying. To my surprise, when I knocked on the door, Elise opened it and pushed me farther in the hall. "We'll be right back," she called over her shoulder. She closed the door and swung in front of me, pressing me up against the wall and murdering me with her lips. When she pulled away she was panting, and still had my shirt fisted in both hands.

"I've needed that all week."

"Uhh...wow." I examined her flushed face. "Does this mean the giving you space thing is finished?"

She kissed me a few more times. "Hell, yeah. We're moving on to Phase Two, where you prove you are really, truly serious about being together."

"Okay. I'm ready for it," I lied.

"You better be. Because I've already decided if you break my heart again, I'm becoming a nun, and I won't look good in a habit." She tugged on my arm. "Come on. Mom and Kyle will be suspicious if we take too long. I haven't told them because, well, frankly Mom's not a fan."

I put the brakes on. "Wait. Your mom doesn't like me?"

"Oh, no. She loves you, pretty much. It's just us she's not so hot on."

As she dragged me into the room behind her, I was still absorbing what she'd said. "We're back. Well, Mom. We should probably get going. Nails aren't going to paint themselves." She gave Kyle a quick peck on the cheek and bolted, her mom in tow.

Kyle stared after them. "Uhh...was she acting a little nutty?"

"Who? Elise?" My voice came out oddly high. "Nah."

He studied me. "I think it's contagious. You're acting a little nutty too. Wait..." He pinched his chin. "Are you guys planning a surprise party for me?"

I sat on the end of the bed. "Dude. Isn't your birthday in the fall?"

He tilted his head. "That's what would make it a surprise, son. You're not the sharpest skate on the ice, are you?"

I laughed. "I've missed this."

"Me too, kid. Now, why don't you tell me how Elise cut her foot instead of the B.S. she was trying to shovel her mom. No way did she cut it by dropping her razor in the shower."

"We can discuss that over some beers."

"Great. Let's go." He moved toward the door, but I didn't follow. "We're not going?"

"Uhh...I could probably use a beer..."

"This isn't about hockey, is it?"

I shook my head.

"Hold on." He crossed to the closet area, fiddled around, and came back with two open beers.

"You're a prince of a guy, Kyle," I said with a smile.

"I know. So, what's up?"

I brought my bottle to my lips and chugged half of it.

"One of those conversations, eh?" His Canadian sometimes came out when he drank. He followed my lead and took a long pull on his Labatt's, sinking onto the opposite bed. "We need to ration. These are my only beers. What can I do ya for?" Before I could start, he waved his hands. "This doesn't concern blackmail, or naked pictures, or assault or anything like that, does it?"

He was referring to some stuff that happened to my sister Zoe in high school. "No, nothing like that."

He exhaled. "Good. I don't think I could take that again. Okay. Proceed."

"So...you know how Elise and I have always been close..."

"Oh, God." His face drained. "I don't have enough beer for this." He took another drink, looking like a man going down on a sinking ship, then set it aside, folding his arms.

"I love her, Uncle Kyle."

"Oh, shit," he mumbled. "He used the L-word."

"You don't like the two of us being together?"

"Well, now. It doesn't really matter what I think does it?"

"It does to me."

He lowered his head and shook it back and forth. "Why do these things always happen to me?" He rubbed his palms on the knees of his jeans. He lifted his gaze and stared at me, the whites of his eyes showing. "What does Elise think of this?"

"Weeell... that's actually why I'm here talking to you. She...kinda wants me to prove myself to her. I need some of your help with my romance skittles. Ha. Ha." I gave him a nervous smile.

"You're not really asking me to help you woo my daughter, are you?"

"No, because I'd never use the word woo. That's so sixteenth century, man."

"I'm just trying to be polite. It sounds better than help you score with my daughter. Help you get into bed with her. Slap the sheets. Get sweaty. Get it on. Screw. Do the horizontal tango. Take the train to pleasure town. Get laid. Go—"

If he weren't pissing me off, I would have laughed at his grocery list of terms. "What's wrong with you, man? That's your daughter. And I'm not talking about that. I'm serious. I love her."

He got to his feet and walked in a circle. "See, here's the thing, Scottie..." He paced, scratching the stubble along his jaw. "I'm in love with your Aunt Sam. She's the best thing that ever happened in my life, bar none. And Elise? You know how special Elise is to me. Kid's got my heart." He stopped before me. "Sam told me you broke Elise's heart once, and I'd pretty much have to be a fool to help you do it again."

"One time. I was a kid! Why does everyone keep throwing that in my face?"

"Because, Scottie... You know what? Stay there, I'll be right back." And like that he was gone, rummaging through stuff in the bathroom.

"No wonder Elise is crazy. They're all crazy."

Kyle returned, looking triumphant, with a tube of toothpaste.

I glanced from it to him. "What are you doing? Washing my mouth out?"

"Shut up." He pulled a rolling chair away from the desk and gestured to it. "Have a seat."

I got to my feet slowly and crossed to it, keeping my gaze on him. "What are you going to do?"

"You'll see." He reached over and slid an ad from a pizzeria in front of me. He gave me the toothpaste. "Squeeze this onto that piece of paper."

"Oookay." I did what he asked.

"All of it."

"All of it?"

"All of it," he insisted.

I shook my head but pressed a huge glob onto the page.

"Okay. Now put it back in."

"What?" I stared at it. "I can't do that."

"Exactly." He grinned, finishing off his beer and nodding.

I studied it again. *What the fuck?* But I knew he was trying to tell me something.

He put his hand on my shoulder. "I know what you did to her when you were kids you didn't do on purpose, but sometimes once things happen..."

he gestured to the paper at my elbow, "...they can't be undone. Want another beer?"

I frowned at him. "I thought you said you didn't have any more."

"Yeah," he winked, "but I was holding out on ya."

We had a long conversation, at the end of which he said, "Scott, I love you like my own son. You know that. But if you hurt Elise..."

"You'll kick my ass."

He clanked his bottle against mine. "I'm glad we understand each other."

When the ladies returned, we had the Avalanche game on. We were playing them on the next night, and they were kicking the Sharks' ass. I loved watching with Kyle because he picked up on things I didn't. Things my coaches didn't even know.

Kyle was sprawled on his side on one bed; I was sitting with my back against the headboard on the other.

"Hey, how'd it go?"

Aunt Sam narrowed her gaze on me as she entered and crossed to Kyle without saying anything.

"Good. Good," Elise said, but it was clear by her pitch she was lying. At least, clear to me. Tension came in the room with them like a third party. We had reservations at six but decided to leave early. The room suddenly seemed too small for us.

"Scott and I will drive separately. That way if you guys decide to go to bed early, we have our own wheels. We'll see you there." Elise rushed us into the hall.

"You told your mom about us, didn't you?" I said after the door closed behind us and we were alone in the hall.

"Uh-huh." Again, her voice gave her away, modulating in a way that showed her unease.

"What did she say?"

She jabbed at the button for the elevator and watched the numbers. "You mean before or after she said, 'Are you out of your friggin' mind?'"

"Huh." I pinched the bridge of my nose. "She was kinder than Kyle."

Her head whipped around. "What? What did he say?"

We entered the elevator. "Before or after he threatened my life?"

"What? No."

I leaned against the back rail. "Yup."

"I can't believe that. What did he say exactly?"

"He mentioned your Uncle Paulie and 'some of his associates' would 'pay me a visit' should I ever do anything to hurt you."

She took in a sharp breath. "He brought Uncle Paulie's name into it?"

I laughed. "I think he was kidding, but he did say, in no uncertain terms, he would take care of business himself if I ever stepped out of line. What did your mom say?"

"I think she called Uncle Paulie, so you may want to lay low for a while." She laughed. Sure she did. It wouldn't be her getting an ass-kicking.

"Great."

Despite the rough start to the evening, dinner was fairly nice. Aunt Sam did make a couple of passive/aggressive comments, but Kyle either defended me or turned it into a joke. I was worried he'd have to pay for that later. Afterward, when Elise not so subtly said something like, "I'm sure you're tired and probably want to get back to the hotel..." Aunt Sam declared she could outlast us any day like we had thrown down the glove, but Kyle convinced her they needed to "leave those kids alone."

I asked Elise to come to my place and open her presents. Sergei was still staying at Blane's. She was surrounded by colorful presents that looked like they'd been wrapped with my hockey gloves on, but she'd told me long ago she preferred it when I "tried" to wrap things myself. She said it was because then they were wrapped with love. I'm pretty sure the real reason was she liked laughing at my attempts. I always had either too small a piece or too big a piece of wrapping paper.

"Scott, this is too much."

I grinned, more excited than she was that she was finally opening the gifts I'd put so much thought into. "No, it's not. It's exactly the right amount."

She flipped her hair. "Well, I'm Goldilocks, and I say you went too crazy here."

"You are *so* not your mom." Aunt Sam often made it clear she liked presents. Lots of them. *Ooh, maybe I can win her over if I buy her one of those expensive purses she likes.*

Elise eyed the presents like they were predators and she was unarmed. "Scott. You know I can't afford to do this for you on your birthday and it makes me feel—"

I cut her off, ready for her objection. "Well, they're not all birthday presents."

She tilted her head with that cute, little skeptical look she liked to give me. "They all have birthday wrapping paper on them...?"

"That's all I had. Come on, pick one."

She chose the smallest one.

"No, not that one. Save that for last."

"You want me to save the one shaped like a jewelry box for last...?"

"Yes. Give it here." I snatched it from her.

"Okay. I guess you're serious." She scanned the gifts again and pulled out one I'd wrapped up like a Tootsie Roll. "You did a good job with this."

I glanced to the side. "Sergei helped me with that one. He said he couldn't stand by while I 'massacred the poor girl's gifts.' That was before you met."

"Oh. Well, it's nicely done."

"Thanks. Open it."

She took an agonizingly slow time, like she was trying to save the paper or something.

"It's a T-shirt."

"Yes. Open it and read what it says."

She smiled. "Okay, okay, I'm getting there."

"That's your Welcome to San Francisco gift, by the way."

She arched her brows. "My Welcome to San Francisco gift?" She held it up. "Cute. I love it."

I was lying on my side resting my head in my hand, watching her. "Which one is that?"

She turned it around. It was gray and had a picture for rock, paper, scissor, violin with violin beating everything. "Just something for fun." I shrugged my free shoulder.

"It's great. And I can always use a new T-shirt. I'm perpetually staining them."

"Wellll...I'm glad to hear that."

She examined the pile and drew out two more Tootsie Rolls, looking at me questioningly.

"I kind of had fun with the T-shirts. Open it."

"Is this a birthday gift?"

"No. This is your Congratulations On Your New Job gift."

"Ahh...I see." She opened it. This one was a dark pink color, like, I don't know, maybe magenta? Mauve? "This is awesome." It said, *Never underestimate a girl who plays the violin.*

"I thought you'd like that."

"I'm sensing a theme here." She held out the other present, waiting expectantly.

"Well, that's your Congratulations For Beating Me In Hockey, You Little Cheater gift."

Her lips curled up. "Oh, I heard those were on sale." Now she was ripping into them, having fun. The third one was black and said, *Treblemaker.* "Oh, this is my favorite right here. I'll wear this all the time." She hugged it to her chest and leaned forward to kiss me. "You're so sweet."

"They're just T-shirts."

She held my chin. "But you put thought into them, that's what makes them special." The goofball got teary-eyed.

"Oh, come on. Don't cry. That's what we're trying to avoid. Open the cube-shaped one."

She searched. "This one?"

"Yep."

She squeezed the sides and shook it. "I think it's a coffee cup."

"Well open it and you'll find out."

She started tearing the paper but stopped. "What is this one for?"

"That's a Congratulations On Your New Apartment gift."

She tilted her head and wrinkled her nose. "Didn't we already have that?"

My arm was falling asleep, so I sat cross-legged in front of her. "No. That was your Welcome to San Francisco gift. This one is about your apartment. Way different."

"I see." She had gotten the paper mostly off and opened the top. "It *is* a coffee cup." She lifted it from its box and laughed. "This is great." It had a violin on it and said, *It's okay if you don't like violin. It's kind of a smart people hobby anyway.* I knew she'd appreciate the sarcasm.

Three gifts were left next to her, and one more waited in my bedroom. We were getting to the good ones. At least I hoped she'd think they were good.

"Where next? Her hands were posed above the gifts.

"Uhh...the biggest one."

"This?"

"Yeah."

"And what kind of gift is this?"

"Oh, this? This is a birthday gift."

"Oh, is it?" She chuckled and opened the box. "What is this?" She slid them out. "Perfection pegs. Oh my gosh. I've always wanted these. These make it so much easier to tune your violin."

"So they told me. We can buy a tool to install them ourselves, or we can take it to them and they'll do it."

"Everybody raves about these. I can't wait to try them."

"Should we have them do it, or do it ourselves?"

"How much is the tool and how much do they charge? Whatever's cheaper."

"I'll have them do it, that way we don't have to mess with it. Open this one." I tapped the one closest to her.

"Scott, you're spoiling me."

"I like spoiling you." I nodded my head at her. "Open it."

She felt and shook it. "Hmm...I'm not sure what this is..."

"I'm pretty sure you won't guess it."

"Okay," she said, clearly curious. She opened the box and parted the tissue, inhaling when she discovered the contents. "Oh, Scott. This is beautiful." She pulled it out and made a cooing noise, her hand going over her heart, her smile becoming dazzling. "You had it engraved." It was a piece of silver molded into what I can only describe as the shape of a comb. It clipped on the top of music books to keep the pages in place when you were playing. It said, *I am Elise. I color the silence.* Came up with that myself. She leaped from the couch and tackled me. I rocked backward with her in my arms as she showered me with kisses.

"You are the best."

"I'm glad you like it." I dumped her off to the side. "Hold on. I have a gift for you in my bedroom."

She hollered after me. "Is that some weird kind of come-on?"

"If you want it to be." I lugged it along the hall but kept it hidden, stepping into the living room to see if she was ready. I caught her messing with the ribbon on the present I had withheld from her. "What are you doing?"

She jumped. "Uhh...merely looking at the ribbon." To make it more believable, she stroked it. "Yes, this is quite some ribbon."

"Put it down or you won't get the one behind me."

"Hmm...do I go with door number one or number two..."

"Get over here."

She hopped to her feet and came to stand in front of me, stretching up on her tiptoes to give me a kiss.

"Okay, are you ready?"

She nodded and I moved aside, waving my arm with a flourish. She stared at it. I'd had a music stand handcrafted for her. It was made of polished mahogany and had a violin cutout in the middle, carved with musical notes and vines rambling across it. In one corner it had her name in script. I thought the artist had done a great job, but maybe I was wrong.

"Uhh...so, I found this little Italian music shop..."

She gazed at me, her eyes glowing. "It's amazing."

I exhaled. "You can adjust it to whatever height you want, and the top switches to different angles too." It had arrived in a huge crate, nestled in some sort of packing grass. It was solid. Like a piece of furniture. "Do you have one already?"

"Not like this," she breathed. "I have some piece of crap dented one they threw away at the school." She circled it slowly, trailing her fingers along the tray. "It's gorgeous." She squeezed her palms together. "Scott...I don't know how to thank you for this..."

I embraced her, kissing her nose. "You just did. Come on, there's more." I dragged her back to the couch.

"You're spoiling me."

"I get to do that since you're my—" I wasn't ready for the g-word yet. Didn't seem right. Me, with a girlfriend? It wasn't like that was a bad thing, it was...well...weird. And best friend clearly wasn't enough anymore because she was more than that. "—special someone." I liked that. That worked.

She stared at me. "It's weird, isn't it? Being 'romantic' with each other after all this time."

I rolled a shoulder. "Weird in a good way." I sat next to her and put my elbow on the top of the couch while I played with her hair. "I like it." I grinned at her. "It makes me happy."

"You're so sweet." She leaned in to kiss me. "Don't get me wrong," she added when she parted from me, "I like it too. It's...crazy. Crazy is definitely what it is. And crazy good." Her lips claimed mine again and she drove me insane. I had remembered her being an amazing kisser when I was a kid, but, she was all woman now, and her skills had somehow gotten even better.

We'd decided to take it slow, and the way she was getting my engine revving I was liable to peel out and leave rubber behind. "Umm..." My voice was pitched too high. "...you should probably open your present."

She laughed. Little tart knew exactly what she was doing to me. Lifting her present, she gave it a slight shake. She guessed wrong when she thought the box I had contained jewelry; this was the jewelry box. Unwrapping it, she said, "Oh, what a beautiful box."

I snorted. "It's not the box, you goofball. It's what's inside the box."

"Oh...?" She cracked the lid. Miniscule LED lights—a feature I loved—showed off the contents like they were in a spotlight. She gawked. "Oh. Oh my gosh. This... Oh." I think I'd made the girl speechless.

"Do you like it? If not, we can maybe have them do some alterations to the design we came up with." It was, of course, a violin, with a diamond nestled in it. I really liked what the designer had done with my rough sketch. I felt it was way better than what I'd put on paper, but still captured the essence of what I was going for—simple and elegant.

"Oh, Scott..." She hid behind her hands and cried. "I...don't want to disappoint you." She got out between sobs.

This was so not what I wanted my gifts to do to her. "Honey." I took her into my arms. "You could never disappoint me? What are you even talking about?"

Her words came muffled from my chest. "They didn't like me..."

"Who didn't? Those people you work with? Don't worry, they will. Give them time to see who you are—how talented you are, and what a wonderful person you are. They'll fall in love with you, just like I did."

She raised her head. "But-but..." she sputtered. "You don't understand. I—"

"I get it. They're being assholes to you." I'd seen it the day when I came to her practice. They'd ruined her. Caged her in. Taken all that beautiful passion she had and tethered it to a chair, trying to make her fit into some kind of standard they had without really seeing what a gem she was. It was like watching a bird with its leg chained to a pole. I cupped her face. "But jobs are always hard when they're new. Give it a little time and they'll lighten up. You're tough. I know you can beat them."

She blinked, gazing at me, pain oozing out of every pore. It must have been hard—Hunter's rejection, Sergei deceiving her, and to have the people she worked with beating her down too. "Sc-cott...you know how much I love you, right? All these gifts, all you've done for me...it's so special. I can't even begin to tell you how much it all means to me... I don't know how to tell you this..." She hesitated.

"Of course, I know it. You've shown me countless times...I was just too stupid to see it. Here..." I took the box she still held. "Let me put this on you." I scooped the necklace off the velvet interior, and she shifted so her back was toward me and lifted her gorgeous hair. I put it on her and when she turned, she stole my breath away. The way the necklace hit, lying between her delicate collarbones. "It...looks good."

She touched it. "It's perfect."

I knew she'd had it rough lately and all I wanted to do was make her feel loved and valued. "I love you, Elise." I brushed my thumb over her bottom lip then peered into her eyes. "I want to show you that."

She froze, the beautiful mouth I'd traced a moment before hanging open. "Scott..." she said slowly, "I want to stay here with you tonight."

"Of course. You can have my bed and I'll take...the other bedroom." I didn't want to mention Sergei's name.

"No, you don't understand. I...I want you to make love to me."

Now it was my mouth that became non-functioning.

She dropped her gaze to the cushion, staring at the space between us. "Oh...I shouldn't have said that. I'm sorry. I—"

I swallowed her words by covering her lips with mine aggressively, and once started, I didn't want to stop. I grabbed the hair at the nape of her neck and stroked her tongue with mine. She slid her hands underneath my shirt and across my skin. Her moan a few seconds later made me tighten in response, desire pulsing through me so strongly it hurt. She pulled back to catch her breath, and I trailed kisses along the column of her neck.

"You have the most perfect body." She tugged at my shirt, and I leaned away and whipped it off over my head, tossing it on one of the chairs. "Mmm." Continuing to explore my abs, chest, and shoulders, she scooted her way into my lap, wrapping her legs around me.

My fingers bracketed her waist as she moved against me. I'd never wanted a woman the way I wanted her. Wanted sex? Yes. But I'd never felt this staggering drive to make someone mine. Claim them. Set them apart from all others and say, yes, this is the one. She was meant to be with me. The more we were together, the more that fact was confirmed and solidified in my brain. I separated from her. "Let's go to my bedroom so I can have the room to do with you what I want to do with you." *So many things.*

She didn't hesitate, getting to her feet and moving in that direction. I stood and bolted for my room. She laughed at my overzealousness and the laughter became a squeal when I swept her into my arms and kissed her as I came to my door. I kicked it in, not caring if I put a hole in the wall. I set her on her feet carefully, twisting to close the door, shutting out the rest of the world. This was me and Elise now, sharing ourselves in a new way. She led me to the bed.

"Sit down."

I lowered myself to the bed, watching her.

She undid the buttons on her shirt. "I want to give myself to you, Scott."

I was totally mesmerized by her.

She got the blouse opened but didn't take it off. Stepping forward, she took my hand, placing it flat against her stomach. "I want you to know me..." She slid it up deliberately to her breast. "All of me." It was the most erotic thing ever. She laced her fingers with mine and it was like she was touching herself at the same time I was caressing her. I about lost my mind. Then she released me and pressed the sides of my face, kissing me long and deep. She had moved between my legs, but she withdrew her mouth, simply staring at me. I got the feeling she wanted me to take control. I had no problem with that.

I stood slowly. "Turn around." A mirror hung on the closet door across from my bed.

This will be our one and only first time. I want to remember this forever.

Unfortunately, that thought spurred on others.

This won't be her first time ever, though. Thanks to Sergei.

Images flashed through my mind. That top on the floor...her bra...in the kitchen. Her slinking along my hallway in his shirt. I needed to let it go. I needed to let it go forever. He would never come between us again. I needed to prove to her, and to myself, she was mine, and I was hers. It had been that way from the beginning, and it would be that way for the rest of our lives.

I studied our image in the mirror, her petite frame against my brawn. "Elise," I said softly, holding her biceps on each arm, "look at me." I jerked my chin toward the mirror. Her gaze met mine in the reflection. "I want you to watch the way I love you. I want you to know..." I nuzzled her, "that I *never* want this to end." I kissed her tenderly from neck to shoulder, drawing away her blouse as I did, and sliding it off until if fell to her feet. "I love you, Elise." My hands glided across her stomach, meeting at her hip level, and ducking under the fabric of her jeans. "And I don't care if I have to tell you that a thousand times, prove it in a million ways, I will keep on loving you until you know the strength and depth of that love."

As I spoke, I was unbuttoning and unzipping her jeans, then working them over her hips. She was quiet, following everything I was doing in the mirror. Brushing her hair behind one shoulder, I brought my lips to her ear. "I've been waiting for this forever." I sat, pulling her between my wide-spread legs. I slipped my hand beneath her underwear and began to stroke her. Slowly. Patiently. "You don't know how many times my mind has gone back to that day we kissed in your bedroom. How many times I've thought of doing this to you." My voice became husky with my restrained need for her. "This...and so much more."

She gasped and twisted to kiss me. I simultaneously inserted a finger between her legs and my tongue into her mouth. She moaned and arched, reaching behind my neck. I placed my other palm under the cup of her bra, feeling the curve of her breast, the weight of it, the velvety skin. Her nipples were hard and begging to be sucked on, but not yet. "You're so beautiful."

"Oh," she cried in desperation. "Oh, Scott."

My movements became stronger, quicker. I nodded to the mirror again. "Watch, baby. I want you to see me taking you over the edge."

Her cries became louder, and I became harder in response. I knew she was close. At the last minute, she rolled her head back against my shoulder and her noises stopped, her body tense and still. A moment later she shuddered then melted, panting in my arms. "Oh." She sighed and laughed, closing her eyes and leaning into me. When she opened them, her face was flushed as she gazed at me. "You're smirking."

"Am I?" I gave her a quick peck on the lips. "Come on." I lifted us enough to work the covers out from under us. "Lie down and rest." She swung her legs up, lying on the pillow. I smiled at her, yanking my belt from its clasp. "You'll need it, because I'm not finished with you." I crossed to the door and locked it, just in case, then dimmed the lights. I got a condom from the dresser drawer and took my jeans off.

Initially she had her eyes shut, then she turned onto her hip, resting on an elbow, her chin in her hand, and watched me. While I was getting my condom on, I pointed out I was completely naked, but she still had clothes on. She gave me an innocent look. "You mean..." She grazed her fingers across her chest tantalizingly. "...this?" Her irises sparkled and she bit her lip provocatively.

I climbed onto the bed, and she rolled onto her back so I could get on top of her. "Yes, I mean that." It opened in the front, so I quickly unsnapped it and filled my hands with her. She had a great body. A *really* great body. I sucked on each breast briefly and she bent her knees.

"Don't make me wait any longer."

I grinned and eased myself into her. I rolled over her in smooth waves, like a freaking merman. An action meant to pleasure her more than myself, but it worked both ways. I brought her up again, then released after her.

Afterward, when we were catching our breath, we spun to face each other. "Holy shit! Why didn't we do this before?"

She giggled, moving closer so she could sprawl across my chest. "Because your mom and my mom could have walked in at any point and would have killed us."

"I'm not sure your mom won't still do that if she finds out." I brushed my hand along her hair lazily. I inclined my head and she responded by tilting hers to peer at me. "I want you to know, I have never made love to a woman before."

Her lips lifted as she pushed onto one arm and slapped my chest. "Liar."

"No, I'm serious." I looked from one of her eyes to the other. "I've had sex before, but I've never made love to anyone until tonight."

"Ohh," she cooed. "You're so sweet." She kissed me, then lay back, snuggling into my side. I stretched to tap the light off.

Sometime in the middle of the night I woke to find her straddling me. "As a professional athlete..." She reached down and took hold of me. "I think it's important to test your stamina."

I chuckled. "Is that so? Somehow I don't think this will be a statistic my agent will share."

"We'll keep it between the two of us," she said with a sexy smile.

Waking next to her in the morning was the best, even though she stole all the covers. After I greeted her, I jumped out of bed. "You never opened your last present." I returned with the little gift and dropped it into her lap.

"What is it?"

"Open it and see."

The wrapping paper practically fell off the box.

"I guess I didn't use enough tape on that one."

She opened it and withdrew a small wooden violin case. "Oh, Scott. This is beautiful." The lid came askew while she was handling it.

"It's special rosin for your bow."

She looked sort of stricken. Had she expected an engagement ring? I was actually planning on getting one, but I would have been surprised if she thought that was a possibility. Maybe I'd built it up too much.

"That's so—" Her voice caught, and she tilted her head. "That's so very thoughtful of you. Really. It's wonderful."

"I got it at that same Italian music shop. But if you don't like it, you can exchange it when we're over there."

"Oh, no. I would never—" She blinked. "Did you say...when we're over there?"

I grinned. "Yep."

"As in, Italy."

"Yep."

Her eyes shone. "You're kidding."

"Nope."

"You're taking me to Italy."

I nodded. "Yes. Didn't I just say that?"

"We're going to Italy? No way."

"Well, if you'd rather not..."

"No!" she shouted, bouncing on her knees in the bed. "I've always wanted to go there. This is awesome." She threw her arms around me, hugging me enthusiastically. Then she became still. "But...I'm not sure I'll be able to get off work. Since I'm new and all."

"That's the beauty of your working for the symphony and me playing hockey. We both have our summers free."

"Oh, yeah. That's true," she said slowly.

Although her reaction seemed kind of strange, I didn't have time to question it. "Well, hon, I need to get dressed. I have practice in approximately twenty-five minutes."

CHAPTER SEVENTEEN

Scott

When I walked in for morning skate a few days later, he was sitting on the bench lacing up. "Faz! You're back?"

He straightened, a kid-coming-down-the-stairs-at-Christmas kind of smile on his face. "Doc said I could skate, so here I am."

I clasped his hand in a bro shake, slapping his shoulder with my other. "Good to have you here, man." I changed into my gear, and we discussed various things, mostly me updating him about the team.

"So, you and The Douche getting along any better? The last time I saw you he was getting under your skin. Didn't he make a bet he could sleep with Elise?"

"Yeah. That's kind of a sore subject...one we probably shouldn't get into."

I could feel him studying me. "Ookay. Uhh...Julie and I were sorry to have missed her at the symphony last night."

I waited until I'd pulled my sweater on before answering. "Oh? You guys didn't go after all?"

"No. We went. She wasn't playing last night, you dork." He shook his head.

I frowned. "What do you mean? She was there. I dropped her off."

"Well, she must have left early then, because she wasn't part of the show. Maybe she was sick."

"No. She wasn't sick. I gave her a ride after the show. You must not have recognized her." I closed my locker.

"No. I thought that was a possibility too, but I went backstage afterward, and they told me she wasn't there."

What the hell? "That's really strange." I'd dropped her off and returned later to get her, and she'd said the show went well. "What time was the show out?"

"Ten."

She'd told me to be there at midnight. Could they have had practice after the show? But she hadn't said anything about practice...

Sergei rounded the lockers. "Mike." His face drained. He'd been playing horribly since his breakup with Elise—if one could even call it a breakup. More like a hookup. All his stats were in the shitter, including a plus/minus of -10. I'd never had a score so low in my entire career. With Faz back, it might mean Sergei'd have to fight for his position on the team.

"Yeah, good to see you too, Duskin," Faz quipped with a grin.

Sergei glared and jerked open his locker with a bang.

Practice was rough. I couldn't stop thinking over what Faz had said regarding Elise. When I'd arrived at the concert hall, the parking lot had been completely empty. She played it off saying she was way too slow packing her stuff, but now I was wondering... I finally shoved it to the back of my mind, reassuring myself I'd uncover what was going on with Elise later.

That night, instead of going to the symphony hall at midnight, like Elise had said, I went at ten. Standing by my car in a stiff wind, I checked every musician who exited the building. I saw her and approached cautiously.

"Hi. Aren't you Carrie Fisher?"

"Yes. Aren't you Elise's hot—" She cleared her throat. "Hoc-key player friend?"

I offered my hand. "That's right. Scott McCord." I nodded toward the building. "Elise still inside?"

"No, she—" It seemed like she was about to tell me something, but she hesitated. "I'm not sure where she is," she ended cagily.

I was getting a bad feeling. "Listen, Carrie." I took a deep breath, glancing to the side for a moment before returning my gaze to hers. I had a hunch, and I had to go with my gut. "You've been a good friend to Elise." Right on cue, those two witches I sensed were causing Elise trouble walked out of the building, cackling. "Unlike some others." I eyed them narrowly, then concentrated on the nervous woman in front of me. "And I think you're trying to be a good friend, aren't you?"

She didn't answer, but she was avoiding looking at me.

"We are on the same page here. I love Elise."

This caused her to lift her head quickly.

"And like you, I want what's best for her. I could use some help here."

She shuffled her feet. "I don't know. If she wanted you to know, she would have told you."

So something is going on. "I think she didn't tell me because she was embarrassed. She thought I'd see her as...less than who she is, somehow. But if she lost her job here, the only one who is less is the person who let her go, because she's one helluva violinist."

She glanced over at the two women, who were talking by a car now, then peered at me, sizing me up. She exhaled, then lowered her voice. "I don't know for sure what happened. All I know is they fired me, then called me later that evening and apologized and asked me to come back. When I did, Elise was gone."

We both watched the two women on the other side of the parking lot.

"I called Elise, of course, and asked her what happened. She said she just decided to quit. But I think she defended me, and they canned her. Then they were down two violinists, so they had to rehire me." Shifting her gaze to me, she added, "And you're right. She's very talented. Way better than Isabella or that diva Angelica."

"What reason did they give you for firing you?"

"They didn't like me 'consorting' with Elise. Said she was a bad influence. I think they were mad because I caught on to their messing with her instrument and her sheet music and doing everything they could to make her look bad, and I told Elise."

I sighed, massaging the bridge of my nose. Why hadn't she told me? "When did this all happen?"

"About ten days ago."

"Ten days?" How had I not figured it out? "Do you know where she is?"

"That day I called her, she told me she saw a help wanted sign in the window of an Italian restaurant near here. I heard some of the others talking tonight...someone said they saw her working as a waitress. But I don't know what the name is."

"Okay. I don't want to hold you up from getting home any longer. Thanks."

She gave me a timid smile. "Sure thing. Good luck." Cutting on a diagonal, she headed to her car.

As I stood going through all of the Italian restaurants I knew in the area, one of the women yelled to the other. "Rossi's?"

"Yes. See you there." They each got in their cars and left.

Rossi's. It was a place to start.

Elise

When I saw them being led to a table in my section, I cringed. Darting around people and tables, I caught Emelia.

"Hey. Any way we could trade tables? Those women at table six...uhh...I know them. And they don't like me."

The hostess, who was walking back to her stand at the front of the restaurant, heard me. "You're wrong, Elise. They asked to sit in your section."

"Just so they can gloat," I said under my breath.

"Do you want me to take them, Elise? Because I can."

I thought about it. "No." I exhaled. "They'd only bitch until someone dragged me over to wait on them. It's fine."

She peered at them. "Well, if you need any help, come get me. Or use Andrea, if you want." Andrea was the busgirl who had been assigned to Emelia.

"Thanks."

But instead of approaching their table, I chose to attend to someone else who had been seated at roughly the same time, a single at a table for two. That always made me sad.

"Good evening. Welcome to Rossi's? Can I get you started off with a drink tonight?"

The tall, black leather-like menu they held in front of them lowered.

"Scott!"

It was clear from his lack of surprise this wasn't a chance meeting. The way he was glowering also kind of gave it away. Not that I could blame him. I'd been lying to him for more than a week now.

I stared at the table, then lifted my gaze to his. "I don't suppose you're here because of our fabulous vodka Bolognese sauce?"

"No," he said shortly. Then his expression softened a fraction. "Why, Elise?"

"I—" I glanced around, sliding the violin on my necklace from side to side. "Uhh...could we maybe do this later? In private?"

He crossed his arms, sitting back. "Will you tell me the truth?"

I felt awful. "I'm sorry."

"Waitress." Isabella was snapping her fingers at me like I was a dog.

Heat rose from my toes to my forehead, flushing through my system like a tidal wave.

Scott rotated to glare at her.

"Umm...I've got to go. We can talk about this in a second."

I plodded toward their table, my ears ringing with the jumbled conversations from the tables I was passing. I inhaled.

I can do this. I can be pleasant and not look as embarrassed as I feel.

"Isabella, Ms. Van Hoof. How good to see you. How are—"

Isabella cut me off. "I'll take a gin and tonic."

I tried to recover. "Oh. Okay." When I turned to Ms. Van Hoof to get her order, she seemed appalled.

"Isabella!" she hissed. "The least you can do is be a gracious winner." She smiled at me. "Good to see you too, Elise. Umm...could I please get a glass of Chardonnay?"

"Of course. I'll get that right up for you."

I left the table feeling slightly better. As I was passing Scott, I threw out a "Do you want a beer?"

He jumped and called after me, "Uhh...yeah. That'd be great."

I knew Scott would want the hoppiest thing we had, which was Dankquator, a collaboration from two of our local breweries. I delivered it. "I'll be right back." I took the glass of wine, along with the gin and tonic, to Ms. Van Hoof and Isabella, who seemed much more subdued now. Once their order was in, I returned to Scott's table.

"I don't want you waiting on me," he said immediately. "In fact, I don't want you waiting on anyone at all. Tell them you quit."

"Scott...I can't do that."

"Yes you can. You can move in with me."

"We've been dating for less than a month. I don't think we're ready for that."

He scowled, tapping his fingers on the table. "Then...stay where you are, and I will pay the rent."

"That's not happening," I said sternly.

"Why the hell not?"

"Because—"

"Elise, is this your young fellow?" Mr. Rossi had snuck up on me from behind.

We looked at each other. "Uhh...yeah. Scott McCord, meet Lorenzo Rossi. Mr. Rossi, Scottie McCord."

Scott sat forward and shook his hand. "Nice to meet you, sir."

He turned to me. "Have you had your lunch break?"

"No, not yet. I—"

"Well, feel free to eat with Scott. But make sure you take off your apron. I'll get Emelia to take your tables."

"Oh...okay." I angled toward Scott. "Maybe I should get your order first."

"No. I was serious. I don't want you to wait on me." He held up his phone. "I ordered the food to-go."

"You ordered...your food to-go...from your table?"

"Yes." He smiled smugly.

"Well, okay. Let me go put an order in for me. It'll only take a minute." On the way to the kitchen, I untied my apron. When I'd placed my order and returned to the table, Mr. Rossi was in an animated conversation with Scott as he opened a bottle of wine." He poured a glass for Scott, then went to pour one for me. I quickly put a hand over my glass. "I'm still on the clock for an hour."

He frowned. "This is fine," he said with his Italian accent. "It's special occasion. I meet your boyfriend." I removed my hand and he poured. "Besides, I am the boss." He winked at me.

I gazed at him warmly. "Thank you."

When we'd finished our meal, during which I manage to distract Scott with questions about his recent road trip, I sighed. "Well, I guess I better get back to work." I rose.

He got to his feet too. "Do you want me to pick you up at the symphony hall or here?" he asked wryly.

I looked at him sheepishly. "Here would be good."

To my surprise, he stepped forward, held my chin, and kissed me. "I am angry with you, but I still love you and I missed you like crazy."

Heat rose from my core. He was still holding my chin, his eyes twinkling with humor, but also with an underlying desire I couldn't wait to explore.

When I walked out to his car an hour later, I started talking the moment my butt hit the seat. I wanted to get our arguing over with so we could get to the makeup sex.

"I'm sorry I kept my losing my job a secret, but here's the whole truth. I heard Isabella and Ms. Van Hoof bullying Carrie and figured they'd fired her because of me. They never wanted me here. They hired me simply because they were afraid to lose Mrs. Prentiss' sponsorship. They wanted to prove to her she didn't know as much as she thought she did about music in hopes she would back off and not try to control them."

He was peering from the road to me frequently, his mouth open and brows raised. "So they hired you, getting you to move across country because they wanted to teach a busybody a lesson?"

"Exactly."

He whistled, staring at the road, and then giving his head a little shake. "What does Carrie have to do with it?"

"Carrie was helping me to piece things together. She knew they switched sheet music on me, overtightened the strings of my violin...basically did everything they could to make me into a fool. They were pissed. So pissed, in fact, they fired her."

He frowned. "But she was there tonight. I talked to her."

"So Carrie was the one who ratted me out?"

"She didn't want to." His voice became soft. "But I told her I loved you and convinced her we were on the same team. We both wanted what was best for you."

"You told her that?"

He glanced at me twice. "Yes. Should I not have?"

"No. It's just...you kissed me tonight, in front of...everyone."

He creased his brow. "Do you not like public displays of affection? Because if you don't, I need to know those kinds of things. I can *try* to keep my hands off you. I'm not making any promises, but—"

"Don't you dare. I live for your hands on me."

A smile slid across his face. He checked his mirror as he changed lanes. "That's good to know." A few seconds later he looked over. "I really did miss you. Like...a lot."

Warmth spread throughout me. I was thrilled we were finally together like I'd always dreamed we'd be. "I missed you too."

He watched the road, trying to absorb the information I'd given him, I guess. "But if they fired Carrie, why was she there tonight?"

"Because I made them unfire her."

He waited for an explanation.

I picked at a crumb stuck in a crack near the stick shift, lowering my voice. "I told them I'd leave if they hired Carrie back."

"So they didn't fire you? You quit?"

"Yes."

He was quiet for a few seconds. "Wow."

I lifted my gaze and studied his profile. "Are you disappointed in me?"

"Hell no. It took a lot of guts to do what you did."

I shrugged. "They were firing me anyway. I simply sped up the process a little."

"Maybe. But still, it takes some balls to put yourself on the ledge like that for a friend."

"Well... It was really the least I could do, considering they fired her because of me."

He had turned into the parking garage below his building and was maneuvering into his spot. As he switched off the ignition, he said, "But that still doesn't answer the biggest question I have." He twisted his body in my direction. "Why didn't you tell me?"

"Because...I was embarrassed. You were so proud of me when you heard about my job here. I didn't want to let you know I'd failed. You're a frigging NHL player. I didn't want you to be embarrassed to introduce your girlfriend by saying, 'This is Elise. She was a concert violinist, but she failed. Now she waits tables.'"

"Nothing's wrong with waiting tables."

I ran a finger along a line in the console between us, not wanting to look him in the eye. "I know. It's just...you were so proud of me." I'd been congratulating myself that I hadn't gotten too emotional with our conversation, but it was slipping. "I wanted to do something special to keep making you proud of me." I gazed at him through the tears blurring my vision.

He put a palm on my face. "Baby...do you really think it matters to me what you do for a living? I was happy for you when you got the job here because I thought that was what you wanted." He skimmed his thumb along my cheek. "But...when I saw you at that first practice..." He took his hand away, facing the wheel again and seeming to search for words. "They'd ruined you."

I had to laugh. "What?"

"I mean, you were chained to that chair, and you seemed so miserable..."

"I didn't know it was that obvious."

He peered at me again. "To me it was."

"I was going to tell you, but you gave me all those wonderful presents..."

He nodded. "All of them violin-themed."

"I didn't want to hurt you. Or disappoint you. I didn't want you to know I wasn't the person you thought I was."

He studied me. "What are you talking about?"

"I'm not, Scott." For some reason, it made me angry. "I'm not some brilliant, talented concert violinist." I ran out of energy and looked down, wiping at the console again. "That's just not who I am."

He covered my hand with his. "You're right. You're not."

I scowled at him. "Well, geez. You don't have to be so brutally honest."

"You're not a brilliant, talented concert violinist, but you are a beautiful, talented violinist. And the woman I'm in love with."

"But I wanted—" I cut myself off, staring at the windshield. What did I want? My gaze bounced from right to left, my body physically mimicking my mental search. "I wanted to...shine. Like you do. Like my mom does. But that's not who I am. And to be honest, I'm not sure I'd be happy that way. The spotlight's never been my thing. I'm awkward and..." I reached for the words. "I'm inadequate. I don't do the whole grownup thing well. I—"

"Stop," he said, sounding angry. "Stop trying to fix yourself when you're not broken. You do shine. Not in any public arena, like me, but...when you're with me, with your friends and family... Not everyone was meant for the spotlight, and that's okay. It doesn't make you any less."

I nodded, saying sarcastically, "Mmm, sure."

"Elise," he huffed. "You really don't get it, do you? What you can do with a violin...it's a rare thing. The way you play, it's extraordinary." He gestured like he was karate chopping the air. "I merely knock a piece of rubber into some twine. You make music. You move people. You offer them a release. You express emotions for them they aren't able to express themselves. You heal people. That's not something small. It's a special gift. Maybe the symphony was not the right place to showcase that, but that doesn't change the fact that you are..." He lifted my chin. "An *amazing* violinist."

I smiled through my tears. "I don't deserve you."

"You're right." I thought he was being cocky, until he added, "You deserve better. But...you're stuck with me. Come on. You look exhausted. Let's get you to bed."

And that's where we left it. Like everything else in his life, he was so damned sure about this. Unfortunately, this was the one time he was wrong.

CHAPTER EIGHTEEN

Scott

I was flying high. Elise was meeting me for lunch, and I had a little surprise for her. We were dining at Le Chateau Lavigne and, while Elise thought we were dining alone, we weren't. I had told the maître d' to expect her, and I stopped mid-sentence when they approached our table. Without even thinking, I rose to my feet. She was just so breathtaking. The three other men at the table also stood.

"Oh, hi."

Her smile trembled and an initial whisper of doubt teased me. Was I doing the right thing? I knew if I had told her about my plan, she would have protested and said she wanted to find her way on her own. But if I had some connections that she hadn't been able to make yet, why not use them to help her out? And I knew for a fact she'd be helping them out too. Anyone would be happy to have a player of her caliber on their team.

She was wearing the black dress she wore the first night she came to San Francisco and her hair was up in similar fashion. The rest of us were dressed in suits. I held her chair for her. "Gentlemen, I'd like you to meet my girlfriend, Elise Scofield."

"Nice to meet you," she mumbled, and shot me a look. I ignored it.

I gestured to the man on her right. "Elise, this is Oliver Lidel, my agent."

She shook his hand. "How do you do?"

"To his left is his friend, a talent agent, Alex...Talent."

He grinned, sitting back and eyeing Elise. "He loves to say that."

She laughed and nodded to him as the round table was too big to span for a handshake.

I glossed over that. "And last but not least, may I introduce Mr. Rich Anderson. Rich is a music producer and owner of the studio across the street from this building."

"Co-owner," he corrected.

"Co-owner." The waiter arrived at the table. "Elise, would you like a glass of wine?"

She cleared her throat, then turned to the waiter. "Yes. Yes, please. Would you have a Riesling?"

"Of course, *mademoiselle*. Would you like me to bring a bottle or a glass?"

She peered at me and seemed to debate. "A glass would be fine. Thank you."

"I was just telling everybody the story of how I became Scott's agent," Oliver said brightly, and launched into the story.

I grabbed Elise's hand under the table and gave it a squeeze. It was ice cold. She did her best to insert pleasant and appropriate remarks. The meal went smoothly enough, but when people were finished, all the guys looked to me and I knew the time had come.

I drummed my fingers on the table, gazing at Elise. "Sooo...as you may have guessed, this group coming together today isn't completely coinciden-tal."

She glanced from me to the others, who smiled and nodded. "Oh?"

It was clear she hadn't put things together. Her earlier surprise and un-ease must have simply been due to the fact that she was expecting only the two of us for lunch, not a posse.

"I...told Oliver you were in town now and how talented a violinist you are."

She bobbed her head slowly, and it was like I could see the gears churning in her mind, trying to figure out what was going on, but being jammed by her anxiety. "Oh, well...Scott is a little biased."

They all laughed. Oliver sat forward. "He told us you'd say that."

Her brow furrowed and she swung to narrow her eyes at me. "I don't un-derstand. What's going on here?"

Before I could answer, Rich Anderson, whom I'd met less than an hour or so ago, addressed her. "Elise, I work with a number of musicians, mostly in the rock genre, and we could use someone of your capabilities, if you'd be willing to work with us."

She sat back, her jaw dropping open for a moment. "Oh, well...of course that would be...incredible, actually, but..." She wet her lips. "Don't you even want to hear me play?"

"I'd love to, but it's not necessary. If Scott says you're good, that's enough for me."

She opened her mouth to say something, then closed it again, blinking. "Not that I'm not grateful for the opportunity—because, believe me, I am—but...like I said, Scott is pretty biased. He's known me since we were ten and his viewpoint is colored by our...relationship. I don't want to run the risk of wasting your gentlemen's time, and I'm not sure—"

Rich leaned toward her. "You are certainly not doing that. You have no idea how hard it is to find a violinist who plays with the kind of...heart you need for rock music. It's hard in general, even, but most of the people we've had in the past have been...talented, for sure, but not the right fit. Too static. Too...precise. But if you'd feel more comfortable auditioning for me, we could take a walk over to my studio, if you'd like?"

She looked from him to me. "I guess this is why you told me to bring my violin. You're not really taking it to get those perfection pegs installed, are you?"

I gripped the edge of the table. "Uhh...no."

Alex Talent spoke up. "What do you say, Elise? We'd all like to hear you play."

"Well..." She glanced at each of the individuals at the table. She exhaled. "Sure. Why not?"

Alex clapped his hands together. "Awesome, let's go?"

I'd taken care of the check before lunch even started, so we all rose and left the restaurant. "I'll just grab my instrument," Elise said once outside.

"We'll meet you there," I added, and they headed across the street. We walked in silence, Elise staring straight in front of her.

"Are you mad because I stepped in and...?" I searched for a diplomatic way to put it.

She swung to face me. "Are you kidding?" She threw her arms around me. "This is great." She covered my mouth with hers in an exuberant kiss, then removed her lips but kept her fingers laced behind my neck. She was glowing.

"Wow. I'm glad you feel that way."

When she bent to get her violin from the car, I caught Alex, Oliver and Rich looking back at us. Then turned to cross the street.

Rich addressed us when we entered, asking us to follow him down a hall. "Elise, we can do this however you want to. Most musicians are more comfortable auditioning from the other side of the glass rather than in the same room with people gawking at you as you play. Plus, I can make adjustments in the sound booth and get a feel for how you would record. Does that sound good?"

"Absolutely."

He got her set up in a room, and the four of us hovered outside the window to listen. At first she seemed a little stiff, but she seemed to realize that and shut her eyes to really get into the music. She played her old standby, "My Immortal." It was almost a theme song for her, and she did it beautifully. As usual, I was drawn in for a bit, forgetting where we were and what we were doing. I checked the others. When we'd started, they were chitchatting some, but now it was completely silent, other than the music Elise was creating. They seemed as riveted as I had been.

"Holy shit," Rich said in a hushed voice. "Where have you been hiding her?"

Warmth flowed through me. So it wasn't just me thinking she was astounding when she played. When she'd played her last note, letting it hang in the air powerfully, she opened her eyes.

Rich cleared his throat and pushed a button. "Umm...Elise? Would you like to join us in here for a moment?" He released the button and spun in his chair. "Thank you, Scott. We've been looking for a player of her caliber for...well, forever."

Elise opened the door and stepped in the room sheepishly, immediately coming to my side and squeezing my hand in a vise grip, waiting expectantly for someone to speak. Rich stared at her, shaking his head in disbelief. "That was...incredible."

"Marvelous," Alex added.

"Absolutely beautiful. Amy will love it."

"Amy? As in Amy Lee? From Evanescence?"

"Yes," he said casually. "I work with her. I can guarantee she'll want you on her next album. You get her music."

She turned to me. "Did you hear that?"

I beamed. "I did."

"Amy Lee. From Evanescence."

I rubbed her arms, chuckling. "Yes, I know. Are you going to pass out?"

"Possibly."

The next hour was spent doing paperwork. I'd asked Alex along because I wanted someone to represent Elise and make sure she got a fair wage, but he didn't have to do anything. Rich's offer was very generous.

That evening, Elise took me to dinner to celebrate.

A couple of weeks later, I returned home and found the place in a shambles. I heard noises coming from Sergei's room, and I crept forward, sliding one of the hockey sticks mounted over my fireplace out of its holder and wielding it like a weapon. When I stepped into the light of Sergei's door, he was sitting on the floor shoving things into a duffle bag.

"Scott. Scott," he said in a panic. "You have to find Elise for me. I've been traded to San Jose, and I have to leave in an hour. I have a game tonight."

I leaned on the stick. "So you want me to find the woman I love—the woman you *slept* with—so you can say goodbye to her?"

"Yes. Come on, man. I just want to say goodbye to her. To wish her well."

Shit. The dude seems like he's about to cry.

"Fine," I huffed.

Elise had gone to the gym but didn't answer their page. I figured she was on the way home, but she wasn't responding to my texts. I went to her place to at least see if her car was there, but it wasn't. Elise had a habit of putting her phone on 'do not disturb' at the gym and forgetting to take it off. She could have gone to the grocery store. She could have been called into work or was laying down a track at the studio... I checked the store she usually went to, and the studio, but no Elise. I came back home to see if she'd gone there, but all I found was a very sad Sergei.

"I'm sorry, man. I looked everywhere."

"That's all right. It's probably for the best anyway." He stuck his hand out, fighting to smile. "Thanks for letting me stay here, and for all the stuff you taught me on the ice. I'm a better player because of you."

I was surprised to find myself a little choked up. "I wish you luck with the Sharks. Except when we're playing you, of course."

And that was pretty much it. The next time I saw him it was on the other side of a face-off.

CHAPTER NINETEEN

Scott

He answered my call without a hello, his voice tight.

"You better not be calling me with some lame-assed excuse for breaking my daughter's heart again."

"And hello to you too, Uncle Kyle."

"What's up?" He wanted to get to the chase. A man of action. That worked for me.

"I need your help...well, I need something else first. I need your permission..."

His voice lightened. "Yeees?"

"You know I love Elise. And I can assure you, I'd rather rip my own heart out than break hers again. I was a kid before, and I've learned my lesson. I can't guarantee I won't do something stupid and piss her off again, but I'm okay with apologizing and will try to do everything in my power not to let it happen again."

"It sounds like you've learned a lot about being a good...partner," he said hesitantly.

"I'm glad to hear you say that, because..." I took a deep breath. "I want to ask for your permission to propose to Elise."

He chuckled. "I had a feeling that's why you were hem-hawing around."

I smiled. "There was no hem-hawing."

"I heard hem-hawing. Have you got a plan?"

"No. That's the other reason I'm calling. You did such a good job of re-proposing to Aunt Sam, I thought maybe you could give me some pointers."

"Okay..." He took a moment to think. "Well, she's not like Sam. You can't do it in public, no cameras, none of that shit. Just you and her. And if you use anyone to help you pull it off, make sure they lay low and *vamonos* immediately afterward."

I knew he'd save me.

"You are so right. See, that's why I called you. I would have ended up doing some huge flash mob she would have hated. Thanks, man."

"No problem. Apparently that's what I'm here for. Zack asked me before he proposed to Zoe too."

"He did? I didn't know that. That's pretty cool."

"Yeah, it was pretty cool."

"Well, I don't want to take any more of your time. I really appreciate your help."

"Glad I could do it. And I'll try to smooth your way with your Aunt Sam too."

He's such a great guy. I will never go wrong asking his advice on anything.

"Oh, gosh. I would be grateful for that too. I'd hate to be in a sniper's sights on my wedding day."

"Well, I'm not making any promises. You may want to rent some Kevlar with your tux."

One side of my mouth lifted. "Good idea. I'm looking forward to your visit next week."

"Me too. And hey, Scott? You've always been part of our family, but I'm happy you'll be an even bigger part of it. You may have made some mistakes in the past, but you're still a great kid."

It made me emotional to hear him say it. "Thanks, Uncle Kyle. I promise, I'll take care of her for you all."

"I know you will. Take it easy, Scott."

I didn't have a plan, but I had a direction.

Elise had gotten a call to come into the studio to lay down a track for a new album they were recording, a call I had arranged. We pulled into the parking lot and Elise grabbed her purse. "He said this wouldn't take too long. Ten minutes, tops. So you may as well wait in the car."

What? No.

"Oh, I want to stretch my legs a little and say hi to Ronnie." Ronnie was a sound mixer and my accomplice in today's events.

"Are you sure? I hate to take more of your time."

I brought her hand to my lips, a hand I hoped would be wearing my ring before we left. "Spending time with you is what makes me happy."

She cocked her head. "You're such a suck-up."

I laughed and got out to forestall any more discussion. She came around the car, and we walked into the building together.

Ronnie appeared to be as excited as I was, almost tipping Elise off.

"Why are you so chipper today?"

"Me? Chipper? I'm not chipper. Well...I'm not *not* chipper, but I'm definitely not more chipper than usual."

She eyed him. "Uh-huh."

He opened the door to the booth for her. "Let's...uhh...just get started then.

He got her set up in a booth and returned. We watched expectantly from the other side of the glass.

He appraised me. "Lookin' good, dude."

I had on a gray suit with a light blue shirt with the collar open and no tie. "Thanks. I assumed it would be better to not wear sweats when I proposed."

He grinned. "Yes. Probably your best bet." He shook my hand. "Good luck. I think you guys are great together."

"Thanks." I leaned forward, my damp palms on the desk area of the mixing board. "Let's hope she thinks so."

In the booth, Elise set her violin case on a stool and opened it. I inhaled and held my breath. She withdrew her instrument and faced us. "Umm...I don't see any sheet music in here."

"Doesn't she see the big honking ring tied to her bow?" Ronnie said haltingly.

"Apparently not." *What now?*

Ronnie pushed the button to talk to her. "Yeah, I'll get that. How about you tune up first and I'll make a few adjustments using that as a baseline."

"Okay."

She brought the bow to the strings.

"How can she not see that?" I murmured.

"You'd think she'd at least feel the weight of it," he added.

Drawing her bow across the neck of her violin sent the ring swinging on the ribbon attached to her instrument, which finally caught her attention. She froze, then slowly lowered both arms, gaping at the ring. Her head rotated in our direction and Ronnie comically ducked out of sight behind the desk and duck-walked to the door, taking my instructions to be as unobtrusive as possible seriously.

"Good luck," he whispered for some reason. He turned in his squat halfway through the doorway. "I'll hide somewhere and give you privacy. I'll shut off the lights and lock up after you leave." With a thumbs-held-high, he backed into the hall, closing the door softly in his wake.

"What's going on?" Elise said hesitantly.

I entered the booth. She was putting her violin away hurriedly.

"Scott? What...?"

I got on one knee in front of her.

Her eyes widened. "Oh my God. What are you doing?"

I had my words written on a piece of paper in my suit pocket, in case I blanked completely, but I wouldn't use them. I took her hand and kissed it. "Elise..." It all came flooding back. Her face red as she concentrated on what I told her and attempted to blow a bubble. The first time I saw her in the cute little polka dot bikini she had. How I held her as she fell apart after Zoe got her butt kicked coming to Elise's aid when some bullies were picking on her. The way my gut clenched seeing her twirl under Sergei's raised arm. A thousand memories swarmed me at once and seemed to push the thoughts from my head and words from my mouth for a moment. "I can't believe we are here..." I finally spit out. "I can't believe you have again allowed me to be part of your life, after all the mistakes I've made."

"We both made mistakes." She always insisted on it, although it was patently untrue.

I didn't argue with her. "Since you've been here, my heart has been so full. Full of joy, confusion, pain, desire..." That thought almost derailed me for an instant. The things we'd done to/with each other in the bedroom, so strangely different from what we'd done before, and yet so right. "...and threaded through it all, my unending love for you. You have been beside all the various versions of me, the goofy, nerdy ten-year-old me, the cocky s.o.b. I was in high school, and...whatever it is I have become now. I hope you'll stay beside me, and I can continue to try to grow into the kind of man you deserve. I want to marry you, Elise. I want to build our lives together, the two of us sharing everything life has to offer, the good times, and the bad times...will you marry me?"

I had never felt this scared in my entire life. I was putting my beating heart in her hands. She could crush it or cradle it. It didn't matter anymore.

I needed to be with her or find some way to make a life without her. My life couldn't go on until I knew what our future held.

"Are you being for real right now?"

I laughed nervously. "Yes. I'm down on my knee here. I love you. I—"

To my surprise, she dropped to her knees in front of me and threw her arms around my neck. "Yes, I'll marry you, you big idiot. You've made me so happy."

The tension rolled out of me as I squeezed her against me, our bodies melting, warmth fusing them. "Oh my God. That was the hardest thing I've ever done."

"What?" She pulled away, smiling through tears. "Why?"

"I just...wanted it so bad. I really want this, Elise. I want to be the best husband for you...make you feel safe and loved."

"Oh, stop it. You're killing me here." She drew me in again. "I love you, Scottie," she whispered in my ear. "I always have and I always will."

Part of me knew that, but it felt so good to hear her say it.

She jerked back, peeking at the window. "Oh, shit. Is Ronnie listening to all of this?"

I laughed. "No." I got to my feet and helped her to hers. "But he is waiting to lock up after us."

She grabbed my face, looking from one of my eyes to the other. "Are we getting married, Scottie?"

"Yes." I chuckled. "I'm pretty sure that's what you agreed to..."

She hugged me again. "I can't believe this!" She took in a sharp breath, leaning back to speak to me. "I can't wait to tell my mom. And Kyle."

"I'm not sure how your mom will feel about this."

"She'll be so excited."

"I'm not so sure."

"Really, Scott. When she sees how happy I am, she'll be over the moon."

I tilted my head. "I hope so. Kyle already knows I was planning on proposing."

"He does?"

"Of course. I had to ask for your hand first."

"You did?" She beamed. "Oh, that's so cute." She gasped and turned away. "Let me check out this rock." She held it to the light and frowned. "I was expecting something more the size of a hockey puck."

"You were? Zoe said you wouldn't want that. I can..."

"Zoe's right. I was joking. She knows?"

"Yeah. I needed someone's help with the ring. But if it's not what you imagined...I want you to have what you want..."

"No. I was kidding." She twisted it to examine it. "It's perfect." She got choked up. "It really is, Scott. I love it."

"Good. Can I put it on you?"

"Oh God, yes."

I untied it and put it on her finger. It was a rectangular-shaped diamond with a lot of fancy scrollwork on the platinum band with a smaller pear-shaped diamond on each side. It looked great on her. "Will it interfere with your playing?"

"Oh no. It will enhance it."

"Do you want to go to dinner and celebrate?"

"Yes. We should go. Especially if we're keeping Ronnie."

I opened the door for her.

"He came in just so he could help with the proposal?"

"Yeah. I offered to pay him, but he refused to take it."

When we were out in the hall, she glanced around. "Where is he?"

"I don't know. He said he would hide so we could have our privacy."

"Oh."

When we got to the car, our private celebration was put off by her video-calling everyone she knew to share the news.

"Mommy! Look!" She held her hand up. "We're getting married!"

Samantha burst into tears.

"Oh, shit. She's crying."

"No," Sam blubbered. "I'm so happy for you guys! Did you hear that, Kyle? Our baby's getting married."

"Yes." He stuck a finger in his ear. "I think she broke my eardrum." He smiled and hugged Sam to his side. "Congratulations, you guys. This is great news!"

That call was followed by one to my Dad and Dani, and some more crying. Then Zoe and Zack, Ryan and Jake, Tabby... By the time we were done, I
was starving.

I'd rented a penthouse with a rooftop that had a hot tub and an area for
dining. Caterers were waiting for my call. It was an unforgettable evening
with an unforgettable woman who had just agreed to become my wife.

EPILOGUE

Scott

I was lying on my stomach on our mattress, half-covered with a sheet. Elise was buried under a fluffy comforter. A tremendous thunderclap shook the windows.

"Three, two..."

The door opened and I cracked an eye. A pair of pink bunny slippers shuffled to my side of the bed. Accompanying them was panting and a loud thumping each time our golden's tail hit the bedside table. "Daddy? Rufus is scared of the storm."

Rufus continued to wag his butt like mad. I worked myself on to my hip. "Really, Soph? Because he doesn't look scared."

"He's trying to hide it." Another peal of thunder, closely followed by a bolt of lightning, had our youngest launching herself onto the bed—leaving a lone bunny behind—crawling over me, and into Elise's arms.

"Couldn't your brothers make...Rufus...feel safe?"

She shook her blonde, curly-haired head, the golden waves tumbling about her face and hiding it. "Nope. *They're* playing video games," she said disgustedly. "A.k.a., Combat Zone." She was very into "a.k.a." at the moment.

"Is that so?" *I need to get out there and take those punks on.* I looked at Rufus. "Well, get up here, you goof." I tapped the bed and immediately he put his paws on the mattress and lumbered over until, he, too, was between Elise and me.

Elise was brushing Sophie's hair and kissing her. Our little angel's hair was always wild, but it suited the munchkin and made me smile.

"So, is Mommy going to get all the lovin's?" I grabbed our daughter by the waist and hoisted a squirming, giggling girl into the air above before lowering her to my chest. She settled in, clutching "Bluie," her worn blanket, in one hand, and sticking the thumb of her other hand into her mouth. We'd curbed that habit quickly with the boys, but with Soph it was so adorable we let it go. Mostly me. Her hair had that wonderful little girl smell.

"You know, sweetheart," I said softly, raking my fingers through her hair, "the rain's outside. And I know it's loud and scary, but I would never let *anything* harm you or your momma, or Ty and Mickey."

"I know. But I wanted to snuggle," she said matter-of-factly.

Elise chuckled and scooted closer, ducking under my arm and putting her cheek on my chest next to Sophie's.

My lips lifted. "I'm being played, aren't I?"

Elise grinned. "Uh-huh."

I kissed her head. "Just like her momma." I took a deep contented breath. I wanted to never leave my bed.

"Daddy?"

"Hmm?"

"Why did that ref call offsides on you? You weren't offsides." She said it like awf-sides.

"I know! Right?" I bent my neck so I could look at her. "Maybe you need to come to the arena with me and talk to Mr. Phillips..."

"No," Elise scolded. "Mr. Phillips made an honest mistake, like we all do sometimes."

"But it's the playoffs," Sophie said indignantly.

We laughed.

"That's why I love this girl, don't I?" I said, tickling her. Elise rubbed her back.

The comforter had fallen away some, and I could see the top of Elise's silky white nightie. "Tell ya what, Soph. You hop on down here and get the big bowl out for me and I'll make you some pancakes, a.k.a. flat waffles. How does that sound?"

She threw her itty-bitty feet over the edge of the bed and slid to the ground. "Yippee! Pancakes!" The dog got up with a bark and leaped off, chasing after her.

This is what my life had come to. Tumbling curls framing an angelic face at whatever ungodly time it was at the moment, the incessant dinging of gunfire from Combat Zone, and a ludicrously sexy wife.

I was a lucky man.

I rolled until I was on top of Elise.

She put her arms around me. "What are you doing?"

I kissed her, my hand finding its way under the covers and lifting her nightie above her hip. "I need about ten minutes alone with Mommy in our own little sin bin."

She giggled, squirming deeper under the covers and kissing me silly.

NOTE FROM THE AUTHOR

Thank you for reading TEN MINUTES IN THE SIN BIN, part of my DEVILISH DESIRES SERIES. I hope you enjoyed it. Now that you've read the book, won't you please consider writing a review? Reviews are one of the best ways readers discover great new books. They don't need to be fancy or long, just a sentence or two honestly describing your opinion of/experience with the book. I would sincerely appreciate it.

Want more from M.J. Schiller?
Page forward for an excerpt from ~
BEATING IN TIME
A Last Chance Beach Romance

BEATING IN TIME

Levi

A crescendo of noise rose from the dance floor, and we looked over. Someone had slid a folding chair over to the blonde and she was up on it, dancing her heart out, facing the other direction. She peeled off the unbuttoned, long-sleeved black blouse she wore over a skimpy black, midriff-baring tank top. The motion of it falling from her shoulders stirred me even more. She swirled it above her head like a lasso before wrapping it around her partner and pulling him into her. She quickly released him and dropped it on the chair then planted her high heel—black, with strings that crisscrossed and wrapped around her leg—on his shoulder with her knee bent, then shoved him away. The crowd had circled around them and was getting into it, whooping and wolf-whistling encouragement. The guy grabbed her legs and whirled around with her then loosened his grip so that she slowly slid to the floor.

"Who is that blonde with the body that won't stop?" I said loudly.

"That's Remi."

It felt like the floor had dropped out from under me. "Remi?"

"How many Remis do you know?" Dak answered. "Remi Lawson."

Wyatt's little sister. So many emotions hit me at once I froze—like a cat walking across a keyboard, the flurry of input jammed up my brain. The level of shock was threefold. One, to see her in the first place. Two, to see her looking so hot. Three, to see her with a guy's hands on her.

As he held her by the hips she bent backward with a hand on her head and whipped her hair around twice. Before she rose, she caught my eye and gave me this sexy smile that shot immediately to my gut. She straightened and spun. Though I couldn't hear her, I could read her lips, and she called out my name, taking a step toward me. Marco yanked her back against him. My gaze zeroed in on his hand, splayed on her pelvis, and... well, I lost it.

I must have gotten rid of my cup, because I didn't have it when I got to her. I heard her say, "Oh, shit," but my focus was on Marco. I grabbed her arm and jerked her away from him.

"What the hell do you think you're doing?"

Marco hauled her back in. "What the hell do you think *you're* doing?" he rejoined. "Get your own."

I snatched her back. "Can't you see she's not old enough?"

Without looking at her, his jaw tight, he said, "You're eighteen, aren't ya, hon? That's what you said."

"Yeah. I'm—"

She's eighteen?

Marco smirked. "A legal adult." He tried to make another move for her, but I shifted to block him.

I licked my lips. "There's more to it than age of consent, you asshole."

"Like what?"

"Levi. Let me go." Remi wrenched herself free but the quick motion caused her to stumble and turn her ankle. She fell against some other guy, whose quick reflexes kept her from hitting the ground.

"Have you been drinking?" I spat, concerned at first, then angry. Before she could deny it, I said, "You've been drinking." I turned on Marco. "Did you get her a drink?"

He blinked. "Uhh..."

I got up in his grill, our chests bumping. "You put anything in that drink, Marco?"

"No," he said a little bit more quickly than I liked. Although a pause would have added even more concern.

I tried to read him, my fists clenching and unclenching. "You sure the hell better not have, or you're going to be in a world of hurt when I get back." I latched on to Remi. "Come on." I started marching with her to the door.

"What are you doing?" she mumbled. She was definitely trashed.

"Taking you home."

"I remember when you used to be fun," she said petulantly. She shook me off.

Pissed, I made an attempt to grab her again.

"Nope." She evaded my hands and tried to rush away from me, but I lunged and latched around her waist. She giggled at first, but started kicking and screaming at about the time we reached the door. "I'm not leaving. You can't tell me what to do."

I tightened my grip. Jerking my head at the door, I barked, "Open it." The couple from earlier scurried out of my way, the guy cracking the door open as he bailed. I was starting to sweat.

Remi stomped her shoe on the ground and flailed. "Stop."

"You stop," I countered maturely, finally getting her out the door and closing it behind me.

"Can't you see I'm not a kid anymore?"

Hell, yeah, I can see that.

I didn't answer her as I dragged her to the truck. Securing her with one arm, I jerked the door open and threw her in, slamming it behind her. I turned, but before I'd even gotten a few steps, I heard the door open and whirled. I banged it closed again and pounded a finger on the window. "Stop."

We glared at each other for a moment. When I moved away, the latch made a noise, and I knew she was trying to make a run for it again. This time I surprised her by swinging it open while at the same time reaching into the bed for a length of rope I kept back there to secure items I was hauling. "Stop or I'm going to hogtie you. And don't think I won't." She jutted her chin out. "You want that, Remi? You want me to tie you up?" For the briefest moment I saw an image of her wrists tied to my bedposts with a silk scarf. I shook my head.

What the hell is wrong with me? This is Remi! She's like my little sister.

"Fine," she spat, breaking up my fantasy further. She crossed her arms and stared straight ahead.

"That's better," I said with an air of triumph. I stomped around to my side and climbed in beside her. Once the door was shut, the party music was muffled, leaving only the sound of our labored breathing. I took a moment to process what had just happened.

"Geez, Remi." My gaze flashed to her and I was ready to lay into her, but I could see she was upset, so I bit it back and just turned on the ignition. In the brief amount of time I had been inside, cars had hemmed me in. Now I was grumpy.

I hardly even finished a beer. It was supposed to be my damn party.

I wondered again over what I'd done with my cup. Did I hand it to Dak? Or set it down somewhere? But I still couldn't remember. And it didn't matter. I looked around. How was I going to get out of my spot? I sighed.

Screw it.

I cranked the wheel to the right and drove across the lawn, the ruts jarring us as the truck bounced over them.

Remi squealed. "Levi, are you crazy?"

TO FIND OUT WHAT HAPPENS NEXT, PICK UP A COPY OF BEATING IN TIME TODAY!

ALSO FROM M.J. SCHILLER

ROMANTIC REALMS COLLECTION:
TAKEN BY STORM
AN UNCOMMON LOVE
LEAP INTO THE KNIGHT
LADY OF THE KNIGHT
A KNIGHT TO REMEMBER

ROCKING ROMANCE COLLECTION:
TRAPPED UNDER ICE
ABANDON ALL HOPE
BETWEEN ROCK AND A HARD PLACE
ROCK ME, GENTLY
MIDNIGHT MELODY

LOVE AND CHAOS SERIES:
ROCKED BY GRACE
ROCKED BY LOVE
ROCK IT TO THE MOON
ROCK OF SALVATION (Coming soon!)

REAL ROMANCE COLLECTION:
UPON A MIDNIGHT CLEAR
THE HEART TEACHES BEST
DAMAGE DONE
BLACKOUT
HOMETOWN HEARTACHE
TAKE A CHANCE ON ME

DEVILISH DIVAS SERIES:
TO HELL IN A COACH BAG
DAMNED IF I DO
THE DEVIL YOU KNOW
SATAN, LINE ONE
PITCHFORK IN THE ROAD
SIN WORTH THE PENANCE
HELL HATH NO FURY

ABOUT THE AUTHOR

Bestselling author M.J. Schiller is a retired lunch lady/romance-romantic suspense writer. She enjoys writing novels whose characters include rock stars, desert princes, teachers, futuristic Knights, construction workers, cops, and a wide variety of others. In her mind everybody has a romance. She is the mother of a twenty-seven-year-old and three twenty-five-year-olds. That's right, triplets! So having recently taught four children to drive, she likes to escape from life on occasion by pretending to be a rock star at karaoke. However...you won't be seeing her name on any record labels soon.

www.ingramcontent.com/pod-product-compliance
Lightning Source LLC
Chambersburg PA
CBHW051430170626
46809CB00006B/2401